Travis Daniel Bow

ISBN: 978-0-9914-6570-5

Mask and Mallet Publishing

To Laura.

PROLOGUE

Verinald had no sword, no knife, no poison, and no noose. He was chained to tent pegs by wrists and ankles, which ruled out breaking his own neck. He had a bowl of soup—tin, not glass—and he had a spoon.

The spoon was his best chance.

But before he could work up the nerve to use it, the tent flap rustled. Verinald relaxed his grip and focused on his soup. He was calm. He was rational. There was no reason to take the spoon from him.

Then a voice spoke. "Let him sit up," it said.

Verinald was not an easily flustered man. He had trained to maintain his composure since he was old enough to talk. He had kept a straight face while in fear for his own life, while lying to generals and kings, and while watching men die. But as he heard that voice—as two Huctan soldiers loosened and extended the chains on his wrists and raised him to a kneeling position—he trembled with a mixture of grief and rage that was beyond his control.

"It's good to see you alive, old friend," the voice said.

Verinald forced himself to raise his gaze, to meet the eyes that belonged to the voice. The trembling would not stop.

"Ricera," he said.

"I know you want to condemn me for my betrayal," Ricera said. "I know you're itching to rail against me, to try to make me grieve for what is lost. Believe me, I grieve already. But I have made my choice, and your judgment is the least of my concerns. So let's skip the shouting and weeping and get on to the reason you're still alive."

Verinald knew the reason he was still alive. His only consolation was that they could torture him until their knives grew dull, and he would not tell them anything. Not because he was strong, but because there was nothing to tell. Everyone else was already dead.

"Certainly," Verinald found himself saying, with a voice that was saner than he felt. "Don't let me inconvenience you. I know how busy you are with treachery and faithlessness."

Ricera sighed. "Or you could replace the shouting and weeping with sarcastic jibes," he said. Then, to the Huctan soldiers, "Leave us, please."

The two soldiers obeyed, and Ricera squatted on his hams so that his eyes were level with Verinald's. He was close, well within reach, and Verinald still had his spoon. This, more than anything, was a measure of Ricera's contempt for him. Verinald might be Ricera's peer in subterfuge and espionage, but in combat he was no better than a common soldier. Even if the spoon in Verinald's hand had been a sword, he would have been no threat to Ricera.

"Stop measuring us against one another," Ricera said. "You have done nothing else your entire life. Focus, just for this moment, on the task at hand."

Verinald's hand shook on the spoon, and he could not stop it.

"I have your son," Ricera said.

Just like that. Ricera's abruptness should have shocked Verinald into showing some emotion, into betraying something, but this deception was so practiced—so ingrained—that Verinald actually managed to raise his eyebrows in confusion.

"My son?" he said. "I have no son."

"You have a son, and you know of him," Ricera said. "Your face has suddenly gone smooth. How many times did we learn that lack of emotion can be just as telling as emotion itself? How old were we when they taught us that? Ten?"

"Who's measuring us against one another now?" said Verinald.

"You're right," said Ricera. "The task at hand. *Your* task, if you care for your son."

"I have no son," Verinald said.

"You have a son," Ricera repeated. "I sent for him as soon as Eoriden fell. His Huctan mother gave him up without a fight, when she learned that you were dead."

Verinald's spoon began trembling again.

Ricera smiled. "And you criticize *my* faithlessness."

"The faithlessness of loving a Huctan woman is *not* the faithlessness of handing your nation over to the Huctan army."

"The task at hand," Ricera said. "The point of this meeting is that you, too, will hand people over to the Huctan army."

"I will not."

"Tomorrow," Ricera continued, "I will set you free. I will have my soldiers wound you, if you wish, so that you can invent a story as to how you escaped capture. You will join your friends, if you still have them, and you will gather the remnants of the Duest to yourself."

"I will not."

"You will. I have found many of them, but there are many that I have not found. They have gone deep into hiding. But you were always a leader of men, Verinald. I have confidence in you. Over the years, you will gather them to yourself. You will organize them. You will form a resistance. Just think: for a time, *you* can be the leader of the Duest. I know it is a position you have long coveted."

"You are mad."

"You will gather them, lead them, even recruit others who wish to rebel. You will make a safe haven for them, a base of operations, a gathering place. The hill country between Suiton and Shadil will do, I think. I even give you permission, as you see fit, to inflict damage on the Huctans. My only condition is that the damage you inflict does *not* lead to your discovery. You will maintain secrecy and safety at all costs."

"You don't have my son," Verinald said. "You may have known of him, but you don't have him. This is a bluff."

"Secrecy and safety," Ricera said, "but watchfulness. Because when I call for you, you *will* respond. You will deliver the remnants of Botan into my hand. You will betray those you have gathered, and in so doing you will earn the life of your son."

"My son is dead," Verinald said.

"Your son is alive," Ricera said. "He is beginning to speak. He is very intelligent; you can see it in his eyes. In that, he is like his father."

Verinald could not stop himself. He was too tired, too full of despair and hate and self-loathing. He dropped his head, dropped his spoon, and began to weep.

"Take comfort," Ricera said. "I may fail. All my plans may crumble around me, and I may never send for you. You may never have to betray those who trust you, as I have. You may even succeed in starting a real resistance. The Huctans may govern poorly. Perhaps, in time, you will throw their shackles off and win independence and freedom for Botan. Maybe your son will hear of your name and come to your throne with open arms."

Ricera's hand touched Verinald's shoulder, and Verinald jerked as if burned. He looked up to find a mirthless smile on Ricera's face.

"But don't count on it," Ricera said. "Don't count on it."

CHAPTER 1

In the northern hills of Botan, where the high desert meets the alpine forests, the sun was rising on the last normal day of Timothy's life.

He had been awake for over an hour. He always got up early, as if his diligence might somehow make up for his uselessness as a fletcher's apprentice. By now, with the pink light of dawn filtering through the pine needles and coloring the mist of his breath, he had already gathered water, spread cracked corn for the chickens, collected the eggs, milked the cow, and cooked breakfast. He was on his way to town for arrowheads.

It was a two mile jog. The air was cool under the pines. The needles that carpeted the steep hill to the northwest damped out the sound of his bare feet, leaving only the gurgling of the stream to break the stillness. Even the stream was silent most of the time, making its way smoothly through a narrow, winding channel of overhung grass and dark loam.

Timothy slowed as he neared town. They called it "town", but there were only six buildings, straddling the path and separated from the stream by a hundred yards of thin alpine grass. The gray wooden structures—the inn, the store, and the homes of the smith, tanner, clothier and carpenter—served as a hub for the canyon people. They came to town when they needed supplies, or news, or social interaction.

Almost no one outside of the canyon knew about town. Occasionally a cowhand would pass through on his way in to Watchton, or a wagoner would bring in supplies, but for the most part, you could count on finding canyon people and only canyon people in town.

And that was what made town worth having. Yes, it was small. Yes, it was probably unnecessary, since Watchton—a *real* town—was only ten or twelve miles up the hill. But it was something that belonged to the canyon people. It was their own.

And to Timothy, it was home. Or, rather, it *had* been home, until a few months ago. Until his father had kicked him out of the smithy. Until his mother had gone to the fletcher and begged him to take Timothy on as an apprentice. Until Timothy had had to bid Robert—the *real* son—goodbye.

No, that was unfair. Only Mother knew which son was her real son, and Father had made the decision. Father could be impartial, because he didn't know which son truly belonged to Mother, and because neither son belonged to him. To him, both boys were adopted. Part of the price of marrying their mother.

No, that was unfair too. Father loved them. Timothy hadn't been sent away because he was unloved or unwanted. He had been sent away because two boys needed trades to survive as men, and because there was not enough work for two smiths, and because Timothy had never shown an ounce of aptitude at the forge.

Or at anything, really.

No. Stop being a baby, he told himself. Don't show Mother even a hint of your pouting. She feels guilty enough already.

But he couldn't help knocking on the door of the smithy and waiting politely for someone to answer it. Robert or Father might miss the gesture—the subtle reminder that they had made him an outsider, that he now *knocked* at the door to the house he had grown up in—but Mother would not miss it. If she answered the door and saw him patiently waiting to come in, she might cry.

But Mother did not answer the door. Robert did. And he did not burst into tears of remorse.

"Your hand broken?" he said. "Or did you forget where the handle is?"

And just like that, Timothy's self-pity evaporated.

"I thought you might be asleep," he said. "After all, it's not even lunch time yet."

"You're letting in the cold," said Robert.

"You're letting out the heat."

Robert shut the door in Timothy's face. Timothy waited. When Robert didn't open the door again, Timothy reached for the handle and went inside.

The front room of the building was the smithy itself. An array of neatly organized tools hung on one wall to the right. An anvil was fixed to a platform in the center of the small room. The forge—a stone structure with a large leather bellows mounted to one side—was built into the bricked chimney on the back wall. The forge fire was lit, but it hadn't yet been stoked and blown to its full heat.

Robert was on the left side of the room, kneeling before a large wooden shelf. He was cleaning it, removing wooden boxes of various buckles, links, and latches so that he could scrub behind and beneath and around the stored goods.

It was unnecessary work. From the tiny amount of dirt on Robert's rag, he had probably cleaned the same shelf yesterday. That was a bad sign. It meant that real work, work that paid, was in short supply.

Timothy stood for a moment, remembering the hours spent in this cramped room, sweating through the summers and relishing the heat in the winters. For a moment he had a strong urge to stride through the smithy and into the house, to see if his old bed was still there, to sit down at the table and eat a breakfast cooked by his mother.

But he couldn't dally. The fletcher would expect him to accomplish his business and be back soon. If he showed that he couldn't be sent to town without spending an hour lingering at his old home, he wouldn't be sent to town anymore.

"The fletcher letting you go to the Jubilee?" Robert asked, not turning away from the shelf.

Timothy felt his mood dampen again. It was a small thing—he had never been to the Spring Jubilee, and it wouldn't hurt him to miss it again this year—but it had been twisting at him. Robert was going this year. Timothy would have liked nothing better than to spend a day with Robert again, to soak up the feeling of peace—without responsibility or self-pity or despair—that came with being around his brother. He would have liked to see Watchton, to really *see* it and explore it and absorb the joy of hundreds of people celebrating another year of planted crops and birthed livestock. In spite of the Huctan guards, who were always at the gates, he would have liked to go.

"Oh," Timothy said, as casually as he could. "Yeah. He said I can go after I finish with the garden. It's going to take a while, though, and I can't start until tomorrow because we're going stave-gathering today. So I'll probably be pretty late."

"How late?" Robert asked, glancing back from the shelf. His blue eyes looked alarmed.

Timothy shrugged. "Probably early afternoon before I can even leave here," he said.

"Early afternoon! It'll all be over by the time you get there."

Timothy shrugged again. It was getting a little harder to act like he didn't care.

Robert shrugged too, turning back to the shelf. "I'll help you," he said. "With the two of us, we can finish the garden mid-morning. Earlier, if we start before the sun's up. The moon was pretty bright last night, wasn't it?"

"No," Timothy said, suddenly feeling guilty for letting his disappointment show and dragging Robert into his problems. "You'll miss half the day. No point in both of us missing it."

Robert waved a dismissive hand.

"Really," Timothy said, "You don't have to come help. I'll get up early. Maybe I'll be able to leave by lunch time."

"Stop whining," Robert said. "I'm coming. What would I do all day without you?"

Something about Robert's matter-of-fact tone made Timothy's throat constrict. He found himself rolling his eyes and hastily changing the subject before a sudden flood of emotion could make his voice crack.

On the next day—the day that everything changed—Timothy was awake and moving even before his usual hour. He donned his heavy wool, then slipped outside to do the morning chores. The chickens, still asleep at their roosts, didn't even notice the corn he scattered. They would find it when they woke.

True to his word, Robert came before the sky had begun to turn gray. They got to work immediately. By the time the fletcher woke up, they were halfway finished with spreading manure and compost from the pit behind the garden.

Robert kept working while Timothy went in to prepare breakfast, and refused two offers by the fletcher before finally joining them around the meal of corn grits and eggs. They ate quickly, and in minutes they were back at work.

As the sun poured down on the garden, sweat began to slick Timothy's arms. By the time full morning had set in, the mixture of compost and manure was worked into the ground and formed into small hills and ridges. The fletcher came out to supervise the planting, pointing to where he wanted pumpkins, beans, squash, onions, and corn. Then the watering began, bucketful by bucketful. As they did with everything, Timothy and Robert turned it into a contest. Robert won, finishing the corn just before Timothy finished the other plants.

By mid-morning the work was finished. The fletcher nodded grudging approval, and after taking a long drink, Timothy and Robert began jogging northeast along the stream.

When the stream turned due east, they chose to cross and cut through the forest instead of following the wagon road. A thin fallen pine spanned the water, and it bounced beneath their bare feet as they ran across. Scrambling up the bank, they settled into a brisk walk as the hill grew steep.

Timothy was breathing heavily now, his shirt and pants damp with sweat, but he felt more alive than he had in months. A tingling excess of energy and excitement made his feet light. There wasn't breath or reason for talking, but the silence was an easy one. The scents and breezes of the morning seemed alive. It felt like the old days.

They came to a place barred by a kind of rooted, earthy embankment that rose like a cliff for some fifteen feet. With unspoken consent they raced to the top, clinging to roots with fingers and toes. It struck Timothy, halfway up, that it would have been quicker and easier to skirt the cliff. If Fenae had been there, she would have rolled her eyes and made a comment about boys and their obsession with doing things the hard way.

But Timothy didn't think about Fenae, not anymore. Quickly he banished her face and the entire train of thought that had led him to remember her, and concentrated on reaching the top. He beat Robert by a nose, and made sure Robert was aware of it.

With the glory of the morning and the woods and the quiet around them, the urgency of actually reaching the festival was beginning to fade. Timothy tried to hurry anyway, for Robert's sake, but when Robert took out his sling and began throwing rocks as they walked, Timothy joined him gladly. After a few minutes of pointing out targets for each other, the ground began to level out again. Putting the slings away, they jogged to make up for lost time.

They reached Watchton in just under two hours.

Even with the streets hidden by a wall of cut and lashed pine trunks, it was obvious that crowds had already gathered within. There was a noise, a dull roar that had grown louder so gradually as they approached that Timothy hadn't even noticed it. Now, as they left the cover of the trees, the rumble of hundreds of voices shouting and talking and laughing struck him all at once.

Only one Huctan manned the guard hut, and he was not questioning those that entered. Timothy kept his eyes averted and his hands at his sides, taking slow, even breaths until they had passed the crimson-cloaked soldier. Robert glanced at him, and Timothy gave a nod that he was OK.

Watchton was jam packed. Everywhere faces turned, legs moved, hands gestured, voices spoke, eyes darted. People with something to sell were yelling their hearts out. Woodspeople and farmers were staring and hanging their mouths open. A group of cowhands was laughing and yelling, a few of them making the strange, yipping cries they used to move cattle. Someone was playing a set of pipes.

Together Timothy and Robert joined the gawkers, pointing things out to each other and pressing tentatively through the crowd. They watched a gangly youth juggling three, four, and then five baggy, faded cloth balls. Mouth hanging a little open in concentration, the boy looked slightly upwards as the balls spun between his hands. Timothy would have watched longer, but an uptilt in the crowd's noise caught his ear. Sliding between the backs of two people and dodging around a woman in a long coat, he strained to see.

A circle had formed as people backed away from the person standing in the center. Pressing forward, Timothy saw that the focus of attention was a grinning, staggering old man.

Holding a finger up, the old man fixed his eyes on someone at the circle's edge.

"What's your name, friend?" he shouted.

The old man tried to touch the stranger, and fell flat when the stranger dodged. A few in the crowd laughed. Most looked grim.

"Sorry! Sorry!" The old man shouted again, scrambling to his feet and grinning about him. "I am not drunk," he announced.

There was more laughter, more frowning. The man whirled, clearly loving the attention, and became wilder with his gesticulations. "I am not drunk!" he repeated. "I am not drunk!"

Timothy's own teeth were gritted, as much at the fact that Botani people were *laughing* as at the man's intoxication. The sight disgusted him, as it should have disgusted them all. As it *would* have disgusted them all, fifteen years ago, before the Huctans came and made alcohol a protected and legal trade.

It wasn't the worst of their trades, but it was a poison to Botan. It was the reason that Fenae's father had...

No. Think of something else. Anything else.

A hush in the crowd started suddenly, spreading like a wave from farther down the street. People pushed each other to make way. Timothy found himself pressed against a counter with Robert.

Someone was shouting for people to move. Timothy recognized the accent, and his jaw clenched harder.

Huctans came into view, two men in gray wool pants and shirts under crimson cloaks. One held a drawn sword in his right hand. The other held a spear and shouted for people to step back.

The drunk, who had stumbled again and gotten himself tangled up in the tongue of a wagon, was the only person still smiling. He reached up a hand toward one of the soldiers for help. Ignoring the hand, the soldiers faced the man coldly.

"Hello," the drunk said, affecting a dignified face that only made the swimming of his eyes more apparent.

"You have been drinking," the Huctan with the sword said. He sounded angry, and Timothy found himself wondering what the Huctans would do. They had made alcohol legal, but they frowned on public intoxication, realizing how it served as a reminder to the Botani people that they were an occupied country ruled by their oldest enemies. In a crowd this size, with so many Botani already hiding clenched fists as they watched the spectacle, the Huctans would be worrying about a riot.

The drunk grinned. "I am not drunk!" he shouted, looking around for those who had laughed at him before. No one was laughing now.

The soldier with a sword said something in Huctan to the one with the spear, who turned to face the crowd.

"This man is disturbing the peace and showing disrespect to a Huctan officer," he announced. "He will be punished accordingly."

The soldier with the sword yanked the old man forward so hard that he fell flat on the ground in the center of the circle. Timothy could only see him in glimpses now, between the shoulders of the crowd, but he saw the soldier's face tighten as he delivered a vicious kick, and he heard the drunk grunt in pain.

The spearman had upended his weapon. Grasping it with both hands near the blade, he lifted the length of the shaft above his head. Then he swung the handle like an axe, hard. The drunk screamed.

People in the crowd gasped. Some nodded in approval, as if the Huctans were somehow doing the right thing, as if the Huctans had not been the very ones to put the liquor in the man's hand in the first place. Timothy felt sick, and his clenched fist trembled.

The soldier raised the spear haft again, and a gap in the crowd allowed Timothy to catch a glimpse of the old man on the ground, turned halfway over and holding his hands up pitifully. The spear handle fell, and Timothy heard a terrible snap that had to be one of the drunken man's wrists.

The crowd, which had already been quiet, grew suddenly silent. Timothy ducked and craned his head, looking for an opening, and caught another glimpse of the old man, lying still, eyes rolled back, body shutting down because of the pain.

The Huctan with the spear struck one final time. The sound of brittle ribs cracking was loud in the unnatural silence.

Timothy was breathing hard out of his nose, now. The Huctans were turning to leave. The crowds were moving, dispersing. Robert was tugging at him.

"Come on," Robert said. When Timothy didn't move, Robert tugged harder, and Timothy allowed himself to be pulled and pushed away from the soldiers and into the open space between two houses.

Robert had pressed him against the wall. Timothy realized that Robert's face was so close that their noses almost touched. "You OK?" Robert was saying. "You alright? Timothy, look at me."

Timothy looked into his friend's blue eyes. In spite of himself, he saw Fenae, saw his own weakness, saw red. With an effort, he shook his head and focused on Robert. His eyes. His blue eyes.

"I'm fine," he said.

Robert looked at him for another minute.

"I'm fine," Timothy repeated.

"Ok," Robert said, "Let's go."

Together, more slowly, they began making their way toward the center of the town, where the festivities would soon begin.

Robert made a valiant effort to distract Timothy from his

brooding, and after a while it began to work. With cheerfulness and energy that was only a little bit strained, they ran back and forth between the contests, trying to see them all. There was an archery shoot, followed by dancing on one side of the square and wrestling on the other. Shepherds had a race to see who could shear a sheep the fastest. Cowhands took turns roping calves. Burly men competed in the caber toss, balancing a ten-foot log upright in their hands, running forward, and flinging the heavy beam as far as they could.

Timothy entered the slinging contest, and although he was better than most of the woodspeople and farmers and *much* better than any of the townspeople, he was far behind the shepherds and cowhands. For them, slinging was a way to protect flocks and herds from the coyotes that roamed the sage. For them, failures with the sling meant dead lambs and maimed calves.

A shepherd won. His prize was a turkey leg and an ear of roast corn. Seeing the food reminded Timothy that, with no money, he would not be eating until they returned home late that night.

A crier shouted something over the crowd, and Robert beckoned to Timothy excitedly. Timothy followed him across town to the field that had been prepared for horse races.

They were early, but the races were what Robert had anticipated the whole day. He was enamored with horses in a way that Timothy would never understand. This was yet another reason why Robert deserved to become a smith, and Timothy did not. Half of a smith's business was making and fitting shoes to the feet of horses. A smith that did not know about horses was like a shepherd that did not know how to shear wool.

They sat for a while on a rail fence in the shade, watching the people swarming and gathering as the racers prepared their mounts. Timothy saw a group of youths from the canyon approaching, and carefully hid his disappointment when Robert stood up and waved them over.

He could feel it happening as his peers came closer, almost like the onset of a disease. With Robert, alone, Timothy could quip and joke and talk as easily as he breathed. Around anyone else—especially around others his age—he was suddenly slow-witted and awkward. His throat tightened. His eyes slid downward. He was reminded, with every second that Robert chatted and laughed easily while Timothy scratched his neck and blushed, that Robert didn't need him nearly as much as he needed Robert.

He hated it.

There were four boys and two girls. One of the boys was unfamiliar, but the rest of the group had lived in the canyon as long as Timothy could remember.

"Come to see how someone stays *on* a horse, Indriana?" Robert shouted. One of the girls laughed and rolled her eyes, and Timothy remembered that she had brought her father's horse to the smithy once when she was younger. A snake had spooked the animal, and she had been thrown. Father had had to bind her ankle.

Trust Robert to remember that, and to be able to make a girl laugh about it.

The group was close now. Chuon, Indriana's older brother, pointed to Robert and looked at his comrades.

"Here's the one I was telling you about," he said, loudly enough for Robert to hear. "The reason half of these horses are going to lose shoes before they reach the finish line."

Robert stepped forward, laughing, and clapped Chuon on the

shoulder as if they were old friends. In fact, Timothy knew, Robert and Chuon despised one another. The fact that Chuon and Indriana's parents had chosen to keep blatantly Botani names for their children, even after the Invasion, spoke for some of the stubborn pride that made their family hard to deal with.

It also made Timothy jealous, that *some* people's parents did not constantly remind their children to bow and scrape to the Huctans at every opportunity.

Thomas, Anne, and their little brother James were farmers from up-canyon. They had always been easier going. Anne, the closest in age to Timothy and Robert, was nowhere near as pretty as Indriana, but she had always struck Timothy as more intelligent. She was also quieter, giving the appearance of shyness, though she seemed to be able to talk easily enough when the time came for it. Timothy couldn't say as much for himself.

Hugs and handshakes were being exchanged—hugs between Robert and the girls, handshakes between the boys. Anne turned away from Robert to meet Timothy. He held his hands out for a hug without thinking, saw what looked like hesitation in her eyes, and tried to turn the gesture into a yawn and stretch. At the same moment, Anne opened her own arms for a hug, but stopped when she realized that he was stretching. Timothy's mortification must have been obvious, then, because Anne laughed and held out a hand. Timothy shook it.

Chuon and Indriana, of course, ignored Timothy completely. The fourth boy—the one Timothy didn't know—had already been engaged in conversation by Robert. Robert was laughing at something he'd said, holding out a hand towards Timothy.

"This is my brother Timothy," he said.

“I’m Peter,” said the boy, holding out a hand to shake.

“I’m Timothy, Robert’s brother,” Timothy said automatically. It was a standard reply, and usually a safe one, when introducing himself to others their age. But of course Robert had already introduced him, and Timothy had just repeated exactly what Robert had said.

Was there any faster way to make it clear how much of an idiot he was?

He probably should have laughed at himself, made some excuse about being distracted, but instead Timothy finished the handshake and then looked past the new boy, towards the horse track, scratching the back of his neck as if he were unaware of the other boy’s presence. It was another automatic reaction. Better to look casual, disinterested and even rude than to writhe and wriggle and make his inability to make conversation obvious.

Luckily Robert had enough conversation for both of them. Gradually everyone turned away from Timothy as Robert talked about the race and told Peter stories about the others. Timothy affected a vacant expression, as if he were only half interested, as if he could have been part of the conversation if he’d felt like it.

Sometimes he hated himself.

After the races, almost all of which Robert had predicted correctly, the two of them split off from the others to explore the town. For almost two hours they wandered, looking at merchandise they could not buy, watching performers they could not tip, and killing time. They were able to avoid the Huctans walking the town, for the most part, and Timothy made an enormous effort to stave off the fury that came over him at the sight of their red cloaks.

The fact that there were too many soldiers for a town like Watchton did not occur to him until it was far too late.

It was getting toward dark when they decided to leave town. Although the festivities were still in full swing, both boys had seen as much as they cared to. It was a long walk back home, and they had been up early, with nothing to eat since breakfast. They were hungry, and tired. The constant presence of so many people, which had been exhilarating at first, was beginning to drain them.

The outskirts of the town were nearly deserted. Only one officer guarded the gate. Timothy, now getting better at keeping his back from stiffening and fists from clenching, fixed his eyes on the forest and walked forward steadily. Soon they would be out of this town, away from the Huctans, and free in the openness of the woods. Soon he could breathe.

Ignoring the soldier became suddenly impossible when the Huctan raised his crossbow and leveled it at Robert's chest. Timothy froze, and another soldier stepped out of the shadows with a crossbow pointed at Timothy.

The boys stood still, not breathing, eyes flickering. Timothy was so surprised that, for a moment, it felt as if his mind had stopped functioning. Then he thought of running, immediately realized that the Huctans were too close, and had to struggle to keep his sudden panic at bay. Then he wondered what was happening, wondered whether something he or Robert had mumbled about the Huctans had been overheard, wondered if he was about to be beaten or killed for a crime he was not even aware of.

Then the second soldier, who had been coming steadily closer, was near enough that Timothy could see the individual blades of the arrowhead on his crossbow quarrel. Suddenly all Timothy could think about was the fact that a simple twitch of the finger could drive that quarrel through him like a gaff through a lake fish.

"Is there something..." Robert began.

"Be quiet," the first soldier—an officer—said. "Move off of the road." He gestured to the left with his crossbow, and Timothy found himself obeying, sidestepping in the direction the Huctan had indicated.

"Sit down, backs against the wall," the officer said. Timothy hesitated, glancing again at Robert, looking for an avenue of escape.

"Sit. Down," the officer repeated, stepping quickly forward and pointing the steel-tipped quarrel at Timothy's face. With the sharp metal arrowhead almost scratching his eyeball, Timothy sat.

The door to the wall they were sitting against opened beside them, and four more soldiers hurried out. Before Timothy could think about getting up, the soldiers were upon them, manhandling them into the building by wrists and throats.

"Help!" Timothy yelled, coming to his senses in time to kick the door frame as he was being shoved through. A fist caught him hard, in the cheek, and dizzying pain cut off his shouts as the door closed behind them.

Panic took over, then, and Timothy found himself jerking violently in the darkness, kicking and thrashing until a heavy blow to the stomach knocked the wind from him.

He doubled over and fell. Opening his mouth, he tried to gasp. Air wouldn't come.

Someone kicked his hip. He was still trying to breathe. Feet appeared in front of his face, then knees. Someone grabbed his hands and forced them behind his back. Timothy kicked, trying to tell them he couldn't *breathe*, but then his chest loosened and he stopped struggling to suck in heaving breaths of sweet, dusty air.

His gasping was cut short as a gag was stuffed into his mouth. Robert, somewhere behind him, cursed. Rough hands yanked Timothy to a sitting position and shoved him against the building's inner wall. The soldiers stepped back, and Timothy's eyes gradually adjusted to the lamplight.

A slender figure was standing near a low table, his back to Timothy and the other boys. There were almost a dozen of them, Timothy realized, tied and stacked against the wall like bundles of firewood. Some were unconscious. He looked for Robert and found him far to the left. Their eyes met, and Timothy's panic lessened by one degree.

Taking a breath, he turned back to the desk where the slender man was standing. The other soldiers seemed to be looking to the man at the desk, and Timothy decided that he was in charge.

The slender man turned and spoke. His voice was calm, pleasant, perfectly enunciated. The Huctan accent was so subtle that Timothy didn't even hear it, at first.

"Hello," the man said. "My name is T'shira."

The voice sounded young. Almost Timothy's age.

Robert said something that was unintelligible through his gag, but the lack of humility in his tone was unmistakable. T'shira stepped forward and kicked Robert hard in the stomach.

Robert doubled over, heaving against the gag, and Timothy found himself half-standing, trying to shout, levelling his head to drive it into the young Huctan's side. T'shira whirled, and his boot struck Timothy's shoulder, smashing him to the ground. Timothy lay where T'shira had knocked him, eyelids squeezed tight against the pain blossoming in his shoulder. His wrists were bleeding against the ropes behind his back.

"Do not speak," T'shira said. His voice was still calm, pleasant, crisp.

The door opened and two soldiers entered, supporting someone between them. The boy was young, only thirteen or fourteen, and he did not struggle. He glanced around with a look of terror on his face as they tied him, and there was something funny about the way his eyes shone in the lamplight. Timothy caught the sight of blood on the back of the boy's head just before he recognized Anne's little brother, James.

The next few hours passed at a slow crawl. The door continued to open and close periodically, sometimes loudly with struggling and muffled shouts, other times quietly as a limp or submissive figure was escorted into the increasingly crowded room. T'shira paced, sat, watched the captives, and then got up to pace again. Timothy tried working at the ropes at his wrists, received several kicks that left him gasping and whimpering in the dirt, and then remained still.

He tried to sleep, but could not. His shoulder throbbed where T'shira had kicked him. His wrists ached and stung where the cords pinched them together. He was hungry, he was thirsty, and he was afraid. He could not figure out why they were here or what was to be done with them, and the uncertainty welled up to a panic that he had to suppress periodically.

The room grew hot, stinking of sweat and fear and blood. No one bothered to look when the door opened yet again, but this time it remained open. The night air, already a little cooler, passed over bodies drenched in discomfort. Heads began to lift.

T'shira had joined another soldier in the doorway, and after a brief conversation in low tones, he gestured to someone outside. Soldiers began to enter, taking up the stiffened bodies of the tied boys, striking those that cried out until they held their silence. Quickly the room emptied.

Timothy's turn came, and he bit back a whimper as a soldier took him by the rope on his wrists and lifted him to his feet, steering him out the door at a painful, stumbling walk.

Horses stood on the road in the night, some with trussed boys already slung across their backs. Timothy was taken to an empty horse, his foot forced into the stirrup. A jab to his ribs encouraged him to step up, and a shove laid him across the saddle blankets.

He felt a cord cinch around his ankles.

"Don't fall off," a Huctan voice advised. Then someone had mounted the horse in front of Timothy, and they were moving.

Every step drove the breath from Timothy's lungs, but after a brutal elbow silenced his first whimper, he did not cry out.

He could not tell how long they rode, or how far they traveled, or even what direction they went. His body slowly bruised against the saddle's edge and the horse's back. His bare feet grew ever colder, and his hands alternately tingled and grew numb behind him. It seemed like dawn should have come a long time ago. He did not sleep, but exhaustion sometimes blurred the pain and the passing of time. He heard someone ask to pee and receive a hard blow in reply. When his own urge became unbearable, he wet himself against the haunches of the horse and was grateful for the warmth.

When the movement stopped and Timothy tried to lift his head, dizziness spun his senses and he almost vomited. Torches and lanterns were lit, and when the spinning stopped, Timothy could see dusty white tents fluttering in the now-cold breeze.

Breath was frosting from the horses, their riders, and their burdens. Someone whimpered. Timothy's rider dismounted, unlashed his feet, and pulled him from the horse. Timothy cried out softly and almost fell as his numb feet struck the ground. Someone grabbed the back of his neck hard, steered him for several steps, and shoved him. Then he did fall, only just managing to twist so that his shoulder struck the ground before his face.

Someone knelt behind him, cutting the bloody ropes away from his wrists. Tightened muscles suddenly released, and Timothy felt a few seconds of relief before the soldier woke the bundles sleeping on the ground and yanked at the chains that bound them.

Seeing the manacles meant for him, Timothy tried to run. He stumbled on his uncooperative feet, rose, and fell again as something heavy struck him in the back. Two more soldiers rushed to help, and he was dragged back to the chains, writhing and shouting. The back of a gloved hand struck him hard across the face, and hot blood poured from his nose. He screamed and freed one of his own hands, swinging back at the figures holding him. Another backhand left his ears ringing and vision blurred.

In a moment, the cold manacles were closed around him, and he was bound between two other boys, wrist to wrist, ankle to ankle.

He wanted to cry, but didn't. Instead he lay still for several minutes, teeth gritted, and tried to get control over his breathing.

Presently someone beside him spoke.

"You OK?"

Timothy didn't answer for a moment. Looking up, he could just make out the shaggy hair of the boy next to him.

"Yeah," he said. "I'm OK."

The boy waited a moment, obviously wanting to ask something, but trying to respect Timothy's shock. Finally he spoke again.

"What village did they get you in?" the boy asked. "Where are we now?"

Timothy felt something trickle down his ear, realized he was still bleeding, and pulled his hand up towards his face. The chain, attached to the other boy's wrist, caught for a moment, but then the boy raised his own wrist so that Timothy could reach his face.

"Watchton," Timothy heard himself say. "I don't know where we are now."

"Watchton," the boy repeated, half to himself. "Still moving us northeast."

Timothy got his nose pinched shut and felt blood start to trickle down his throat. He tried to swallow, but his throat was so dry that he was unable to do so.

"Us?" he said. "Still? What is this? Where are we?"

"Shh," the boy said. Timothy realized that most of the torches were gone, moved farther toward the tents, and that a quiet had fallen over the mass of boys on the ground. The clouds were covering the moon, and it was hard to see much farther than his own hand.

"Where are we?" Timothy asked again, in a whisper. This time the boy answered.

"I don't know," he said. "There are about a hundred and fifty of us, all boys, all older than twelve or thirteen. They've been marching us along the edge of the desert, kidnapping as they go. The popular theories are that they're going to kill us, make us into death-slaves, or force us to fight in their army."

Timothy had the sudden feeling that the boy had explained all this before.

"How long have you been..." he asked.

"Two weeks," the boy replied. "Almost since the beginning."

Timothy was quiet for a moment, trying to stave off his exhaustion long enough to collect his thoughts. The jingling of chains and the whimpering of boys grew steadily quieter. The air grew steadily colder.

"I'm Garret," the boy said.

"Timothy," said Timothy.

He wondered where Robert was, how far away he was chained, whether he had fought as they manacled him. He hoped Robert had not had to wet himself, as he had. The stink was already wrinkling his nose, and the wet was cold on his legs.

"How many soldiers?" he whispered. Garret did not answer. Timothy nudged the boy with his elbow. "Hey. Hey."

"What?" Garret whispered.

"How many soldiers are there?" Timothy asked.

"I dunno. Fifty maybe."

"And you said there are a hundred and fifty of us?"

"About," said Garret.

Timothy lay back again on the hard ground, looking at the stars. After a moment, Garret spoke.

"Look over there," he said.

"Where?"

"There." Garret was pointing with their chained hands. Timothy sat up, grimacing, and then saw what Garret was pointing at. About fifty feet away, something stood in a pool of light cast by a lamp that had been left burning.

"What is it?" he asked.

"Two people that tried to escape. Got out of their chains

somehow. They tied them there this morning."

Timothy leaned forward, blinking to clear his eyes, and suddenly realized what he was seeing. Two naked figures hung limp, strung up by wrists and ankles below a wooden beam like the carcasses of two animals. Timothy shuddered as he made out the silhouette of the boys' heads, lolled back at an unnatural angle and hanging limp. He wondered how long it had taken for the weight of their heads to become too much for their necks to hold anymore.

A sudden thought crossed his mind, and he turned sharply to Garret.

"Are they..." he whispered.

"No, they're alive." Garret said. The way he said it made it sound like an unfortunate truth. Garret rolled over, turning his back to Timothy. Slowly Timothy laid his head back on the grass and stared up at the stars.

For a long time he could not sleep. He was cold, and the boys huddling close on either side only helped a little. He was also afraid. His fear shamed him, his shame angered him, and when that wore off he was afraid again.

But something was happening, deep in his gut. Something was... *opening.* The trembling was slowly being replaced with something harder. Something hotter. As if his life, before this, was wax. As if the molten iron was ready, and was beginning to be poured.

When Timothy finally fell asleep, his knuckles were white on the chains, and blood trickled from his palms.

CHAPTER 2

SELENA

Selena was physically shaking.

She had done this sort of thing before, but it had always been a game. Her mentor had always been watching. Her opponents had never been real Huctan soldiers who might actually kill her.

She asked herself, for the hundredth time, why she was going through with this. She had only met the boy once. Why was he her responsibility?

Because she had opened her big mouth, that was why. She had had pity on him, seen potential in him, and had promised to help him. And now that things had gone bad, she could not bring herself to let him die.

Hesitating at the bottom of the stairs, Selena tried to calm herself. Pressing her forehead against the cool stone, she took a deep breath and exhaled slowly. Then she pursed her lips, opened the door, and walked out into the open moonlight.

The storm last night had drenched the courtyard, and now a slow drizzle was speckling the silver surfaces of the puddles. The rain was a warm one, this late in the spring, and she was glad to have it. With luck, it would rain harder.

As Selena crossed the courtyard, she tried to find the balance between skulking and parading. She had an excuse to be out this late, but the guards that knew about her and Ibara—which, hopefully, was all of them—would enjoy stopping her. Even that she couldn't afford. Not tonight, when timing was crucial, when a few moments could ruin everything.

She was practically running. Deliberately Selena slowed her steps. Staying mostly in the shadows, but not hugging them, she kept her back erect and walked quietly. When she came to the guardhouse door she took a deep breath, stilled her trembling, and knocked.

A chair scraped inside. That was good. Ibara was here.

Then a voice said something Selena couldn't quite catch, and was answered with laughter.

Selena froze, and the shaking started again.

Ibara was not supposed to have company. He knew she was bringing him dinner tonight. She had been painfully obvious about her intentions. Why, then, was he not alone?

Run, Selena's instinct said. You don't owe the boy anything.

But didn't she, now? Hadn't this been *her* plan? Wasn't this plan the reason T'shira had readied a gallows?

Please, Selena said silently, mouthing the word and closing her eyes briefly as she waited for the door.

The latch turned. Selena opened her eyes, and Ibara stood before her. His Huctan cloak was missing—she saw it hanging on the wall inside—and his bare chain mail was bulging around the meat of his shoulders. Selena, who had placed her feet close together and lowered her head demurely, looked up at him from the tops of her eyes and affected a smile that she hoped was both inviting and afraid. The afraid part was easy.

"What do you want?" Ibara said.

Selena did not wince, and it was one of the most difficult things she had done. This was the worst possible beginning to what she had hoped would be the easy part of tonight's mission. She *had* to get into this guardhouse.

She had counted on Ibara inviting her in. That was the obvious part of her plan. But he was not inviting her in. He was not alone—she could see his companion watching from the table—and he was not in a good mood. Did her entire mission, and the lives of those boys, depend on the temper of one idiot soldier?

"I brought dinner," Selena said in Huctan, being careful to struggle with the vowels and retain the heavy Botani accent Ibara seemed to like. She put a slight tremble in her voice, as if hurt by Ibara's tone, and looked down at his feet as she spoke.

"Give it to me," Ibara said, taking the dish from Selena's outstretched hands and lifting the corner of the cloth to inspect the contents. Selena glanced up, and saw the corner of Ibara's mouth twitch upward as he tried to frown at the dinner dish.

This was a *joke* to him. Selena found it difficult to keep her shoulders from slumping with sudden relief. She could use this.

"Was there something else?" Ibara asked, pressing his lips together and glowering. Selena maintained the confusion on her face and increased the hurt in her eyes. She even managed to make her lip tremble a little.

"No," she said. "I..."

Whirling suddenly, she turned and began to leave. She had only gone three steps when Ibara laughed out loud.

"Selena!" he called, and Selena winced at the noise. The idiot was going to wake everyone in Northelm.

She glanced back, over her shoulder, but kept walking. She forced herself to hurry, taking quick little steps as if she actually intended on leaving. It was difficult—so much depended on his inviting her in—but Selena had learned long ago that you had to be confident. You had to commit, act, and trust your judgment.

"Wait," Ibara said, now in a loud whisper. He ran after her suddenly, and Selena let him catch her. She gave a tiny cry as he seized her arm.

"Please," Ibara said, affecting earnestness. "Come in. I was only joking."

Selena hesitated. Ibara tugged at her arm, and she resisted the urge to smile. This was good. Now she had a grievance. It might be a small one, and Huctan soldiers might not care about the grievances of Botani scullery maids, but it was better than nothing.

As Ibara ushered her into the guardhouse, he dropped the apologetic look and wiggled his eyebrows at his friend. The quick, appraising glance at Selena was obvious and insulting, but of course Selena pretended not to notice.

"Good evening," said Ibara's friend, standing and giving Selena a small nod. "I am Lieutenant Byon."

Selena did not miss the apologetic flick of Lieutenant Byon's eyes toward Ibara, as if he were embarrassed by his companion's behavior. Nor did she miss the emphasis of his rank, which was higher than Ibara's. The sharpness in Lieutenant Byon's eyes was obvious. He was significantly more intelligent than Ibara, Selena thought. His presence was going to make her job a lot harder.

"Of course, of course," said Ibara. "My friend, Byon! He is joining us tonight. I hope you do not find him too ugly?" Ibara laughed again, sweeping a heavy chair across the room with one thick hand and scooting it up to the table.

Selena did not change her expression, only continued appraising Byon, but she could see that this was enough. The lieutenant took her appraisal to mean that she was fascinated by his suave manner and high rank, and he preened under her gaze.

Selena took the seat Ibara offered her, keeping her head slightly lowered and her arms submissively at her sides. She had never known a Huctan who minded an overly humble Botaña.

"I brought beef, and gravy," she said, timidly reaching out to withdraw the cloth from the dinner dish on the table. She nearly jumped as Ibara made a sudden movement, but she managed to hold still as the man grabbed her wrist and held it, his fingers easily encompassing the bone of her wrist.

"Time for that later," he said, and then sniggered, as if somewhat surprised by his own boldness.

Selena looked at Ibara, who was only partially joking, and then at the lieutenant, whose gaze held no mirth at all. Suddenly she realized, deep and cold in her gut, exactly how much danger she was in.

She had been in this guard hut twice before, and both times she had escaped without giving Ibara anything but hints and promises. She had pegged him as stupid, yet having some measure of honor, and so far she had found him easy to manipulate. But now he was drunk, and the burning look in his friend's eyes was both shrewder and more sordid than Ibara's had ever been.

Never play the seduction game, Haberd had told her, unless

you're prepared to lose.

Suppressing a swallow, Selena continued, as if her heart were not thrashing in her chest, as if she were not a status-less Botani maid in the power of two smoldering Huctan soldiers.

"And I also found good wine," she said, raising one eyebrow and giving the small smile she had practiced. The smile was designed for Ibara—shy and submissive with a generous touch of mischief—but she hoped it was a good one for the lieutenant as well.

Neither man responded. Selena used her free hand to withdraw the wine from within her cloak. Focusing her full attention on the bottle—trying to feel enough lust for the drink to draw the two soldiers' attention along with her own—she slid it onto the table. As she released it, she allowed her fingers to accidentally catch on the glass, causing the sanguine liquid within to slosh.

Ibara looked at the wine, but did not remove his hand from Selena's arm.

"As you may have noticed," he said, hooding his eyelids and clearly thinking himself very funny, "I have already had a few drinks, myself."

It would have been very easy, at this point, if Ibara had been alone. Selena would have met his eyes out of the tops of her own and asked if the wine was too much for him, if he couldn't handle a little more. There would have been shyness in her voice, but also a bit of a challenge, and Ibara, as surely as water flows downhill, would have swept the bottle from the table, popped the cork, and drunk deep.

But Ibara was not alone, and Lieutenant Byon was intelligent enough to grow suspicious at such obvious coaxing. Selena now had to say or do something that was both subtle enough to slip under

Byon's guard and obvious enough for Ibara not to miss it completely.

It was difficult.

Selena settled for a demure shrug, and reached for the bottle herself. "Good," she said, again with the smile that she hoped she was not overusing. "More for me."

She lifted the bottle with her free hand, and Ibara instinctively released her wrist so that she could work at the cork. She struggled with it, deliberately. After a moment, Ibara snatched the bottle from her hand, seized the cork in his teeth, and pulled it free with a small pop. Selena noted that his lips had touched the neck of the bottle and knew that she had to hurry.

Taking the wine from Ibara, Selena lifted it to her mouth. Carefully clamping her teeth onto the bottle neck and pursing her lips as close to the glass as she dared, she tilted her head back and took a long drink. Her lips and tongue quivered with the effort of not touching the glass, but she managed to take three swallows before lowering the bottle and giving a breathy sigh of satisfaction. It *was* good wine.

She slid the bottle to the center of the table, not so close to Byon as to be offering it to him, but not so far that he couldn't easily reach it. Then she closed her eyelids as if enjoying the ecstasy of the liquor.

Outwardly she was calm, but inside, down in her toes, she was shaking again. She needed the lieutenant to drink, now, but he was not moving. She could feel his eyes on her even with her own eyes closed. She prepared to praise the wine, to tell them whose special case it had come from, to do *anything* to get the lieutenant to drink.

But Ibara beat her to it.

Snatching up the bottle again, Ibara closed his lips well around the glass and took several long, gulping swallows before slamming the bottle down on the table. Selena noted with dismay that he had left a sheen of saliva on the bottle neck, and that there was a slight set of distaste to Lieutenant Byon's face.

But Ibara's exclamation couldn't have been more perfect.

"Now that," he said, "is *wine*."

Still the lieutenant did not reach for the wine. Still he looked at Selena, eyes burning, only as interested in the wine as it had relationship to her. Selena willed herself to meet the lieutenant's eyes coolly. She twisted her mouth, smiling and pursing her lips in the same motion, and raised her eyebrows a fraction of an inch.

It was a subtle challenge, and it was a gamble. Selena hadn't had time to study the lieutenant, had no idea whether he had the same competitive, not-to-be-bested streak that ran so strongly in Ibara. She had no idea whether a challenge was the right temptation for him. She was flying by instinct.

But tonight she was lucky.

The lieutenant hesitated, then took the bottle from the table. He glanced back at Selena as he lifted the wine, raising his own eyebrows in reply.

Well, why should she be surprised? He and Ibara were both men, weren't they?

Selena sighed inwardly as the lieutenant touched his bottom lip to the glass.

Then Ibara stumbled, and the lieutenant paused.

Too soon, Selena thought, but she kept her face smooth. She forced herself to stop staring at the lieutenant's lips and looked with a sudden grin at Ibara, as if his stumble was simply the effect of too much alcohol. Drink, she willed the lieutenant, even as she covered her mouth and pretended to giggle at Ibara.

But the lieutenant was not drinking. His bottom lip was still touching the bottle, which was good, but Selena wasn't sure that Ibara had left enough oil on the glass to make one lip enough.

Ibara had stumbled again and was on his knees now, feeling for the floor as if looking for a good place to lie down. Lieutenant Byon was looking at Ibara with an expression of amusement that was fast becoming alarm. Selena saw the lieutenant's eyelids droop momentarily as whatever had seeped into his lower lip began to take effect, and then the confusion and alarm on his face turned to sudden realization. His eyes met Selena's.

He knew.

It happened in an instant. The lieutenant stood suddenly, dropped the bottle, and lunged for her.

Selena dropped her shy pose like a mask and sprang up, dancing backward as her chair fell over behind her. The lieutenant followed her, much more quickly than she had expected, and caught her cloak in one fist.

Desperate, knowing exactly how helpless she would be if the larger and stronger man got a good grip on her, Selena twisted. Throwing her arms back and her body forward, she left the cloak in the lieutenant's hands and vaulted over the table.

The lieutenant paused to draw his sword, and she saw him stumble on unsteady feet. Good. At least some of the liquid had gotten into his system.

Selena looked for something to defend herself with, snatched up a chair, and only just deflected the lieutenant's first swing as he came around the table. The steel broke two slats from between the chair legs, and the magnitude of being attacked with a real sword that would really kill her hit Selena like a blow to the stomach. She felt panic trying to rise and struggled against it, trying to remain calm and remember her training as she fled around the table again.

The lieutenant swung a second time. In this small space, there wasn't much Selena could do to dodge him, and only the clumsiness of his hand saved her from a torn shoulder. Desperately, she swung the chair, and though it bounced uselessly off of the lieutenant's armor, it was enough to upset his already weakening balance. He fell, and dropped his sword.

As the lieutenant rolled over, Selena saw a swimming movement of his eyes and knew that the drug was now taking hold. He sat up part way, reached for his sword, and then slumped down again. Rolling onto his side and panting, he looked up at Selena with vicious hate.

Then he opened his mouth to shout.

Selena rushed forward and landed a brutal kick in the Huctan's stomach. As his wind left him, she dropped on his shoulders, picked up her fallen cloak, and shoved the cloth into his gasping mouth.

The lieutenant struggled, but only with the weakening muscles of his neck and a useless flopping of his arms. Selena pressed down hard, clamping cloth over both mouth and nose. The soldier's struggling slowed.

Then, as his body's desire for air momentarily overcame the working of the drug, the lieutenant's resistance grew frantic. Selena held fast, clenching her teeth and shutting her eyes and throwing her full weight on the man's face as he bucked and pushed at her body with arms that had lost their strength.

In a moment the struggling slowed again, and then it stopped.

Selena continued to hold the cloak, breathing heavily through her nose, shaking through her entire body. At last, with a swift, frightened effort, she withdrew her hands and lunged to her feet, dropping the cloth like something unclean.

Straightening, trembling, she saw the blood she had wrung from the Huctan's nose as she pressed his face. She gagged. Swallowing, feeling weak, she took several quick breaths and then several deep ones.

Then, clenching her teeth and swallowing, she nodded to herself once. Putting out the light, she went to the door.

Pausing in the darkness to thumb a tear from her eye, Selena quietly crept into the barracks where the boys were.

CHAPTER 3

Timothy was beaten, and half naked, and still trembled a little when he stood up, but he felt strong. A change had come over him. He wasn't the barefooted woodsboy of a few months ago.

Pushing his body up to a sitting position, he prodded at the bruises. There was no good reason to prod at them—it wasn't as if they would have healed in the last five minutes—but he had never been able to leave his wounds alone. Besides, the pain reminded him of what he had done. For once in his life he was nursing wounds of honor instead of shame and self-loathing.

Soon it would be over. If the girl was to be trusted, they would escape within the week. If she was not to be trusted, Timothy would find a way on his own, and this time they wouldn't be taken alive.

Timothy stood up and went to the door of his cell, and for probably the tenth time that day he felt at the lock and the bars and the crack where the hinges were. After a moment he stood on his toes and put his face to the barred window, trying to get a look at the cell just across the hall from his.

It was infuriating, being so close to Robert and yet so

impenetrably separated. Timothy thought of calling out to Robert again, but decided against it. All his previous attempts had brought nothing but laughter from the boys down the hallway and threats from the guard at the barracks entrance.

Timothy closed his eyes and saw Robert as he had been this morning, limp and ghastly, dangling between four soldiers as he was carried down the hallway. His head, streaked with blood, had been lolled back. His mouth had been open.

Timothy's knuckles went white on the bars at the memory. The rational part of his mind said that it was good, that it was according to plan, that the girl had relayed his message and Robert had been brave enough to see it through. The rest of his mind, and his hands on the bars, said that it was terrible, that Robert might be dead or crippled in that cell, and that it was Timothy's fault.

Both were true. It was good, and it was terrible.

Timothy left the window and returned to the floor of his cell. The stones were hard, and he hissed as he laid his battered skin against them, but he forced his body to be still. After a minute he closed his eyes and tried to get some sleep.

He woke suddenly with the impression that he had heard something. His eyes snapped open in the darkness, but he could see no more with them open than he could with them closed.

He listened, and the noise came again: a metallic scratch from the direction of the door. Quietly Timothy rose to a crouch and crept forward, holding one hand in front of his face to keep from running into a wall. He opened his eyes wide, trying to catch any light he could, but the darkness was heavy.

There was a snap that made him jump. The door moved—he

couldn't see it move, but he felt the draft when it opened—and Timothy scuttled backward.

"Timothy." The word was spoken in a whisper, a tiny breath of air just strong enough to form each syllable.

For a moment Timothy didn't answer. Finally he whispered back. "What?"

"Shh... come on."

It was the girl.

Suddenly Timothy was no longer cold and stiff. He grinned in the darkness. The feeling of strength came back, and an energy that bordered on giddiness shuddered down his rib cage. He felt warm, and alive, and almost free.

The girl had kept her word. His cell door was open. They were escaping.

"I can't see," he said.

"Shh!" the girl repeated. "This way. Slow... it's lighter out here."

Timothy rose. His finger met the door, then a warm hand, and then he was in the hallway.

"Follow me," the girl said, and Timothy followed the shadow of the girl on the balls of his bare feet. They reached Robert's cell almost immediately.

"I already opened it," the girl said, pressing the door and widening the shadow around its edges. Timothy slipped inside and peered into the darkness.

"Robert?" he whispered.

"Hey."

A weight lifted from Timothy's shoulders at the sound of his brother's voice. Robert was alive, and if his voice was hoarse, so had Timothy's been. Timothy recognized the lighter spot in the blackness and knelt beside it.

"Hey," he whispered. "How's it going?"

Robert sniffed a laugh. Timothy grinned again in the darkness, then wrinkled his nose. The smell of vomit was in the air, and the sharp scent of it brought back the memory of his own beating. Coming to consciousness of such pain, all at once, had left him dizzy and heaving as well. All things considered, it was surprising that Robert was still awake. This was good.

Then the girl said something terrible.

"He can't walk," she said.

The soaring, dizzy excitement in Timothy's veins stopped dead and shattered, like an arrow against a rock. Part of him wondered if he had heard correctly, while the muscles in his gut knotted in the terrible certainty that he had.

"What?" he said, a bit too loudly.

"Shh!" the girl said again, and Timothy felt a hot flare of anger. He knelt by Robert, certain that he had done the unthinkable, that his friend was a cripple because of him.

"Can you move at all?" he whispered, feeling for Robert's legs.

"I might be able to, now," Robert said. There was a shuffling noise, and Timothy felt Robert's leg move a small distance. Then there was a catching of breath and a very low moan, and the leg relaxed.

Robert's pain was palpable, but Timothy felt sudden relief. Robert could move. He wasn't crippled. It was just the pain, and hadn't Timothy himself felt that? In a few days, Robert would be fine. The girl would come back. They would try this all again.

But why had she come and unlocked him, tonight, if Robert couldn't walk?

"See?" the girl said. "We have to leave him."

Timothy turned again to face the girl's voice, and a sudden cold rage spread inside him. The girl was trying to manipulate him. She had opened his cell door and gotten him excited about escaping, and now she was showing him Robert, lying here unable to move. She would probably say that this was their chance, that she was sorry, that they had no choice.

She had to have known that Robert had been beaten today. She had to have known that he would need a couple days to recover. Yet she had deliberately chosen tonight.

She had never wanted to bring Robert in the first place.

"I told you," Timothy said, "I am *not leaving without him.* That's the reason he's here in the first place. Take me back to my cell. We'll try again in a couple days."

"We don't *have* a couple days," the girl said, and there was something almost frantic in her voice. "This is it. Tonight. T'shira put up the gallows this afternoon. He's going to make an example of you both in the morning."

All three of them, squatting there in the darkness and the silence, were still and quiet for several long seconds.

She could be lying. Timothy knew that. It would be a terrible thing to do, just to get someone to leave his brother to die. Almost unthinkably terrible. But he didn't know the girl. She could be that kind of person.

But Timothy also knew that she was their only chance of really escaping. Without her, his best plan was making a run for it during a courtyard drill, and even he knew how that plan was likely to end.

Finally Timothy spoke.

"I'll carry him," he said.

"Too dangerous," the girl replied, dismissively, as if she had already considered and discarded this option.

"I'll *carry* him," Timothy repeated, turning away from her and feeling for Robert's body.

"We'll all get caught," the girl said. "I'm sorry... you don't know how sorry I am, but we have to leave him."

"Go for it," Robert whispered, batting Timothy's hand away.

"I'll carry you," Timothy repeated again.

"Hey!" Robert grabbed Timothy's arm and pulled him close. "It's not worth it. They'll just get both of us. At least give me the satisfaction that you got away."

Timothy sniffed a laugh.

"I'm serious," Robert said, in a tone that Timothy hadn't heard from him before. "I'm not going. If you try to carry me, I'll yell and wake everyone up. I swear I will."

Timothy felt the sudden urge to hit something, or to cry. This was not the way he had imagined things. They were supposed to either die together, defiant and proud and strong, or to escape together and look back at the Huctans laughing. He wasn't ready for this possibility, that he would escape and Robert would die. He wasn't ready for Robert to threaten him. He wasn't ready for that deadly serious tone in Robert's voice.

Something came back to him, a memory, as vivid as if it had been yesterday.

"Stop whining," he said. "You're coming. What would I do all day without you?"

Robert's hand continued to grip Timothy's arm for a moment longer. Then it slackened, and Timothy heard Robert sigh. He closed his eyes in relief.

Robert remembered, and he understood.

"I'm going to carry him," Timothy said, his voice stronger.

"We can't..." the girl began.

"He's going to carry me," Robert repeated. Timothy was already groping for Robert's other arm and turning.

"It's fine if you can't help us anymore," Timothy said. "Thanks for unlocking the doors. We'll find our own way out."

"Don't be an idiot," the girl said, and he could hear something between rage and crying in her voice. It suddenly occurred to him that she was as scared and desperate as he was. Possibly more so. He had nothing to lose, but she was risking everything.

Robert heard it too.

"Thank you for helping us," he said, quietly and sincerely. Timothy nodded agreement in the darkness.

The girl sniffed, and then spoke in a very low whisper.

"You're welcome," she said.

There was a moment of silence. Then Robert began trying to pull himself up onto Timothy's shoulders. His attempts were pitiful, as if he could barely lift the weight of his own hands, and Timothy looked for the girl.

"Help him?" he asked. The girl hesitated, then knelt, and Robert was bravely quiet as they pushed and pulled him up to Timothy's shoulders. Timothy could feel the welted pattern of Robert's chest on his back.

He stood, with the girl's help, and felt Robert's weight. Robert wrapped his arms around Timothy's neck, but they were almost limp. His body began slipping, and Timothy's own legs trembled.

"Hold on," Timothy whispered, and then jumped Robert higher up on his shoulders. Robert's teeth clacked together, and a low whine escaped his lips, right by Timothy's ear.

"Sorry," Timothy said.

Robert swallowed, audibly, and then tapped Timothy's arm with a weak hand.

"Giddy up," he whispered.

Timothy grinned in the darkness. They were going to get out of here. They were going to get out together.

The journey down the long hallway of the barracks was excruciating. It took about ten steps to wear down the energy and excitement that had made Robert's weight seem tolerable, and Timothy was soon gripping Robert's legs with trembling arms and trying not to admit to himself that he already needed to rest.

More agonizing than Robert's weight, though, was the thought of the boys. There were scores of cells on either side, each filled with several sleeping Botaños on cots, each separated from the hall by nothing but an iron grating and the darkness. Timothy had spent his nights in such a cell for weeks before his punishment, and he knew well how exposed he was.

He also knew how many of the boys had already turned, and how many would love to gain a fingernail of favor by raising the alarm and preventing an escape.

Robert slipped, gradually, and carrying him grew even more difficult. Timothy desperately needed to bounce Robert's body higher up on his back, but he wasn't sure that Robert could keep quiet if he did.

Six times they froze at noises in the darkness-shrouded cells around them. Each time, after waiting, the girl finally continued, and Timothy, breathing once more, followed. The tension was hot and slick.

Either the light grew steadily better or Timothy's eyes grew more adjusted to the darkness, because when they arrived at the door, Timothy could distinguish the wood from the stone.

The girl put a hand on Timothy's arm and put her lips inches from his ear.

"Quiet," she whispered, so softly that Timothy could not even feel her breath.

He nodded.

The girl crept to the door, lifted the handle, and opened it.

Moonlight cascaded into the blackness. The guardhouse room was filled with the silver light, which poured through the window and overflowed into the hallway.

The girl seemed surprised at the light, and she spun her arm, hurrying Timothy inside and using her body to keep the nearest cell in shadow. Timothy was through the door in three steps.

But it was too late.

"Hey," someone said. The voice was loud and profane in the silence.

Timothy swiveled, already inside the guardhouse, and saw one of the boys with his face to the grate of his cell. He was sleepy, and confused, and squinting in the moonlight, but as the situation dawned on him, his eyes grew wider.

"Take me with you!" the boy whispered, loud enough to wake the dead.

The girl jerked, holding up a hand for silence. She floated to the cell and leaned close to the boy, who was several years younger than Timothy or Robert. She whispered something Timothy could not quite make out.

"Take me *with* you!" the boy repeated, just as loudly. This time someone heard him.

"Berrin, shut up," an older voice said, and even though it only took a second for the girl to dance back through the guardroom door, that second was enough for Timothy to recognize the voice. And for the owner of the voice to see someone escaping.

"Hey," Chuon said aloud. Then, as the girl closed the door, Chuon repeated in a full-throated, all-out shout. "Hey!"

The door snicked shut. They were alone in the guardroom, with only one more door separating them from the open night air.

But Timothy wasn't looking at the outside door, or at the light-filled window. He was looking at the larger of two forms on the floor. It had stirred at the shout in the hallway. It was a soldier.

The Huctan sniffed, and shook his head, but did not open his eyes.

The girl had already bent to pick up one of the swords. As more people in the barracks woke and shouts from within came muffled through the heavy door, she stood over the man on the floor.

"What are you doing?" Robert hissed, as the girl put the tip of the sword to the Huctan's throat. She jerked her head, and glared at Robert, and in the stark lighting her face looked wild. The calm she had had, when she visited Timothy's cell two days ago, was gone. Her hand was trembling.

Timothy looked at the form of the second Huctan on the floor, the one who had not moved a muscle since they came in, and realized the reason for the girl's crazed look. The second Huctan was in no danger of waking up. Ever.

"Don't," Robert said. "Let's just go."

It would be smart to kill the Huctan, Timothy knew. The yelling in the barracks was getting louder. Soon the boys that had turned were going to organize, to find a way to yell together and increase their volume, and the Huctan was going to wake up.

Besides, he deserved it. For all that the Huctans had done, this one deserved whatever came to him.

"Do it," Timothy said.

"Let's just go," Robert repeated.

The girl hesitated a moment longer, and then seemed to come to a decision. She snatched the sword away from the Huctan's throat and marched to the inner door they had just come through. Throwing it open, so that the confused yelling thundered into the room and light spilled into the barracks, she knelt and took hold of the soldier's ankles.

He was stirring again, turning his head as if trying to wake up. The girl gave a mighty pull at his ankles, and he slid several feet across the floor. Still he did not wake. She pulled again, twice more, and the Huctan slid through the door and into the barracks. Timothy could hear Chuon yelling at the top of his lungs for the soldier to wake up.

Chuon was the one who deserved a sword.

The dragging and shouting was beginning to bring the Huctan to full consciousness. His eyes fluttered, and his left hand moved.

The girl paused to fling something skittering down the hallway—the keys, Timothy realized—and then leapt back through the door. Slamming it shut, she threw the bolt and leaned against it, panting.

That was smart. Someone was going to figure out a way to get those keys. There was going to be a riot.

The girl ran across the room to the outer door and opened it a crack. Timothy could hear, soft and muffled in the night air, the same noise that was coming through the barracks door. It was muted, but clearly audible.

Then a Huctan voice split the night air, calling down to the guardhouse door. The language was Huctan, but apparently the girl understood it. Drawing herself up and cocking her head strangely, she shouted back.

Robert jerked on Timothy's back at the sound of her voice. It was loud, and deep, and if Timothy hadn't seen her mouth moving with the syllables, he would never have guessed that the bellowing, masculine, Huctan shout had come from the lips of a young Botani girl.

"What did you say?" Timothy hissed, but the girl shook her head and darted back across the room. Snatching the two crimson cloaks from their hooks on the wall, she threw one over Robert and Timothy and wrapped the other around herself.

"I told him I was handling it, but I had to take the Lieutenant across to the infirmary," she said.

"What?"

"Stick to the shadows on the right side, and follow me. Run!"

Timothy ran.

It had been raining in the courtyard, and the air still had a wet smell to it. The moon was almost full, shining through a break in the clouds. The night air was warm and still, as if the clouds were wrapping the night in a blanket.

Timothy caught this in a glance as he left the guardhouse. Then he lowered his head and saw nothing but the girl's feet. Desperation gave him strength as the Huctan above yelled again from the outer ramparts. He crossed the courtyard at an awkward gallop, expecting any moment to hear the twang of a crossbow.

But he did not feel a quarrel in his back, and they made it safely across the open courtyard. They entered a small side-door to the main fort, and a short flight of stairs robbed him of his wind.

The girl glided ahead of them, now vanishing from sight in the darkness, now reappearing as they rounded a corner. Timothy hiked Robert farther up on his back again, and this time Robert let out a small cry. As Timothy began panting audibly, Robert started making small, whimpering noises between breaths.

They came to another flight of stairs, and Timothy had to close his eyes and hold his breath to gain the last few steps. His eyes would not focus. He staggered as he reached the top of the stairs and had to release one of Robert's legs to catch himself against the wall. Robert slipped, and the change in his weight pulled Timothy down. Timothy sank to his knees, and Robert slid from his back.

The girl crouched beside them, peering about and throwing nervous glances at them both. Timothy was in the midst of a heaving gasp when she turned sharply and threw up a warning hand.

Timothy tried to hold his breath and could not. He breathed slowly, trembling for more air, and listened.

There was shouting, outside, barely audible through the thick stone walls of the keep. The girl listened, as if she could understand the Huctan, and then looked despairingly at the boys slumped on the floor.

"They're sounding the alarm," she said. "We have to go."

Timothy shook his head that he could not, but got to his knees anyway. The girl knelt and grabbed Robert under the arms, straining to lift him high enough to wrap his flopping arms around Timothy's neck. When Timothy couldn't get up from his knees, she got under his arm and pushed until he was standing.

Timothy took several quick breaths, gritted his teeth, and hiked Robert up once more. Robert let out another whimper.

"Maybe thirty yards through the hallway, then a ladder, and we'll be on the battlements," the girl said.

"A ladder?" Timothy gasped.

"Shh... yes. Come on!"

Timothy went, as if in a dream, sure at each step that he was going to collapse. He followed the unfocused shadow of the girl through the dark stone passageway. Through the haze of his pounding pulse, he could hear shouting and the peals of the alarm bell, but the sounds seemed irrelevant. The important thing was the next step, the next step, and then the ladder.

The girl opened the door to a small room. Moonlight shone through a hole in the ceiling. The open sky was only ten feet up.

But opening the door let the full volume of the alarm bell directly into the hallway, and as she shut it again behind them, Timothy heard shouts in the hallway they had come from.

"The ladder comes out next to a short wall," the girl said. "When you get up, get into the shadow as quick as you can. I'll come behind and try to help with Robert."

Timothy had not paused to listen, was already putting foot and hand to the ladder rungs and setting his teeth to climb. His resolution and momentum carried him upward for three rungs, and for a moment he thought he would make it.

Then, on the fourth rung, his knee buckled. His right hand slipped, and he nearly fell to the floor.

"Push!" the girl hissed, and Timothy felt her underneath him. Robert's weight lessened as she threw her shoulder into helping them, and Timothy set his jaw and pulled again. Slowly he rose, air escaping his lips in a hiss. His thigh trembled with the effort. With a heave and a jerk, Timothy got his foot on the next rung and planted, gasping.

"Again!" the girl said, and Timothy strained, baring his teeth and shaking. He pulled as hard as he could, rose four inches, and could rise no farther.

Voices sounded close, in the hallway, and the girl scampered down the ladder to lock the door. Timothy dropped the four inches he had risen and barely stopped himself from falling further.

The girl reached the lock and threw it just before someone tried the door handle, rattled it, and then began shouting something in Huctan. There was a pounding at the door, and the hinges shook.

They were going to get through. They were going to get through, and Timothy could not lift himself one more rung.

"Let me go," Robert whispered.

CHAPTER 4

"Don't you *dare*," Timothy said, as Robert loosened his hold on Timothy's neck and made as if to fall down. Trembling with the effort of holding himself up, Timothy tried to pin Robert against the stone of the ladder shaft. "Don't you dare."

"Don't be stupid," Robert said.

"If you slide down," Timothy rasped, "I'm coming down to pick you up again. I swear I am."

Robert sighed, as if Timothy was dooming them both to death, but he stopped trying to wriggle himself free. There was more yelling in the hallway, more banging at the small door. The girl shouted something in Huctan, again in the deep, masculine voice, and then she was slamming upward with her shoulder and Timothy was pulling and pushing and wondering through the haze whether this was all really worth it.

They made another rung, and Timothy's head was almost in the open. The girl groaned in exertion, pushing at Robert, and Timothy held still as Robert got his arms and chest onto the stone floor above. With a last effort, Timothy thrust his shoulder upward, and

Robert rolled out of the ladder shaft.

The girl then threw her shoulder against Timothy, helping him upward, and he crawled into the night air like a wretched animal from its hole. Feeling dizzy, breathing as if he had been drowning, Timothy squinted through the sweat-tears.

They were sitting by an arched stone bridge that spanned the distance between the fort and the outer ramparts. They were on the fort side of the bridge, some thirty feet away from the wall and the river. Timothy could hear the water.

He could also hear booted feet and Huctan shouting all along the wall to their left.

"Too close," the girl muttered, raising her head just enough to peak over the low stone railing of the bridge. "Get ready."

"Can't... we wait a little longer?" Robert gasped, but the girl dropped suddenly and shushed him frantically, pushing them both down into the shadow.

Boots sounded close on the ramparts, and Timothy closed his eyes, trying to still the heaving of his chest and shrink his body into the stone of the wall. There was nothing to hide behind but the shadows. If the soldiers turned and looked hard, the three of them would be found.

But the soldiers ran past the bridge without pausing. The girl stood up enough to peek over the stone handrail again, then dropped down.

"Let's go," she hissed. "Everything you've got... you're almost free."

Timothy turned his back for Robert to climb up again, but the girl indicated that she could help. Between them they got Robert up, suspended with one arm around each of their necks. Then, together, they ran across the bridge.

The girl shrugged out from under Robert as they reached the wall, withdrawing a rope from her belt and wedging what looked like a hay-hook into the corner of the stone. With a wide sweep of her arm she threw the rope over the edge, and before it had finished falling she was back with Timothy and Robert, pushing and helping them towards the rope.

"Here," she whispered, "Slide down. There's water, thirty feet down, and a boat to the right... go!"

"I can't hold us both..." Timothy said.

"I can lower myself," Robert said.

Timothy doubted this, but he didn't hesitate. Turning, he heaved Robert up onto the wall top. The girl helped him over the edge, and without looking down, Robert began to slide.

"Quick!" the girl said, shooing Timothy after Robert. Timothy climbed up onto the stone, took the rope in his quivering hands, and with an effort allowed himself to slide over the wall.

The rope burned. He tried to squeeze harder to slow his descent, and for a moment he succeeded. Then the rope caught and the skin on one hand tore. He began to slip, and barely caught himself with bare feet and hooked arms. He heard a splash below as Robert fell, and managed to slide painfully for another ten feet before plummeting to the water himself.

The water was icy cold, and Timothy's breath, already short, left him completely. His bare feet struck mud at the bottom, and he fought for the surface in panic. When he broke into the air, the Huctan shouting was closer and the sound of boots on the wall was coming from both directions. Someone grabbed his shoulder, and he jerked before he realized that it was Robert.

Shivering, the two of them held the bottom of the rope against the sweep of the current.

Above them, the girl was sliding down the rope without a sound. She entered the water silently just as two silhouettes appeared above.

Something was said in Huctan that Timothy could not understand. The girl held her finger to her lips, then suddenly released the rope, motioning for them to do the same. They obeyed and began floating down the river in the shadow of the fortress wall.

Timothy still couldn't find his breath.

The rope jerked upwards, and the voices above rose to shouts that Timothy did not need to understand.

"There's a boat," the girl whispered. "Swim!" She shot out before them, smooth and silent in the water. Robert and Timothy struggled to follow her.

There was another shout above. More soldiers had joined the two above, and they were arguing. A twang that sounded like a crossbow was followed by a hissing splash in the water.

Timothy saw the boat now, tied next to the drawbridge. The girl was climbing in. Robert was struggling to swim. Timothy was struggling to keep them both afloat.

He was so tired.

More shouts from above: more soldiers. The girl was reaching out a hand to Timothy. He gave her Robert's hand instead, pushing as much as he could from the water. The boat nearly capsized.

The girl offered her hand again, hissing for him to hurry. Timothy stared at the hand a moment, shivering and feeling foggy. The girl hissed, waved, slapped Timothy's face. He took the hand. The girl pulled, and with a heave Timothy managed to roll into the boat.

He lay on his back. Splinters prickled. The girl was cutting a rope. The wall and stars and flaring torches began slowly drifting.

Robert was next to him, his half-naked body glistening wet in the moonlight. Hisses in the water around them were followed by a loud snap, which the back of Timothy's mind identified as a quarrel piercing the boat's edge. The girl was ducking and cursing.

But somehow Timothy couldn't bring himself to worry, just then. His eyes closed, and before the sounds of Huctan voices had completely faded from hearing, he fell asleep.

When he opened his eyes, the stars were blurred. He squeezed his eyes shut again and blinked twice, then used the back of his wrist to rub out the sleep. The stars came into focus. The night was clear.

His back hurt. Groaning a little, Timothy sat up and scooted over to lean against the boat side. The girl was sitting on the rowing bench across from him, looking out over the water. She turned, as he stirred, and raised her fingers in greeting without lifting her hand from her thigh. Timothy nodded back.

Robert was lying in the other side of the boat. The Huctan cloak the girl had stolen was draped over his body. His mouth was half open, and with the bruises and the slack expression on his face, he was almost unrecognizable.

Timothy shivered and hugged his knees, wondering where he and Robert had dropped *their* Huctan cloak. His pants were still damp, and the breeze was cold on his bare arms. Clouds were covering and uncovering the moon. It was starting to drizzle.

"Sorry," the girl said, "I meant to bring clothes and supplies, but I ran out of time."

Timothy looked at her and shrugged.

"No," he said. "You saved us. Thank you."

He noticed that the girl was not shivering, and that her clothes were also damp. With an effort he stilled himself.

"How... long have we been floating?" he asked.

"A couple hours."

"Are they coming after us?"

The girl shrugged. "Probably. The river's pretty fast, though."

There was an awkward silence. Timothy felt some of the old awkwardness, the throat constriction that had not bothered him since being captured by the Huctans, come back. Thinking of nothing to say, he pretended a casual disinterest and looked out over the water. It was too dark to see anything of the shore but the silhouettes of the low bushes.

Finally he asked her name.

"Selena," she said.

A Botani name. There was a lot that was strange about this girl. When she had offered to help him escape, he had been reckless and desperate. He'd discussed plans with her without believing that anything would come of them. He'd even made demands, insisting that Robert come with them. Only after she'd left his cell with a message for Robert had he started wondering why an obviously Botani scullery maid was working for the Huctans, or why she would want to help him.

Until earlier this morning, when Timothy had seen the soldiers carrying Robert, it hadn't seemed real. When the girl had come and picked the lock on his cell door, things had begun happening quickly. He hadn't had time to wonder how this girl could impersonate a Huctan or put guards to sleep or shimmy down ropes.

Or kill Huctan soldiers.

The memory of the soldier the girl had not bothered to lock in the barracks flooded back to Timothy all at once, and he turned sharply from surveying the darkness.

"Good job carrying Robert," she said. "I didn't think you were going to make it."

"Oh," said Timothy. He looked down at his hands and shrugged again.

"Are you two brothers?" she asked.

Timothy sniffed a laugh.

"What?" she asked.

Timothy shrugged again. "Do we look alike?"

"No. Just something about the way you talk or something. Just good friends, then?"

Timothy shrugged, and looked out at the water again.

"We were raised together," he said. "We're brothers."

Selena paused. "I see," she said.

They were quiet for a while. The girl cleared her throat. Timothy tried to think of how to ask her who she really was, but before he'd quite decided, she spoke again.

"I was surprised you convinced Robert to let you carry him."

Timothy looked at Robert, and remembered how the girl had tried to manipulate him into leaving Robert behind. It was hard to be angry with her, now that they had gotten out, but he still frowned.

"Yeah," he said.

"What was that you said to him?"

Timothy looked up. Raised an eyebrow.

"Something about having nothing to do all day," Selena said.

"Oh," Timothy said. "Just... something he said to me earlier."

Selena bit her lip and looked at him. Timothy realized that it sounded like some big secret he was trying to keep, laughed at himself, and shrugged. He opened his mouth to explain, but could not think of a way that would make it sound anything but stupid.

"Some things are between brothers," Selena said finally.

Timothy shrugged again.

Selena opened her mouth again to say something else, but before she could speak, Timothy spit out the question he'd been trying to ask.

"So who are *you*?" he asked.

The girl cocked her head at him. "Selena," she said, as if he had just asked her name again, and as if he were being a little rude by interrupting. "How did they capture you?"

"Just grabbed us," he said. "I mean, I know your name, but who *are* you?"

"Just grabbed you?"

"Yes. There was a festival. I think they were waiting at the gates for anyone our age to try leaving." Timothy realized suddenly what the girl was doing, and decided to be more blunt.

"Are you a spy?" he asked.

The girl gave him a quizzical look. Timothy tried not to look away, tried to hold her eyes for an answer, and she laughed.

"Right now," she said, looking out over the water, "I'm a scullery maid on the run from the Huctans with a couple of half-naked boys. Which reminds me, we're going to have to get you two some clothes as soon as we get to town."

"But you used to be a spy," Timothy said, trying not to let her be slippery. "And what town?"

"Dellin," she said. "I have a friend there that can get you some clothes and hide us until they stop looking."

"A spy-friend?" he asked.

She gave him that look again, and again he had the feeling that he was being insufferably rude. He almost fell for it, almost dismissed his own question, but with an effort he endured the awkward silence and let the question stand.

Selena ignored it for a moment. He was about to press her when she seemed to come to a decision.

"We've got to trust each other," she said.

Timothy nodded.

Selena chewed on her lip, and looked out over the water. Timothy got the distinct feeling that there was a lot she *could* tell him, but that she was deciding at that moment to tell him very little. He was not mistaken.

"Listen," she said. "I can't tell you much."

"OK," Timothy said.

"Actually I can't really tell you anything, except that... that I'm against the Huctans." It seemed to take an effort for her to say this, and she clamped her mouth shut and looked at him as if daring him to try to pry more out of her.

"OK..." Timothy said slowly. "I had... kind of figured that part out. When you helped us escape, and killed that soldier..."

The girl jerked, when he mentioned killing the soldier, but she said nothing, only looked at Timothy with her lips clamped between her teeth.

"Are there more of you?" Timothy asked.

The girl hesitated, moved her eyes as if she were about to nod, and then froze and continued glaring at Timothy. It was as good as a yes, and Timothy pursed his lips. For several seconds he wondered how to ask more, but could not bring himself to be rude enough to press her.

Finally he settled for acting disinterested again. He looked out at the silhouettes of the scrubby little trees crowding the river's edge and pretended that it made no difference to him whether this girl was part of what sounded like a resistance. He tried, in the silence, to act as though the thought of someone fighting back didn't make his pulse grow pointed, as if he hadn't been dreaming about it ever since he could remember.

Don't get your hopes up, he told himself. Yet he did hope, so hard that he didn't have room to worry about the pursuit or their lack of clothes or Robert's condition. If there were people trying to fight the Huctans—people actually trying to *do* something—the only thing that mattered to Timothy was finding those people and becoming one of them.

Someone shook him awake, and he gasped. A finger touched his lips, and he opened his eyes to see the girl crouching right in front of him, her face inches from his. When she saw that he wasn't going to speak, she took her finger from his lips and leaned close to his ear.

"You were snoring," she said. "Be very quiet. There are horses."

It was a testament to how tired Timothy was that he spent several seconds thinking how nice it was to have a beautiful girl whispering in his ear before the meaning of her words sank in. When they finally did—'There are horses', she had said—he sat up very quietly and looked at the shore.

The girl pointed. They both listened.

A twig snapped, and Timothy's head swiveled to face the spot the noise had come from. Suddenly the sound of hooves in soft loam distinguished itself from the rustling of the trees. The sound of several horses, trotting, punctuated by the low rhythm of clinking chain mail.

Timothy strained in the darkness to see the soldiers. The trotting grew louder, then faded as it passed them. Soon Timothy realized that he was not hearing actual hoof beats anymore and leaned back into the boat with a slow exhalation.

Selena was getting the oars out of the bottom of the boat. Thrusting one into Timothy's hand, she began sliding the other into the oarlock.

"What're you doing?" Timothy whispered.

"There's a bridge ahead," she replied. "We have to get past it before they get to it."

Timothy hobbled to the other side of the boat and fumbled with his own oar.

"Won't they hear us?" he whispered back.

"I don't think the road comes that close to the water again. Not for a while. Not until the bridge. Anyway, it'd be better for them to hear us out here in the dark than to catch us under the bridge."

"OK," Timothy said.

After a minute of splashing and spinning, they managed to get a rhythm between them. The water was frustratingly still, and their oars were loud in the darkness. Timothy's feeling of strength was almost completely gone now, but he wasn't afraid. They had made it this far, and they weren't going to be caught again.

"Can't we just pull to shore and hide?" he asked between strokes. The girl shook her head.

"If we can get past the bridge, we'll be safer. They'll have dogs out tomorrow, and if Robert can't run..."

She said the last with an accusing tone, as if to imply that things would have been better, easier, if Timothy hadn't insisted on bringing Robert. Some of the old anger came back, and Timothy thought of saying something. But he was exhausted, and breathing heavily already from the rowing. He decided to save his breath.

A long while later, Selena stopped suddenly, holding out a hand to stay Timothy. Quivering and sweating, he held his oar up out of the water and tried to quiet his breathing.

They listened.

There were voices on the north bank. Selena twisted in her seat, and Timothy followed her gaze to see the silhouette of the bridge. Horsemen stood at one end, dark against the moon. They were talking, in Huctan.

"They just got here," Selena breathed.

Hooves on wood punctured the blanket of stillness covering the night, and Timothy watched the outline of a horseman riding up the long arch of the bridge. The hooves slowed and came to a halt over the center of the water.

Timothy looked at the moon. It was low on the horizon, behind the horseman and the bridge, casting a long shadow over the water. The boat was in that shadow now, which was the only reason the horseman hadn't seen them. When the boat reached the edge of the shadow—and the light shining under the bridge—they would be in clear view and exposed some fifteen feet below a Huctan who almost certainly had a crossbow.

"Hold my oar," Selena whispered. Timothy reached out and took the end. Selena pushed down on his hand, making sure he had the oar tilted well out of the water, and then wriggled out from under it. She knelt, for a moment, in the bottom of the boat next to Robert's sleeping form.

"What are you doing?" Timothy whispered back, but she was too far to hear and he dared not whisper louder. He tried to turn his head to see how close they were to the bridge, but in doing so he almost dipped one of the oars to splash in the water. Grimly he concentrated on holding the oars and sat with his back to the danger, floating nearer with every passing second.

Selena straightened to her knees, looked behind Timothy, looked over to the shore, and gauged the shadow. She held something in her hand.

Orange light flared to the left. The soldiers had lit torches. One of them said something in Huctan. Hooves clattered on the bridge, which sounded much closer. Timothy could see the edge of the shadow in his periphery now. He chewed his lips and tingled.

The girl poised herself to throw whatever was in her hand, then waited. They floated. The hooves on the bridge grew louder. The voices were very close.

Suddenly Selena leaned back and hurled whatever she held. It was lost in the darkness immediately, and for a moment there was no sound.

Then there was a splash, loud and near the northern shore.

The Huctan voices stopped dead, and then, suddenly, the sound of hooves was like thunder on the planks above. A second later the moonlight washed over the boat, and Timothy looked up to see a soldier leaning over the bridge rail not fifteen feet above them. His face was turned toward the shore and the splash.

Slowly, agonizingly, the boat drifted through the light and under the bridge. Timothy was close enough to see the moonlight glistening on the whites of the soldier's eyes. He held his breath.

Selena raised a finger to her lips and made a motion. Timothy held her oar steady while she stepped up onto the bench and then slid her legs beneath the oar to sit. Leaning close to his ear again, she whispered.

"We only row if I say," she said.

Timothy nodded.

The river gently pushed them out from under the bridge. They were in full moonlight now, exposed and obvious to anyone who looked out over the water. Torches were shining, garish and orange on the left bank, and shouts Timothy did not understand were echoing over the water.

They floated, and Timothy cursed the river for its slowness. He could see the horseman in the center of the bridge, now, facing out over the way they'd come. The moonlight shone on his back, and Timothy could distinguish the crimson of the soldier's cloak from the silver of his mail.

All it would take was a backwards glance.

But the soldier did not glance back, and they continued to drift. Slowly, like a leaf before a breeze on a still lake, the boat passed away from the bridge. The soldier and the torches receded into darkness. Timothy found himself shaking, and realized that he was alternately shivering and chuckling.

He looked at the girl. She was smiling.

"It's better this way," she said, as they quietly slid the oars back into the boat's hull.

"What way?"

"That they didn't see us."

Timothy sniffed a laugh.

"No, I mean, obviously, it's better that they didn't see us, but we probably could have made it under even if we'd just rowed. It's harder to hit a moving target than you'd think. But this way they won't be following us down the river. With any luck, they'll spend a week patrolling the shores and watching the bridge before they realize we got through."

Timothy nodded.

"That was close," he said after a minute.

"Yeah."

"What was that you threw?"

Selena giggled, a sound that Timothy had not heard in a long time. A sound that reminded him of Fenae.

"What?" he asked.

"A potato," she said. "I guess we'll have to share the other two."

Timothy slept until the morning and woke feeling significantly stiffer and significantly more free. Robert woke as well, and managed to sit himself up in the hull of the boat without help. He laughed as Timothy told him about the bridge and the potato, laughed loud, and despite the bruises and the chill that was beginning to get to him, Timothy thought he had never felt better in his life.

They were free. He had been caught by Huctans, failed two escape attempts, been beaten and hung by his ankles overnight, attacked a Huctan soldier, been beaten and sentenced to death... and now he was laughing in a boat on the open water with his old friend and a pretty girl who was "against the Huctans". It was late spring, and blossoms were turning to bursts of green on the low scrub willows at the water's edge. Everything was beautiful and alive and full of color.

Raw potatoes for breakfast dampened his mood a little, but soon the taste of the cold starch faded and they were passing the morning telling Selena about their childhood. Robert did most of the telling—he always did—but Timothy's silence wasn't awkward, and he found himself nodding and smiling and offering the occasional reminder. "Tell her how the farmer caught us rolling rocks down into his squash plants," he said. "Tell her how you cried when lightning struck that old tree we used to climb in." "You didn't mention that *I* knew nothing about it..."

The sun slowly heated the air, and by midday their clothes were nearly dry and it was warm enough to swim. While Selena slept, Timothy undressed and slipped into the water to float alongside the boat. The water was cold, but it felt good to not be sitting on hard wood.

Robert leaned over the side of the boat, resting his discolored arms on the wooden edge.

"Your face is hideous," Timothy said.

Robert feigned concern and looked down into the water to catch his reflection. He brought a hand to his face and touched the purple knot on his right cheekbone.

"Oh, I don't know," he said. "I think it looks pretty nice."

"You're right," Timothy said. "Yes. It does. You should try it more often."

"You think so?"

"I do. And I'm always available, if you need someone to give you a good punch in the eye."

"Thanks," Robert said. "I can always count on you."

"What'd you do, anyway? You were supposed to get just a little beaten, not disabled."

"Well," Robert said, "I didn't want to have to go to all the work of running away myself. I figured you could probably use the exercise, and I could use the sleep."

"So what'd you do?"

"Oh, you know. Told a soldier what I thought of his mother. That got him to hit me once. Then I told him what his mother thought of me, loud enough for everyone to hear. That just about did it."

"Subtle," Timothy said.

"I bet old T'shira is a little cranky this morning," said Robert.

Timothy smirked. T'shira had commanded the kidnapping party that swept through the northern villages of Botan. He had only been a few years older than Timothy and Robert, but he had been cold and arrogant and cruel. He had taken command of Northelm on their arrival. It was he that had hung them from their ankles after their second escape attempt, and probably he that had issued their death sentence. The thought of his pale, smug face going gray when he heard that they'd made a clean escape brought joy to Timothy's heart.

For a while they were silent. Floating there, in the warm sun with the cold water and Robert leaning against the boat side, it was almost like the happy days of summers past. Timothy had been content then, and ignorant. The Huctans had been a distant and unfamiliar evil. Fenae had still been alive.

"I was just thinking," Robert said.

"Mm-hm?'

"About a couple summers ago, when Dad let us go up to the lake for a couple days, and we were so excited that we got to go by ourselves. And we made that raft, remember?"

Timothy smiled, realizing that they had been thinking of the same thing, and looked at the shade at the edge of the water. "Yeah," he said. "That was a good time."

They were quiet for a while. The water lapped at the boat and at Timothy's shoulders. The trees, which were thicker now and spread up the banks for some distance away from the river, passed slowly by. Timothy got cold and climbed back into the boat. In a minute he had his mostly-dry-now pants back on and the warm sun was making the water droplets run in streams down his chest.

"So," Robert said, a little more quietly. Timothy opened his eyes and climbed over the bench to sit closer to Robert. They eyed Selena where she lay. Her chest was rising and falling slowly.

"So," Robert repeated. "Who is this girl?"

Timothy shook his head and gave a 'beats me' expression.

"She says her name's Selena," he said. "She was some kind of scullery maid at the fort.

"So she's some kind of spy?"

"I guess. I asked her about it last night. She said she couldn't tell us anything except that she was 'against the Huctans'. When I asked her whether there were more of them, she didn't say anything, but you could tell that the answer was yes.

"So where are we going?" Robert asked.

"Dellin, she said. She has a friend there that can give us clothes and hide us until they stop looking for us."

Robert frowned and leaned back. Timothy watched him, and

realized suddenly that Robert was not as excited about all this as he was.

This realization hurt, more deeply than he would have imagined.

It was cloudy and cold that night, and Timothy shared the cloak with Robert. Without the weight of weariness, the rocking, splintery hull of the boat was not as comfortable on his bare back as it had felt on that first night of utter exhaustion. He woke up in the morning badly sunburnt, and spent half of the next day trying to hide in the shade of the boat's short sides. Robert was able to stand up a little, and spent some time stretching and trying to massage out the kinks in his muscles. If Timothy's experience with his own injuries was any indicator, Robert would be able to walk tomorrow.

The boredom grew worse. Timothy picked threads from the hem of his pants and managed to piece together some ten feet of fishing line. Selena let him use her belt knife to carve a piece of wood from the boat edge into a double-pointed sort of hook.

If there were any fish in the river, they had no appetite for the soggy square of potato Timothy used as bait. After a couple of hours Selena noted that they wouldn't be able to cook a fish anyway, and Timothy broke the string into several short pieces and put them very gently into the river. It was a little tense in the boat for a while after.

Just as it was getting dark, they passed a ford shallow enough to scrape the bottom of the boat. Selena said they were as close to Dellin as the river went. After arguing for a minute about whether it was safer to sleep in the boat or in the forest, they decided to go ashore, drop Robert off, and then try to sink the boat somewhere in the middle of the river.

Robert managed to climb out of the boat and hobble over to a rock by himself. Timothy and Selena rowed back out towards the middle, then jumped out of the boat and pulled down on one side. After several minutes of hissing at each other and shivering, Timothy climbed up on one side of the boat and sat on it while Selena swam around and pushed from the other side. The boat capsized with a smack like a beaver's tail, and after some more pulling and climbing they managed to start it sinking to the muddy bottom of the river.

Timothy was tired and sullen by the time they had reached the shore and trudged back upstream to join Robert. His pants were wet again, and the night was chilly, and Selena had insisted they sink the crimson Huctan cloak with the boat. She made them hike several hundred yards away from the river before bedding down, and while Timothy knew it was the smart thing to do, he was too tired to be rational. He just wanted to sleep.

Robert made it, with Timothy's help, and at last they found a sort of hollow in a stand of willows that ran up a gully from the river. Timothy bedded down and spent the night tossing and turning in wet pants and the constant itch of sunburn.

But he dreamt of a resistance that sent out girls like Selena. Girls who could speak Huctan and pick locks and rescue prisoners.

And kill soldiers.

CHAPTER 5

SELENA

The Huctans came over the north wall. Clothed in darkness, they threw padded hooks over the ramparts and ascended on soft ropes. The sentries of the north wall did not stop them; they were already dead, slain at their posts, warm blood still seeping from their backs.

The Huctans swept the west wall, and many of Botan's soldiers died in silence. Then one brave sentry chose to spend the last seconds of his life reaching for his horn instead of his sword, and he sounded the alarm for two long seconds before the Huctans cut him down.

If there was ever a crucial moment in that battle, it was then. Answering horns rang throughout the city. The mass of the Huctan army, now thundering down the Great Road, was still a thousand yards distant. The Huctans on the ramparts threw themselves at the gatekeepers, but the gatekeepers gave ground slowly and dearly.

If the gatehouse had held for ten seconds longer, or if reinforcements from the other walls had run ten seconds faster, or if the Huctan cavalry had been ten seconds slower, the assault would

have shattered on the barred gates of the city. Eoriden would have stood. Botan would not have been lost.

Selena let the boys sleep. They were starting to get over the shock of escaping and the sense of danger, and if she pushed them too hard they were going to start pushing back.

The leaves were itchy, but she made herself be still and wait as light started filtering through the forest of willow saplings surrounding them. The first boy, Timothy, stirred not long after she'd woken. Selena heard him sit up, lay back down, then stand suddenly and loudly, brushing the leaves and dirt off and tramping out of the hollow to sit on a rock. She slitted her eyes and saw him hugging his chest and looking towards the sun.

"Stop being such a pansy," Robert mumbled. Selena realized he was talking to Timothy, who immediately stopped shivering and sniffed a laugh.

"Not everyone gets to be all crippled and warm under the driest leaves," he said.

"You want to come cuddle?"

"I'd rather die."

The two of them were quiet for a while. Finally Robert groaned a little and stirred. The leaves crackled around him, and with a grunt he got up. His footsteps were heavy and a little irregular, but he seemed to have no trouble joining Timothy on the rock. That was good. They would have to walk several miles today, and she had been worried that they could not carry him.

Selena felt a sudden surge of guilt for thinking of Robert this way. If she had had her way, they would have left him behind. He would be dead. Was she so cold, so calculating, that even now that they had escaped she was watching his steps, analyzing his ability to keep up, looking at him as a liability rather than a person?

"So we're going to Dellin today," Robert said to Timothy.

"Guess so," Timothy replied.

Both of the boys were still speaking in the kind of low, slurred voices people use when they don't want to wake someone.

"So, what are we going to do?" Robert said.

There was a brief pause.

"Get some clothes first, I guess."

"They're just going to give us clothes and hide us and then let us go?"

Selena imagined Timothy shrugging. There was silence again.

"I wonder," Timothy said after a while. He hesitated, then continued very carefully. "I wonder if they would let us join them."

Robert sniffed, and Selena could see Timothy deflate without needing to slit her eyes at all.

"Not me," Robert said. "I'm going home."

There was a shifting noise: pants on wood. A series of small snaps: a stick being broken by nervous hands.

"You don't want to join," Timothy said.

"Join what?" The edge in Robert's voice contrasted sharply with Timothy's flat, careful tone. "We don't have any idea what they are."

"They're against the Huctans," Timothy said.

"Whatever that means."

Selena hadn't known the boys long, but she knew enough to feel that they had rarely, if ever, spoken to one another like this. The unfamiliarity was palpable.

"Doesn't it bother you at all?" Timothy said. There was an edge to his voice, now.

"What?"

"The Huctans. What they do."

"What do you mean 'does it bother me at all'?" There was no guard on Robert's voice now. It was flat and cold and angry. "Does it bother *you* that Selena was about to kill a person in cold blood?"

A pause. Selena felt a surge of guilt again, and it was not lessened by the knowledge that Timothy, at least, had noticed Lieutenant Byon.

"It wasn't cold blood," Timothy said.

"She was about to *kill* him. Kill. Him."

"We'd be dead if he had woken up."

"I forgot," Robert said, with sudden venom. "*You* told her to go ahead and do it."

There was a rustle, and a very long pause. Selena found herself feeling very uncomfortable. They must have fought before—how could two people live in the same house and not fight?—but she doubted that they had ever fought like this. This wasn't about who was shirking their chores or using the other's things. This was about principles and dreams.

"I miss Dad. And Mom," Robert said finally. Selena did not miss the implication, and neither did Timothy.

"You think I don't miss them?" he said, and the flatness was gone from his voice. "You think I wouldn't rather go home and sleep in a nice bed and pretend nothing's happening?"

"No," Robert said. "You wouldn't. You'd rather kill you some Huctans."

Selena decided it was time to wake up. She stirred.

"Morning, sunshine," Robert said, a bit too loudly. The sound of Timothy's teeth clacking shut was loud.

Selena yawned, rubbed her eyes, and sat up. The boys were sitting side by side, arms folded, looking at her. Timothy had very little expression on his face. Robert was overly cheerful. She pretended not to notice.

"Who's hungry?" she said, and laughed out loud at the way they both perked up. They hadn't eaten anything for almost two days. No one had complained yet—she thought it was some sort of contest between the two of them to see who would crack first—but they were all very hungry. Selena was starting to feel faint at times. No doubt the boys were doing worse on their bruises and prison-rations.

"Berness makes the best biscuits," she said. "I'm hoping we can get there in time for lunch."

"Berness," Robert said, a little aggressively. "Is that your friend in Dellin?"

"Yep," Selena said, again pretending not to notice the palpable tension in the air. She gave a little groan as she stood up, yawned, and began stretching.

"There's a road where we crossed that ford," she said. "It goes straight to Dellin. We can't walk on the road, in case they're looking for you, but there are trees and bushes alongside most of it. We can follow those. We should be able to duck down and hide if we need to."

"How far is it?" Robert asked.

"About three miles," she answered.

Those three miles took all morning. Robert calmed down a little, and there was a period of about ten minutes when he and Selena talked easily about blacksmithing and horses. Then he began puffing and fell silent to concentrate on walking. Timothy spoke very little.

By midmorning the hunger and weariness were starting to get to them. They complained, snapped at each other for complaining, and wondered aloud why the day had to be so hot and why there had to be so many flies. The thirst began, dry and sticky, and the cheat grass prickled beneath bare feet. Dust and bits of brush stuck to exposed skin, and Timothy began scratching furiously at his badly sunburned back. Robert's breath took on a raspy tone, and they had to rest often.

Just as Selena began to fear that the boys would mutiny, the sage and willow and aspen began to thin. Over the top of the next rise, she began to catch glimpses of the gardens and the low buildings beyond. She slowed, and the boys came to a halt beside her. They stood watching, Robert rasping, Timothy breathing heavily. When Robert saw that they were really pausing, he sat down.

"This is it," Selena said. "These gardens surround the whole town."

"Berness lives in the town?" Robert said.

"Yep," Selena replied. "And her biscuits, too."

As soon as the last words were out of Selena's mouth, before Timothy's shoulders had even stiffened, Selena knew that she had made a mistake. She nearly slapped herself in the forehead.

'And her biscuits, too'. Could she have been any more obvious? She had wanted to remind the hungry boys that there was food in the town, to quell any second thoughts they were having about following her. This wasn't a bad idea, in principle, but making it so blatant was a bad thing indeed. Robert was too tired to notice, but

Timothy had caught the scent of coaxing in the air. He was giving her a look, now, like a deer recognizing a hunter.

"It'll be hard to get you two in," Selena said quickly, trying to roll over the mistake. "They could have gotten word down by now—the Huctans, I mean—they could be watching for a couple half-naked, purplish boys. I was thinking it would be best if I went in first..."

"I'm not going in," Timothy interrupted.

Inwardly Selena cursed. Outwardly, she looked confused and a little perturbed at being interrupted.

"What?" she said.

"I'm not going in," Timothy repeated, without even a hint of abashment, "until you tell us more about who you are."

There it was. Timothy had caught her mistake, knew he had an advantage, and was pressing it hard.

This was what she had seen in him, she reminded herself. This was why she had rescued him.

Mustering a semblance of confusion on her face, Selena looked at Robert as if to say, He's *your* friend, what is this about? Robert looked back at her, then to Timothy, then back to her. She saw his hunger for the biscuits, for a moment, and hoped for some support. Then Robert looked at Timothy again, folded his arms, and waited.

"Come on," Selena said, turning to Timothy again. "I told you, I can't tell you anything else. I'm going to be in trouble already." That was true. She would be. Never mind acting on her own to help them escape, revealing her position, and killing a soldier in the middle of a Huctan fort. Never mind starting a riot that had probably gotten several Botani boys killed. Never mind the way she had let Timothy know there were more rebels by pretending to accidentally betray the fact.

All of that was objectionable, punishable, even deplorable. But telling two untested boys about the Band, in any detail whatsoever, would be unforgivable.

"Will you be in more trouble," Timothy said, "if we walk away right now, or if you tell us a little more and bring us in to your friend safe and sound?"

Suddenly Selena hated that sharpness in that boy's eyes. Even if it was what had set her on this whole course of action in the first place, even if that sharpness was what could make him valuable in the Band, right now she hated it.

"Bring you in?" she said, going for a hurt look. "I saved your lives. You act like I'm trying to trap you somehow."

He faltered—she could see him falter—but with a stubborn shake of his head he silenced the apology and waited. Robert was looking uncomfortable, but he seemed to have decided that he'd fought enough with Timothy for today. There was no help coming from him.

Selena wanted to growl in frustration. It wasn't like she was trying to do them wrong. She'd sacrificed to save their lives. All she wanted now was to get them to someone with more authority to decide what to do. But no, Timothy wasn't going anywhere until she told him more.

Was he bluffing? She knew how much he wanted to join them, but she had also heard the hurt in his voice this morning. Was he having a change of heart? Would he walk away, for his brother?

Salt, she hated that look in his eyes.

"Fine," she said, letting the sweet and wounded expression give way to acid. "You want a little honesty? I saved you. I went against all orders of keeping quiet and not acting without permission, brought Robert into it because you wouldn't leave without him, killed a soldier right there in the fort, and even *told* you that I'm against the Huctans. All I want now is to get you to Berness's house and get you safe so you don't get caught again and tell some Huctan everything you've heard. How *dare* you lay conditions on me?"

Timothy shifted his feet, but he kept his eyes trained on her.

"We'll come," he said, "if you tell us what this group is."

Selena didn't have to fake a look of shock and outrage. She was a *Thane*! She had spent most of her life learning how to keep secrets and control conversations. She shouldn't be having this much trouble with some exhausted, half-naked, half-starving woodsboy.

But Haberd had warned her, hadn't he? Pulling the wool over someone's eyes is a fine art, he'd said, but sometimes all it takes is plain, sheep-headed stubbornness to keep the wool off.

Well, Timothy was full to the gills with sheep-headed stubbornness. All the guile in the world was not going to convince him, right now. He had set his condition, and he was sticking to it.

Worse, there was nothing Selena could do about it. She couldn't just let them go, and she couldn't drag them both into town by force.

A lifetime of training, and she was being beaten by a *woodsboy*.

"Alright," she said. "Fine. But after this you had better follow my instructions *exactly*. You will *not* get caught on the way in because you're too good to be careful. Deal?"

Timothy shrugged, and nodded.

"Deal?" Selena repeated.

"Deal," Timothy said.

"Fine." Selena calmed herself, took a deep breath. For a second she considered lying about the Band, trying to satisfy them with some misleading explanation, but Timothy was watching her and she was too angry to come up with something convincing right now. Robert had his arms crossed over his knees and was looking back and forth between them. The amused grin that he was trying very hard to hide was infuriating.

Selena clenched her fists behind her back.

"It's called the Band," she said. "It's a group of Botani that do whatever we can against the Huctans. We don't want them raping and taxing and abusing Botani people. We don't want their trades—or *them*—in Botan. I can't tell you where we are, obviously. OK?"

"But what do you *do*?" Timothy asked.

"So how is murdering a soldier and helping a couple boys escape going to change anything?" Robert asked, at the same time.

Selena held up her hands. "I can't... first off, I didn't *murder* anyone. Second, what I did is not at all what the Band usually does. The Band's policy is mostly to watch, wait, and plan."

"So that someday you can start a rebellion," Timothy said.

"Plan what?" Robert said.

Selena clapped her hands and held them up. "No more," she said. "I've told you absolutely all I'm going to. No more."

For a moment she thought Timothy was going to press her. She felt her muscles preparing to hit him. But he hesitated. Maybe he saw the look in her eye, or maybe he was excited enough about what she had told him to be satisfied for now, but he did not open his mouth to ask more.

"We had a deal," she pressed.

Timothy and Robert exchanged looks. Robert slapped his hands on his knees, pushed, and stood with an effort.

"Lead on," he said. Timothy nodded in agreement.

It gave Selena some satisfaction, two hours later, to see the two boys stumble into the dark, herb-smelling front room of Berness's house wearing dresses and sun-bonnets. She smirked at them, but they didn't seem to notice. Both of them had swiveled on entering to face the loaf of bread on the little table in the corner.

"Go ahead, don't be shy," Berness said, pressing them both toward the bread. "Are you thirsty?"

"Yes ma'am," Robert said, already tearing off a chunk of bread and handing the loaf to Timothy. The two of them looked absurd, wearing Berness's dresses and cramming bread into their bruise-splotched faces, and Selena had to remind herself that she was angry with them both.

"I'm sure you are," Berness said. "I'll make some tea. I have just the thing to help those terrible bruises. Selena? Selena." Selena stopped watching the boys and faced the old woman. "Go in the back room and find me that little dark bag with the small leaves in it. The small leaves, not the crushed ones."

"Yes ma'am," Selena said, mocking the little bit of woodsboy twang Robert had when he spoke. He didn't notice.

She went to the back room and stood there waiting. She knew, and Berness knew, that there was no bag of herbs in the back room. Berness hadn't sent her back here for herbs.

Selena waited for a good minute, while Berness fussed over the boys, before she called out to the front room.

"Did you say a brown bag?"

"What's that, dear?"

"A brown bag," Selena repeated. "I don't see it."

“A *dark* bag, I said. Oh, I’ll get it...” Berness bustled into the back room, accidentally kicking the door shut as she came through. When the door closed, she dropped her fussy demeanor like a mask.

“I talked with Kialo,” she said in a low voice. “He’s going to get help and be here in the morning.”

“Lucky that he was on his way through,” Selena said.

“Lucky indeed. Can you keep them here if I go to buy them some clothes?”

“Yes.”

“Good.”

Berness bent and scooted a chair loudly, banging it against the wall a couple times. She glanced at the door. Satisfied that the boys didn’t suspect anything, she looked at Selena and pursed her lips.

“What were you *thinking*, girl?”

Selena shrugged, opened her mouth. Berness wasn’t waiting.

“Well, I suppose I *see* what you were thinking, with those eyes—I see very well—but it hadn’t occurred to me that... well, you’ve grown up some since I saw you last. That’s for certain. But I’d expected better out of you. I’d expected better.

“Robert?” Selena said, stinging. “I wasn’t even going to *bring* him! Timothy wouldn’t leave without him...”

Berness waved as if she had heard enough, gave Selena one last disappointed shake of the head, and then bustled out into the front room again.

“Oh dear,” Selena heard her saying, “where have I... oh! Here it was, the whole time...”

Selena waited a moment before following, trying to get her emotions under control. Berness had rarely dropped her grandmotherly guise around her, and certainly never to rebuke her.

It hurt, in the way only someone who was never cross could hurt you.

And it rankled. Selena realized, suddenly, the assumption that everyone was going to make. No matter how hard she stressed that it was *Timothy* she had decided to save, *Timothy* who had insisted on bringing Robert, people were going to see Robert's blue eyes and handsome face and nod knowingly and say that they had thought better of Selena.

It wasn't fair. She had saved two Botani boys from death, and she was going to be blamed and punished and shamed for it.

Shuffling her feet, Selena went back out into the front room. Berness was taking the bonnets off of the boys.

"You'll have to wear the dresses for now," she was saying. "Besides, those britches were filthy. I'll clean them up right away, and then I'll go out and see if I can't get some shirts, and maybe some cloaks. Although," she stepped back and held Robert's shoulders with both hands, "You *do* look quite becoming in my floral."

Timothy snorted, Robert turned red and shuffled his feet, Berness laughed, and as quick as that, Berness had the two boys completely disarmed. Selena felt, on top of everything else, a sudden deflating of her own pride. She found it hard not to sulk the rest of the night.

She didn't sleep well. The floor was hard in Berness's front room. The boys, both clothed in shirts and pants now, were crammed into a corner between the table and the fireplace. Selena slept on the other side of the table, in the narrow walkway by the shelf of pots. Ostensibly she had to sleep on the floor with the boys because Berness snored dreadfully and didn't want to keep her up all night. Really she was supposed to make sure they didn't try to leave in the night. Being a guard dog did not make sleep any easier.

Robert stirred. Selena slitted her eyes and saw the gray light of dawn seeping through the small wax-paper window near the ceiling.

"Think you could be any louder?" Timothy whispered. Robert responded by kicking his heels on the floor and thrashing about.

Timothy snickered. "What time is it?"

"I dunno, but I need to pee," Robert replied, standing up. Selena decided to drop her sleep guise and stirred, squinting. She heard Robert bang into something, hiss, and start hopping on what sounded like one foot.

"What are you *doing*?" she said, in a tired voice.

"Hey," Robert said. "Where do we, uh..."

"Um. There's a bucket in Berness's room, I think."

There was a brief pause.

"I'll go outside."

Selena started to protest, then decided to keep her mouth shut. He wasn't going to leave, not without Timothy. Besides, she had no plausible reason ready why he shouldn't go outside. And part of her got a little satisfaction out of flouting her guard duty. She could admit that.

Robert fumbled for a second in the dark, and cold gray air filtered in. The door banged shut.

Timothy sat up, popped his neck, and rose to the balls of his feet. Selena sat up as well, yawning and rubbing her eyes. There was an awkward silence. Timothy popped his thumbs.

The door opened suddenly, and Selena realized immediately that something was wrong. A short, thin boy slipped in. When two others followed, one holding Robert in a choke-hold, Timothy gave a shout and jumped up. Selena groaned.

Timothy swung a stool.

"Stop it," Selena said, "Timothy, they're friends!"

Timothy wasn't listening. He swung the stool again.

The scuffle was brief. Kialo hit Timothy in the stomach, got his neck in the crook of an elbow, and leaned heavily on his back. Timothy struggled, kicked at Kialo's shins, then slowed. His eyes started rolling up in his head, and he sank slowly to the floor.

Kialo released Timothy's throat almost immediately, but kept a knee in his back. His small head swiveled, taking in the room. His eyes settled on Selena. He winked.

Timothy stirred. Kialo leaned down to his head and spoke brightly, as if he were a mother talking to a sulky toddler.

"Good morning!" he said. "Now, if I let you up, are you going to start swinging chairs around again?"

Timothy tried to head-butt him.

"Tell them who you are," Selena advised. "They probably still think you're Huctans."

At this, Robert stopped trying to pry Lutho's arm off of his neck. Timothy slowed a little.

"We're not Huctans," Kialo said. "And while Lutho may smell like one from time to time, and Tolede has been known to throw knives at them, I, frankly am a little hurt at the implication. Offended, even."

There was a brief pause.

"Relax, Timothy," Selena said. "They're from the Band."

Kialo dropped every cheery note from his voice and looked at her with sudden sharpness.

"Selena, do not speak again," he said.

The comfortable, jovial mood that always came with being around Kialo dissipated, and Selena felt the sudden and insane urge to cry. Then anger swept a heat through her cheeks—Kialo did not have any authority over her, not really—and just as quickly she wanted to cry again. Then she realized how sensitive she was being, how spoiled she must be for anything but praise to upset her, and felt even worse. It wasn't fair, or right. Selena folded her arms and didn't care if she looked like she was sulking.

"I won't swing a stool at you," Timothy said.

"Thanks!" Kialo said, standing up immediately. Lutho let Robert go, and Robert went to stand beside Timothy. The boys faced each other, and for a moment no one spoke.

Berness's bedroom door opened suddenly. Selena realized that everything had happened in a matter of less than a minute.

All eyes turned to face the old woman. Her hair was down, unbraided and thin over her shoulders. Her baggy nightgown was wrinkled from sleep, but her face was awake and her eyes sparkling.

"Oh good," she said, beaming at everyone. "I'll make breakfast."

CHAPTER 6

If Timothy was annoyed at their lack of choice in the whole matter, Robert was something close to furious. He didn't scowl or snap at people or slam doors or sulk in the corner, but Timothy knew him well enough to see the perfection of his posture, his pointed courtesy, and the way his hands were deliberately unclenched. Timothy wanted everything about the Band to be true and couldn't quite believe that it was. Robert didn't care if it was true; he wanted no part of it and certainly did not want to be a prisoner again.

Selena was sulky. Timothy didn't know her well, but he didn't have to be a genius to interpret the sarcastic sweetness in her tone and the stiffness in her shoulders when she obeyed Kialo's orders. He wondered why she *did* obey Kialo's orders. Kialo didn't seem to be any older than the rest of them, and was certainly the smallest, but both of the other boys obeyed him with alacrity.

Berness had her biscuits cooking by the time Timothy and Robert finished their talk with Kialo in the bedroom. The smell of the baking bread was glorious, and the food went a long way toward dispelling the tension in the tiny house.

It did not, of course, decrease Robert's anger at being 'taken somewhere safe' against his will.

After breakfast, Kialo and Berness left to make some sort of arrangements. Lutho, the big boy whose face had not changed since he arrived, stayed with Tolede to make sure Robert and Timothy didn't try to leave.

They were prisoners, again, but this time Timothy was glad. He'd been afraid Selena would cut them loose and let them go. She'd saved them, and deserved their thanks for that, but now that Timothy knew there was someone out there doing something against the Huctans—whatever that something might be—he did not think he could go back to working in the garden and fastening arrowheads and tying bow-staves to dry.

Robert, of course, was furious. When Kialo had told them they were not yet free to go home, that they would be taken to the Band so that a decision could be made, his face had gone smooth and hard. And his anger, when Timothy felt like pumping a fist in relief, twisted at Timothy's gut. Almost always, growing up, they had wanted the same things, got in the same trouble, endured the same pain. Only when Timothy had been sent to the fletcher had there been any divergence in their lives, and that had been a necessity.

But now, on the matter of the Band, Robert had made it plain that he saw only one right thing to do, and it was exactly the thing Timothy could not bear. It set Timothy's teeth on edge to think about their argument by the river, about Robert's implication that Timothy didn't love the people back home. It was *because* he loved and missed them that he couldn't pass up an opportunity to do something.

Of course, his motives weren't all selfless and sacrificial. He knew that. There was a childish part too, a part whose eyes popped and hands shook at the idea of being whatever kind of spy Selena was, of rescuing prisoners, fighting soldiers, running through the night with some sort of purpose. That was what he was made for, what he had dreamed of since he had been a little boy with his toes in the stream.

But that childish part was a small part. Most of it was about helping Botan and getting rid of the Huctans. Of doing something so that people like Fenae, and her brother, and her father, didn't have to...

Robert snapped his fingers. Timothy realized that he was holding the jar they had been rolling back and forth, twirling it in his hands and staring at it. He rolled it back to Robert, and the slow ritual of passing time and waiting began again.

Finally Kialo and Berness returned, and Berness started a stew cooking. Lutho, who had not said a single word the entire day, perked up and helped her chop some vegetables. Tolede, as he had done the entire day, continued to twirl and balance and shift his knife around in his hands. Robert, who had dropped some of his stiffness while Kialo was gone, went rigid and polite again and stopped rolling the jar.

Timothy was glad when dinner was over and Kialo told them they would have an early start in the morning. He wasn't sleepy, but sleeping was at least something to do.

Timothy woke to the sound of Kialo whistling. Sitting up, he rubbed his eyes and squinted in the flaring lamplight. Robert was lying on his stomach. As Kialo's whistling grew obnoxiously loud, Robert got up on his elbows and turned his head to give the boy a sleepy scowl. Kialo stopped whistling and made a deep bow.

"Good morning, sirs," he said gravely. "Breakfast is served, at your convenience."

Timothy stared, still squinting, as Kialo went to the front door and went out, letting in a draft of chilly morning air. It was still dark outside.

Before the door had shut all the way, Kialo peeked back in.

"We're leaving in ten minutes," he said, in a less grandiloquent tone. "If you want food, you may want to hurry."

Timothy thought he would have liked Kialo, if Robert hadn't hated him.

His muscles were tight, but most of the soreness was gone. There was some hard fruit and cheese and a couple half-loaves of bread on the table. The bedroom door was open, and as Timothy began helping himself, Selena emerged, chewing on a little green pear. She nodded, scowling almost as much as Robert, and went outside.

"Hey," Timothy said, nudging Robert with his foot. He was a little wary of being too playful, with Robert both sleepy and upset, so he kept it simple and spoke quietly. "Better get some food."

Robert groaned something and got up. He was moving a lot better now. The bruises were healing. He wrapped the blanket Berness had lent him around his shoulders, ruffled the creases out of his hair, and stumbled over to join Timothy by the table. They ate in silence, and Timothy poured some milk into a tin cup.

He had only half finished his cup when the door opened and Kialo stepped in with the cold air again, affecting a formal posture.

"The carriage," he said, "awaits."

Then he shut the door and dropped his playfulness like a mask.

"Before we go," he said, looking them both in the eyes, "I want to make something very clear. We are traveling in secrecy. There have already been soldiers through town, looking for you. If they find you, they'll kill us, which would be upsetting. Therefore, you will obey all orders immediately. If you don't, I swear in all seriousness that you will regret it."

Kialo looked at them both, nodded to see that they understood, and then smiled.

"We have a wagon full of straw waiting outside," he said. "It has a false bottom, which leaves a small space beneath the straw where you'll ride. It'll be cramped and bumpy, but until we get out of town, you'll have to be very quiet. When one of us up top gives you three knocks, you can move around and talk in low voices. But if we knock again, you have to be completely silent. Understand?"

Timothy and Robert nodded.

"And don't worry. Everything should be fine," Kialo said. Grinning again, he opened the door and bowed. "After you."

They went outside. The wind was blowing through the dark alley, and it was cold. Lutho was standing behind a wagon, which was hitched to two mules. Tolede was nowhere to be seen.

"Wait," Berness said, behind them suddenly. Timothy turned and saw her bustle back to the bedroom, then come out into the light carrying a gray cloak. She held it out between Robert and Timothy.

"We finally found you something to keep you warm," she said. "You'll have to share, though."

Robert took the cloak and thanked the old woman. Timothy felt something like fondness for her. It was a good cloak, of thick wool. It would help, in the nights.

Robert had already disappeared into the wagon. From the

outside it was no more than a box on wheels, piled high with musty smelling hay. In the back, where Lutho stood, a board had been swiveled to reveal a slot below the hay. The opening was maybe a foot high and as wide as the wagon.

As Timothy slithered in on his belly, the ceiling grew slightly higher until he was able to roll over on his back between Robert and Selena. When he lay down, the wooden boards above his face were about eight inches from his nose. He could see almost nothing in the darkness.

A moment passed in stillness. Timothy mulled over how singularly uncomfortable the ride was going to be, but he felt something like joy or excitement, too. He was hidden and safe in here, and it was warmer, and even if it already smelled like the breath of three people in a small space, there was something nice about being pressed shoulder to shoulder with a girl as pretty as Selena was.

The novelty would soon wear off.

Kialo's voice whispered near their feet. "It'll be three hours before we can stop. Anyone need anything?" He was answered with silence, and a moment later the board was replaced. It grew dark, and the cool wind on Timothy's bare feet was stilled. The wood above them creaked, someone clicked his tongue, and the cart began to move.

For a few seconds it didn't seem so bad. Then the cart turned a corner and sped up, and Timothy's shoulder blades began to grind into the wooden floor with every jolting bounce. He started to sweat where Robert's arm pressed up against his shoulder. The air was stuffy and oppressive.

The cart sped up again when they left Dellin, and Timothy's

neck started to cramp from trying to hold his head off the bouncing wagon bottom. When the road grew smoother, Kialo sped up yet again, as if determined to make up for fewer bumps by making each one count.

Timothy got used to the bouncing and swaying, after a while. He also got Robert to roll up their cloak and put it behind their heads, which took the bite out of the worst shocks. What he couldn't stand, though, were the long stretches of downhill. Blood rushing to his head, combined with the swaying, made Timothy dizzy and nauseous. Swallowing hard and breathing slowly was barely enough to keep him from vomiting.

The three knocks came eventually, but on that first day, no one was in a very talkative mood. The conversation was limited to rather touchy instructions on the positioning of elbows and knees. Dust began to filter through the cracks in the wagon bottom, and the air grew very dry. Another hour passed, and Timothy wished aloud that the Huctans had caught and killed them already. Robert graced him with a chuckle.

At some point the cart slowed to a stop and the board was removed. Pushing and shoving, the three of them scrambled out of the wagon into the midday light, gulping fresh air and water and relieving themselves in the trees. They ate a short meal in the shade of some bushes not directly visible from the road. Tolede was still nowhere to be seen.

Lutho was almost unrecognizable. He looked older, by decades. Timothy realized, after a moment, that the boy had disguised himself somehow, and that he and Kialo were posing as a father and son. Timothy stared at Lutho's face, searching for the paints or dyes he must have used, trying to figure out what had so completely changed the boy's appearance.

His staring must have been obvious, because Kialo laughed. "Doesn't do us much good to hide you in the wagon hold, if the Huctans decide that *we* are the two Botani boys they're looking for. Lutho makes a pretty good father, don't you think?"

Fifteen minutes later, Robert, Timothy and Selena slithered back into the wagon. Robert suggested that the middle person ride with his head by the feet of the others, to help make it more roomy inside. Selena volunteered to be the odd person out.

It didn't help much.

All told, they rode twelve hours that day. They made camp in a stand of scrubby pines, and Lutho stayed with the wagon. Timothy was so tired that the ground, littered with pinecones and sharp rocks, felt like he had always imagined a feather mattress would. He slept without dreaming and woke feeling almost refreshed.

Robert and Selena's moodiness faded, on the second day, and the hours began to pass more quickly. Something about the situation, and the fact that they had to endure it together, encouraged a sort of cavalier attitude toward the whole thing. Robert and Timothy joked almost like they were back home, and by lunch time they were even bantering with Kialo through the sides of the wagon. Timothy knew it was stupid, but it felt *good*, almost, to be trapped in the wagon with Robert and Selena. It made the whole thing more like a game, or a task, and those Timothy was good at.

The other kids had always complained, when they were little, when the mothers made them play traditional games at birth-festivals. They hated the enforced rules, the structure, the guidelines. Timothy, of course, pretended to hate them as well—he could complain and shuffle his feet with the best of them—but secretly he loved everything about the games. Outside of the games, he was shy and awkward, but in them he was bold and strong.

When Timothy got a little older, he realized it wasn't just the games he liked. He liked knowing what to do. Casual conversation terrified him, but if he was running the smithy and getting instructions from customers—even if the customers were his peers—he had no trouble. If he met a girl his age in passing, he never knew what to say, but if they were playing the game where you had to ask questions to find out who had the bean pod, his tongue and mind loosened.

So when the situation in the wagon shifted from being a situation to being a mutually borne burden, Timothy found his fear and timidity turn to confidence and contentment. He still didn't talk much, and was still more awkward than Robert, but he made his own jokes, and spoke to Selena some. When he complained, it felt like the birth-festival games; he was pretending to hate the situation, but in his heart he was glad. This wagon ride was something they were going through together. Something that nobody else could lay claim to.

The air outside was getting colder every morning. The leaves, which had been turning colors, were starting to fall. Timothy judged, from what he could see on their short stops, that they were travelling south or west. Of course Kialo would say nothing about their destination, Lutho would say nothing about anything, and while Selena surely knew where they were going, she was even more closemouthed than the boys.

On the morning of the sixth day, Timothy woke to find Kialo gone with the wagon and Lutho speaking with two men astride horses. Timothy sat up. One of the men saw him and nodded in his direction, and the conversation came to a close.

The horsemen rode closer, and Timothy realized that they had brought an extra mount with them. Robert and Selena woke as the horses approached, and Lutho fetched a quick breakfast from one of the sacks that had previously been under the wagon seat.

"Morning," Robert said in a friendly tone, trying to break the awkward silence as the two riders watched them eat. The riders replied by nodding, but it was clear that they did not want to speak. Robert, probably annoyed by their silence, kept talking.

"Nice day, don't you think?" he said, biting off a piece of bread and smiling. One of the men shrugged, while the other ignored Robert completely.

When they had finished their breakfast, the ruder of the two riders produced two blindfolds, which Lutho tied onto Timothy and Robert's eyes. With help they mounted behind the riders, received their warnings not to peek, and began the long ride.

For some reason Timothy had it in his head that he would only have to endure the blind, silent bouncing for an hour or two. When, after six hours, they stopped to eat fruit and dried beef and Timothy was allowed to pee blindly before being hustled back onto the horse, his mood had grown black.

He woke from a sort of dozing half sleep many hours later, and the cold air told him that night had fallen. The horse had stopped, and the rider was sliding off the saddle in front of him. Voices were speaking in low tones.

"We're here," the rider said. "You can get down now."

It took Timothy a moment to realize that the rider was addressing him. Then he pointed to his blindfold, carefully keeping his hand a good six inches away to show that he wasn't trying to peek.

“Can I take this off?” he said.

“Go ahead.”

Timothy pulled the cloth over the top of his head, squinting in the moonlight. He could make out buildings before them and trees behind. Robert was beside him, apparently asleep, slumped forward on his horse.

The rider reminded Timothy that he had been told to get down. The other rider woke Robert, who also dismounted, looking disoriented without the blindfold on. Selena was already gone.

The riders seemed to be waiting for something. After a minute, a light came swinging towards them from the buildings and a young boy of about ten approached with a lantern. He bowed and held the lantern to the side so they could see him in the darkness.

“I am Rian,” he said, very distinctly. “I have come to show the two young men to their rooms. Please follow me.”

With a glance at the riders, who nodded, Timothy and Robert followed the boy. They made their way between the low wooden houses, following Rian’s light until he turned and opened one of the doors. He held the lantern at the door so Timothy could see as he entered. Robert followed.

The cabin was furnished with two straw mattresses, a small table, two stools, and a lamp, which Rian lit with a short splinter from his lantern.

“Please stay here and make yourselves comfortable, sirs,” Rian went on, as if he had rehearsed his speech. “I will get you some dinner and be back soon.” They nodded and told him they would wait, and with another small bow the boy shut the door quietly and was gone.

Timothy exchanged a glance with Robert, who flopped down on

one of the mattresses, put his hands behind his head, and imitated Rian's falsetto voice.

"This mattress is very nice, please," he said, "please, make yourself comfortable, Tim-o-thy."

Timothy laughed. Dropping on his own mattress, he heaved a sigh. After many weeks of sleeping on the ground on the march to Northelm, followed by the hard bunks in the communal cells, followed by the stone floor of the solitary cell, followed by another week of the ground and the wagon, the softness of the thin straw pallet was almost intolerably comfortable.

Rian arrived with a cloth-wrapped dinner and a pitcher full of water. Timothy rose and took the bundle from him, managed to accept the boy's formal good-night without laughing, and closed the door behind him. Lying down again, he set the bundle between Robert and himself. They ate, drank, snuggled into their respective mattresses, and went to sleep.

It was past midnight when they came for him.

CHAPTER 7

It took one second to sit up and squint against the torchlight, and by that time they had him.

Timothy fought, of course. He fought hard. He didn't stop to wonder who could be attacking him *here*, or why, or how they'd gotten to him. He remembered well, in those months of chains, how he'd cursed himself for not fighting at the beginning, when all that separated him from freedom had been a couple of soldiers with crossbows.

This time, if he were taken, it wouldn't be for lack of fighting.

But it was already too late. There were too many hands. They had already lifted him from his bed, pinned his joints. Timothy thrashed, freed a leg, landed a kick, and was deliberately dropped. His head struck the hardwood floor and bounced. A concussion of pain spread through his skull, and his vision sparked. By the time his eyes had refocused, his wrists were bound and his attackers had raised him to their shoulders.

"Robert!" Timothy yelled, but he was already outside, the cabin door already shutting behind him, Robert already trussed and gagged in his bed.

They didn't carry Timothy far. The door was open in the cabin adjacent to his, spilling lamplight in a golden patch on the gravel road. Timothy's captors carried him up the steps and dropped him on the bench inside, closing the door behind them. Timothy took the opportunity to fight again. He heaved and almost succeeded in rolling off of the bench before someone hit him again, hard in the stomach. For a moment he could do nothing but gasp for breath that wouldn't come while someone stretched his bound hands above his head and someone else began stripping off his clothes.

What was happening?

He was naked, his shirt rolled up around his hands, his back stretched tight against the grain of the wooden bench. His lungs finally opened and he took a huge breath that left him coughing, then another. Someone scooted a chair up to his head, and he turned enough to see an old man and a small table.

There were pliers and a knife on the table.

"I'm going to ask you some questions," the old man said, "and you're going to answer them."

Timothy felt sweat on his forehead in spite of the cold room and his naked body. He began to buck against the bonds, throwing his hips forward and backward with every muscle in his body. The bench jumped off of the ground, and he twisted, trying to upend it. Then two sets of hands grabbed the bench ends and held them as he continued to twist and thrash. His own spit flecked his lips. His breath was coming fast through his teeth.

And then he heard Robert.

It was a low moan. The sound was muffled by two cabin walls and a gag, dulled as if it had escaped Robert's mouth through a clenched jaw, but it cut straight through Timothy's panic.

Robert never moaned. Timothy had seen Robert smash his thumb on the anvil, look at the bleeding gash, and calmly go for a rag as if the pain didn't touch him. He had heard Robert trade banter while they hung together by their ankles. He had felt Robert suppress whimpers after a Huctan beating that left him unable to walk.

And now Robert was moaning in pain.

Timothy stopped struggling for a moment. The old man spoke again.

"Your turn will come next," he said. "For now, you talk. If you talk quickly, you will shorten Robert's suffering. Maybe he'll do the same for you when your turn comes. Do you understand?"

Timothy stared for a moment, unable to respond, his mind still struggling to catch up to the present.

What was *happening*? Who were these people?

He had assumed that they were Huctans. Who else would attack him in the middle of the night like this? Who else would threaten to torture his brother while they questioned him?

But they weren't Huctans. None of them wore a scrap of Huctan crimson, or held a slightly curved Huctan sword, or even wore a shirt of chain mail.

Of course they didn't. This was a safe place. This was where Selena's friends had brought him, sheltered him, given him a cabin to sleep in, dinner to eat, water to drink. This was the rebel headquarters. Hours of secret forest paths separated Timothy from the nearest Huctan soldier.

But that meant that the *rebels* had woken Timothy up, bound him, stripped him, stretched him on a bench, and threatened him with torture. The *rebels* were doing this. The *rebels,* his supposed friends, were hurting Robert.

"Do you understand?" the old man repeated.

No, Timothy didn't understand. *Where's Selena?* he wanted to ask. *Why did she rescue us to bring us to a place like this?*

But he couldn't ask. He couldn't waste any more time thinking, because every second he delayed was another second for them to hurt Robert.

"Ask," he said. Then, as another groan met his ears, "Ask!"

The old man sat back on his chair. "Good," he said. "Let's start simple. What is your name?"

"Timothy."

"And your friend's name?"

"Robert."

"Are you related?"

"Yes. No. Not by blood. We grew up together."

This time Robert screamed. Not groaned. Not yelled. Screamed, like a polecat.

Timothy screamed back, and bucked again, but the bench was firm, held down by rebels on either side. The bonds were tight. Skin tore where the ropes held his wrists and ankles to the wood. The old man sat with arms folded, waiting calmly as Timothy thrashed against his bonds.

Timothy forced himself to be still, tried to remember the last question, breathed in short gasps.

"Please, hurry," he said. "Ask your real questions. I'll answer. You don't have to hurt Robert."

The old man glanced at one of the others, then turned back to Timothy.

"Tell us about your escape," he said.

You already know about my escape, Timothy thought, why are you wasting time, why are you *hurting Robert* to ask me these stupid questions?

"Selena helped us," he said, trying to make his mind and lips and tongue work together even though his body was shaking with the effort it took to keep from thrashing again. "She picked the locks on our cells. We got into the water and escaped on a boat."

"She said you carried Robert."

"Yes."

"All the way out of the fort."

"Yes. He couldn't walk."

"Why not?"

Robert screamed again, sudden and loud and long.

"Because he'd been beaten!" Timothy yelled. "Selena told him to get beaten, so they'd put him in a cell by himself, so we could get him out. Because I told her I wasn't leaving without him. You know this! I'll tell you the whole story again, if you want, frontwards and backwards. I'll act it out for you. I'll draw you *pictures*. You don't have to *hurt* him for me to tell you!"

The old man leaned forward, elbows to knees, and looked Timothy directly in the face. His eyes were sharp, and hard. "Let's get to the point, then," he said. "Why were you alone, when all the other cells had groups of boys in them?"

This was the point?

"Because I hit a Huctan soldier," Timothy said.

"Why?"

"Because he was taunting one of the younger boys."

"Taunting him?"

"Yes!"

Timothy was so tired of this. He wanted to lash out, to hit someone again, to *kill* someone. He was trembling. But the old man's arms were folded on his knees, and he was waiting. Waiting, while they hurt Robert.

Thrashing and yelling again would help nothing. The only thing Timothy could do now was talk faster.

He closed his eyes and tried to maintain control. To focus.

"One of the younger boys was crying," he said. "At the fort. In the parade grounds. He'd dropped out of line again. The Huctans had been cutting his rations every time he dropped out of line, which made him so weak that he dropped out of line the next day. And the next. They were making an example out of him. He could barely walk. He was going to die, and he was crying a little. Not loud, just tears, but one of the soldiers saw him."

Timothy could feel the warm air in the parade ground wicking away his sweat. He could see the soldier, cloaked in crimson, stalking over to the weeping boy. He could see the triumph in the Huctan's eyes.

"Don't cry," the Huctan said. Timothy could still hear the reassurance in that voice, the terrible calmness. "Don't cry. Don't you remember what happened to your mother, because she cried?"

The Huctan was close enough to Timothy for the smell of his chain mail to be sharp in Timothy's nose. The other boys–the hundreds of other Botaños that had been stolen from their homes, placed in chains, and marched to the fort to train in the Huctan army–stood rigidly at attention. No one turned his head to look at the soldier talking to boy.

There was silk in the Huctan's voice as he leaned close to the weeping boy's ear.

"You were strong, that day we took you," the soldier whispered to the boy. "You didn't know it, but we saw the strength in you. We saw that, deep down, you hated your mother's tears. *Hated* that weakness, in her and in yourself. That's why we wanted you. That's why *you* had to be the one to stop her crying. Because stopping her weakness was the first step to driving the weakness from yourself."

Timothy felt his stomach rise in his throat as he realized what they had forced the boy to do. He trembled, but he did not move. He stood in the parade ground, with columns of Botani boys all around him, and clenched his fists. But he did not lose control.

Not until the boy sniffed, and nodded, and leaned forward with his head lowered to let the soldier embrace him and pat his shoulder.

Robert's scream snapped Timothy's eyes open. A series of screams, short shrieks of increasing volume capped by a long, animal howl.

Timothy's reason began to leave him. He bucked again, and this time he did not stop when the skin on his wrists tore further and his head struck the wood and his ankles bruised against the sides of the wooden bench. The old man was talking, but Timothy wasn't listening, wasn't fully sane. He was thinking of the boy, and of Fenae, and of Robert. He was seeing the faces in the room around him, the pliers, the knife, spinning and bouncing and blurring into the raw parts of fear and hate and hopelessness and helplessness.

"What did you swear?" the old man shouted, for what Timothy was suddenly certain was the third time. Had Timothy been talking? What had he been saying—no, screaming—as he thrashed and bled and listened to Robert howling?

"Won't break me!" Timothy heard himself shouting. Like they'd broken Fenae. Like they'd broken the boy. "Won't," he screamed, "break,"—he was punctuating his words now with the thud of his body against the bench—"me!"

And suddenly they were loosening the bonds, wrapping his clothes around him, holding him still, murmuring in soothing voices, talking amongst themselves in a language he did not know but that, in his stupor, seemed almost familiar. Comforting.

The door was opening. Robert was rushing in, touching Timothy's shoulder, sitting next to him and glaring at the rebels around them as if daring them to touch Timothy again. The old man was asking where Verinald was. The boy at the door, Timothy's age, was saying that he didn't know.

And then it was quiet, except for Timothy's labored breathing and the scuffing of feet on the wooden floor. Timothy and Robert sat on a bench, surrounded by rebels in a small room filled with flickering lamp-light, and waited for something to happen.

"Since no one else is going to say it," said the boy at the door, "we're really sorry about this. All of us."

People nodded. Someone began to explain what Timothy had realized the moment Robert had come in the door, that Robert had never been hurt, that the rebels had never intended to torture either one of them. Someone—the boy at the door, who was named Jesher—had been impersonating Robert's screams while the old man questioned Timothy. It had all been a performance. A sham. An act.

They'd had to make sure that Timothy wasn't a spy, they said. They'd had to convince themselves that he hadn't been *pretending* to be a prisoner, that he hadn't tricked Selena into rescuing him, that he wasn't working for the Huctans in some elaborate scheme to learn the secret location of their headquarters.

Of course he wasn't. It sounded ludicrous when they said it out loud. He'd been scheduled for execution. He'd been beaten so badly that it had taken him days to walk without a limp. Robert's beating had nearly been fatal. Had the rebels really thought it possible to fake all of that? Were there really spies in existence who would withstand such beatings and put their lives at such risk without ever giving a hint of their true loyalty?

Well, maybe there were. Maybe, for the rebels, such performances were commonplace. But Timothy could see that a few of them seemed embarrassed, now, to have ever thought it a possibility. The boy especially. He was frowning to himself, looking back and forth between the torn skin on Timothy's wrists and the obvious rage in Robert's blue eyes.

Timothy knew that he himself should be angry, at least as angry as Robert was. More so. Wasn't *he* the one who had been stripped and tied and questioned? He should be furious at the injustice of the accusation, furious at the pain in his battered body, furious at the deceit, the humiliation, the manipulation.

But he wasn't.

Partly he was too tired to be angry. Partly his body was still recovering from the shock and strain of remembering Northelm while he listened to what he thought were his friend's screams. But most of it was understanding. Somewhere, in the back of his mind, behind the choking residue of emotion, Timothy understood exactly why the rebels had done what they had done. This was the *Band*. This was the only place in Botan that still resisted Huctan rule, and it was a place to protect, to keep secret, at all costs. Ten minutes of emotional trauma were a small price to pay for that secrecy. It was a price Timothy was glad to pay.

Glad! Robert was trembling with anger on his behalf, but Timothy was glad. Glad that the Huctans had such enemies as these. Glad that he was *here*, that he had made it, that he was going to join these dangerous men.

But he couldn't show his gladness, not now, because doing so would be to betray Robert. Robert was looking at the torn skin on Timothy's wrists and the trickle of blood dripping on the bench. His rage was barely contained.

Robert always saw the consequences. Never the purpose.

"We believe you are both innocent," said Verinald. Somewhere in his mid-fifties, Verinald had entered the cabin after five minutes of awkward silence, in which Robert never stopped unclenching his jaw and the boy at the door—Jesher—never stopped shifting his feet and looking ashamed. Verinald's hair was iron-gray and long, held behind his head in a well-combed ponytail. His voice was calm and courteous, but like T'shira's voice, the courtesy seemed to be hiding an edge of coldness and condescension.

"Your sincerity, at least, is evident," Verinald continued. "Your questioner is satisfied that you are not Huctan spies. He believes that your story is, in large part, accurate. You were kidnapped from your homes by the Huctans, rescued by one of our Thanes, and now brought to us for safekeeping."

The old man who had questioned Timothy, who had held a whispered conversation with Verinald when he entered, nodded.

“We did not order your rescue,” Verinald said. “Selena acted without permission or help from us. She will be punished accordingly. But you are here, now, and we must decide what to do with you.”

Verinald took another sip of his tea, set it down on the floor, and leaned forward on his chair in what he obviously thought was a friendly and confiding posture.

“We are left,” he said, “with three, or rather *four*, options.”

If there was one thing Timothy hated, it was people that said, ‘three, or rather, *four*” when they had obviously known from the beginning that there were four.

“The first option,” Verinald said, “is to kill you both.” He paused for effect, obviously hoping for some visible sign of fear. When Timothy scratched his bleeding wrist and Robert continued clenching that muscle above his cheek bone, Verinald smiled.

“We would, of course, like to avoid that option,” he said. “If possible.”

This was when everyone was supposed to give a nervous chuckle. Fortunately, no one did.

“The second option,” Verinald said, “Is to simply let you go. Of course we cannot do this. However sincere you may be, you know too much, and we know too little.”

“Of course,” said Robert. His tone was overly sweet, but the acid beneath the honey cut at Timothy. He suddenly wished with all his heart that the rebels had chosen someone less condescending and obnoxious than Verinald to explain things to them.

“The third option is, for us, most desirable,” Verinald said. “The third option—and don’t worry, you will not be harmed or thought a coward if you choose not to take the oath—”

Verinald paused again, bending for his cup of tea, taking another dainty sip.

"The third option," Verinald said for the third time, "Is for you to join the Band."

He looked at them both like children, like he was offering them sweets, like they might start jumping up and down. An hour ago, Timothy might have. Now he was watching Robert, whose blue eyes had gone, if anything, flatter.

"And if we don't want to join the Band?" he asked.

"That is the fourth, and most difficult, choice," Verinald said. "If you do not join the Band, you will be kept here for a time. Perhaps in a month a place will be found for you, perhaps in a year. Perhaps you will be released one day." Yet again he sipped at his tea. Timothy had the sudden urge to lean forward and knock the cup from the man's hand. Any chance there had been of Robert changing his mind was slipping away with every infuriating gesture Verinald made.

"You understand, of course," Verinald said. "It is difficult. We cannot simply set you free."

Robert smiled. "Of course," he said again, with the same sickly sweetness as before.

"You mentioned an oath," Timothy said. "What's that?"

Verinald sat forward, dropping his voice a little. The false drama was unbearable, yet Timothy found himself listening intently.

"The oath," he said, "is more than an oath. It's a new birth. A wedding vow."

He wanted Timothy to look incredulous, to ask what he could possibly mean, but Timothy gritted his teeth and waited.

"A wedding vow," Verinald repeated, "and the bride is Botan.

When you take the oath, you swear fealty and service to Botan, forsaking all others. That means your friends, your family, the girl you left back home... everyone and everything comes second to Botan. You serve her, protect her, and honor her. As a man honors his bride. As a son honors his mother."

The boy at the door—Jesher—shifted. There was a look of barely-contained frustration on his face, the look a person gets when someone tells their favorite joke, but says all the lines wrong. Jesher believed what Verinald was saying, but hated the way he was saying it.

"Choose well," Verinald said, sitting back on his chair. "Once taken, the oath is binding. There is no turning back."

Robert's voice, when he spoke, had lost a little of its sweetness. There was something in his tone—or maybe it was the straightness of his back, or the clarity of his eyes—that made him look taller than Verinald. Above him, somehow.

"Forsaking all others?" he said. "Abandoning all others, for the sake of *Botan*? What's Botan, if it isn't the same people you're abandoning?"

Verinald raised his eyebrows and took another sip of his tea. "Botan is bigger than any one person," he said.

"Oh, yes," Robert said, his voice dripping poison now. "Bigger than any one person. It doesn't really matter what happens to *one person*, does it? You can do whatever you want, kill whoever you want, as long as it's for *Botan*."

"We do not kill Botani," Verinald said. A little of the condescension in his tone had been replaced with coolness.

"Oh no, you don't kill them personally," Robert said, "but you kill them anyway. Do you think me and Timothy got out of

Northelm without Botani people dying? Do you have any idea how many of the boys they probably beat and killed in the riot we caused when we escaped? Or how many more were killed when they found us missing?"

Timothy felt like he had been punched in the stomach.

"No, of course you haven't thought about it," Robert said, and suddenly it wasn't entirely clear whether he was talking to Verinald or to Timothy. "Why should you? If a few *individuals* die, what does it matter? It's for *Botan.* You've forsaken all *others.*"

Verinald stood abruptly. Some of his composure was gone, but his voice was still even.

"We," he said, "are the only reason you two are alive today. If you feel no gratitude, that is your concern. You have until sunset tomorrow to decide which path you will take. Choose well."

And with that, he was gone.

The boy—Jesher—led them back to their room, replaced the lamp on their table, and helped them get their bedding back in order. Timothy moved numbly, torn between the offer he had hoped the rebels would make and the rage he had feared would consume Robert. When they were finished, Jesher lingered at the door for a minute, as if looking for something to say.

"I'm really sorry about everything tonight," he said, as Robert lay down stiffly on his bed and Timothy used a wet rag to wipe the blood from his face. He turned to leave, then paused once more.

"Not all of us are like Verinald," Jesher said.

Then he shut the door and left, and Timothy was left alone with Robert.

Without Robert, Timothy would have grown up as an outcast. Before he had become shy, before he had learned to hold his passion in check and pretend casual disinterest, he had been a nuisance to the other children, boisterous and rough when he should have been temperate, enthusiastic when he should have held back. If it hadn't been for Robert, in those years before Timothy had learned to hide himself, the other children would have hated him rather than tolerating or ignoring him.

Timothy hadn't cared that Robert was always at the head of the crowd. He certainly hadn't intended to use Robert to raise his own social status or shield himself from being teased. But Robert's presence had had those effects, and, willingly or not, Timothy had reaped their benefits.

Until, one day, Timothy had realized what was happening. He saw himself following Robert like a shadow, clinging like a leech, and it occurred to him that Robert might not always *want* Timothy tagging on. It occurred to him that he might be doing the same thing with their friendship that he had done with everything as a child, that he might be trying too hard, caring too much.

So, despising himself, Timothy withdrew. He pretended aloofness, acted as if he didn't care where Robert went, as if he would be happy whether they were together or not, as if he were independent, dispassionate, self-sufficient. Strong.

This was his life; a constant charade of pretending not to care about what he cared about, of pretending to dislike what he liked, of covering his passion with a sheen of indifference. He was a liar, a fraud, one who wanted to run and leap and fly but settled for trudging so that he would not stand out, would not be mocked, would not be thought strange.

This was why, when they were captured, when the fear had worn off enough for Timothy to begin understanding the openness he felt, a small and guilty and almost unconscious part of Timothy had been relieved.

Relieved. Yes, Huctan bondage was cruel and miserable and dangerous. Yes, he hated every hour that he had to bow and scrape before his enemies, every minute of knowing that he could not go anywhere without the boys chained to his wrists and ankles like anchors to a ship. Yes, he chafed under Huctan brutality and despised every second that he was in their power.

But he knew what to do. He had a goal—*fight*—and he was able to pour every thought and effort into that goal. He didn't have to hide his passion. He didn't have to feel helpless, useless, impotent.

And now they were free. Now Timothy could rebel against the Huctans with the Band at his side. Now, lying on a straw pallet in his cabin with his wrists throbbing and Robert seething beside him, Timothy had to admit that he was fiercely glad.

"You're joining them, aren't you," Robert said. It wasn't a question. Timothy didn't answer.

Of course he was joining them. He was going to train with the rebels, to learn to hold a sword and pick locks and speak languages and kill Huctans. He was diving in head-first, all in, ships burned. This was what he was born for.

But Robert could only see home. Robert could only see Timothy betraying their family. Robert could only see the consequences, the deaths, the futility.

"You're not joining them, are you," Timothy said. It wasn't a question. Robert didn't answer.

They lay still in the night, not speaking, and Timothy vowed not to let this come between them. But as hard as he tried, as desperately as he and Robert acted out the old familiarity and mouthed the old jokes, things would never be the same.

Two people can't walk two paths together.

CHAPTER 8

HABERD

"You're really going to keep him here, as a prisoner?" Haberd asked. "Is that what we are now?"

"You know we have no choice," Verinald said. "Would you do anything else, if the decision were yours?"

A subtle reminder that the decision was *not* his. After all this time, it was still hard to hear that tone from an old student.

"I would not have revealed the Band to them so thoroughly." Haberd said. "They came here blindfolded. They had not seen any of our faces. We could have blindfolded them again and released them halfway across Botan. The most they could have told anyone was that a few boys carried them in a wagon, a few riders led them through some trees, and they spent a night in a cabin."

"They could have revealed the fact that we exist."

"That who exists? A few children who managed to sneak them out of a loosely guarded Huctan fort? They don't know who we are."

"They know now," Verinald said, "or close enough. They cannot leave. My mind is clear on that."

Haberd had been planning to tell Verinald about what he had seen in the first boy's face, but something about Verinald's voice—which was pointedly *not* sharp or defensive—stayed him.

Then Verinald took his shoulder, and bid him good night, and Haberd forgot whatever intangible cue had broken through to him. The blanket of dullness and despair that had clouded his mind for fifteen years returned, like a cataract. With a shrug, he turned and went to his own cabin.

CHAPTER 9

ROBERT

"Take him," the queen said, the tears still contained in the corners of her eyes.

"My Lady..."

"Take him!" the queen almost shouted. Clarena jerked as if from a blow, and could no longer keep her own tears in check. The queen took Clarena's shoulders.

"Take him," she whispered. "Be strong for me, Clarena. Go."

Clarena went, the child strangely quiet in her arms. He sucked his fingers, then waved as he recognized his mother behind them. Clarena gave the queen one last glance from the doorway, suppressed a sob, and went.

In the hallway she began to run. It was still quiet in the Keep, but there was a flickering glow in the windows. The city was burning.

Clarena's apartments were below the Keep, and it was not so quiet at the bottom of the stairs. Men were running. Loud voices were shouting. Clarena's husband was somewhere among them, she knew, but she did not see him. The tears started blurring her vision, and Clarena pushed her husband from her mind. The only things in her power now were her own life, that of the queen's child, and that of her own son.

She found him in his bed. In one motion she took him up into her other arm and held both boys close. The queen's child recognized her child, who was rubbing his eyes, and smiled. Clarena hoped to see them play together again.

"Hold my neck, babies," she said. Steeling her arms, wiping her tears on her son's downy hair, Clarena began running again. Behind her she heard swords clash, and only the gasping of her breath stayed her sobs.

It still felt like the middle of the night when Robert heard the scrunch of Timothy's straw mattress and the small, soft sounds of getting dressed. There was a little scrape—Timothy moving the stool—and then quiet.

Robert slitted an eye, but could see nothing. It was still dark outside.

He dozed. About half an hour later a quiet knock at the door woke him up. He slitted his eyes again. It was still dark outside. Timothy opened the door and Robert heard Selena's voice.

"You ready?" she asked.

"Yeah," Timothy said. He was all keyed up; you could hear it in his voice.

"Let's go then," Selena said.

"Have fun," Robert called out at them as Timothy turned to

close the door. "I think I'm gonna sleep a little longer."

Timothy laughed. Robert heard them jogging down the gravel path, and then it was quiet again.

He tried to go back to sleep, but he had been sleeping too much lately. Two nights ago, when the boy Jesher had pinned him and gagged him and pretended to scream his screams while they questioned Timothy, he hadn't slept well at all. Last night, after watching Timothy swear the oath and prepare for his training and try to hide his enthusiasm so that Robert wouldn't get angry, he hadn't slept much better.

But he couldn't sleep now, either. He had been indoors too much, cooped up in the cell, cooped up in the boat, cooped up in the wagon, now cooped up in this cabin. He had to get out.

Robert got up and got dressed. There was a little gray light showing through the window. He went out to the latrine, then back to the cabin, dancing across the hard gravel on cold feet.

Rian showed up with breakfast. There were boiled eggs, some more of the little green pears, and bread. As the kid restacked the dishes from last night, Robert tossed an egg back and forth between his hands.

"Am I supposed to stay in here all day, or is it OK to wander around?" he asked.

Rian looked up at him. "I do not know, sir," he said.

"Is there someone you could ask?"

"Yes sir."

"I'd appreciate it," Robert said.

"Yes sir."

Robert pulled up the stool and cracked the egg against the table, rolling it under his palm until all the shell was broken. He peeled it.

The shell stuck badly, taking pieces of egg with it no matter how careful he was.

He finished his food and picked up the razor Rian had left him. Leaning over the bowl of water, he caught a glimpse of his reflection and saw that he had quite a bit of scraggly-looking fluff on his face. The Huctans had shaved them all upon their arrival at Northelm, and each morning afterward, but it had been almost two weeks since the night of their escape. The hair was long enough to tug a little as Robert wet the razor and began scraping.

Rian knocked again.

"Yeah," Robert said.

"May I come in, sir?"

"Yeah," Robert repeated.

Rian opened the door and stepped inside. "Verinald says you may walk around, sir. Only he says to stay in the camp. Sir."

He added the last 'sir' hastily, as if he had almost forgotten and thought Robert might tell on him or something. Being served and called "sir" was awkward enough, without the kid being so scared all the time. Robert wished he knew how to put him at ease.

"Thanks buddy," he said, swishing the razor in the warm water.

"You're welcome, sir." Rian went to the door, then turned again. "Do you need anything else, sir?"

"If I do, I'll let you know," Robert said.

"Good bye, sir."

"Good bye, Rian."

Robert finished shaving, wiped his face off with a towel, and ran a hand over his cheek. The smoothness felt good.

Shrugging his cloak around his shoulders, he went outside.

People were already up. Robert glanced into wax-paper windows as he made his way down the street. A few lamps were lit. A door opened and someone walked down the street a ways before going into a larger building.

Robert looked around for a while, trying to guess how many people lived in the compound of cabins and low buildings. Then he made his way to the far edge of the little town and looked at the mountains around him.

He was in a low basin, surrounded by trees that had gathered where the moisture would collect when it rained. Sage and granite boulders covered the mountains above the trees, and a stand of aspens ran up a gully on the far northern side. Robert had the sense that they were very secluded, that beyond the pink and gray of the basin edge there were many more steep, desert hills with stands of aspen and granite boulders and waves of rolling sage.

It was warmer here than it would be back home, even this early in the morning. Today would be a hot one.

Robert was standing there, feeling the breeze and watching the leaves shake, when he heard something familiar. He cocked his head, listened again, and immediately made his way back into town.

He found the smithy set back a little from the cabins, close to the big building he had seen several people going into and coming out of. The smithy door was closed, but inside he could hear someone working iron. After a few minutes of listening, Robert reached for the door handle, hesitated, and then knocked.

He had waited for a lull between hammer sounds, and a tall man in a leather apron opened the door almost immediately. Robert thought he looked familiar.

"Yes?" the man said.

"Hi," Robert said. "My name's Robert."

"Gerard," the man said. "What can I do for you? Come inside a minute, I need to get this out before it burns up."

"Sure," Robert said, letting himself in as Gerard went back to the fire. Giving the bellows a couple pumps, Gerard pulled a long pair of tongs from the loop at his belt and took what looked like a buckle from the flame.

Timothy's ceremony last night, that's where Robert recognized Gerard from. He was the one who had been up on the platform with Timothy, taking his oath, proclaiming Timothy a man of Botan.

Gerard worked the buckle and put it back into the fire. While he slipped his tongs back into the loop at his belt and used his apron to brush a few flakes from the anvil, Robert began pumping the bellows. Gerard glanced up, watching him.

"You've done that before," he said.

"Yeah," Robert laughed, thinking of how many years he and Timothy had spent working the bellows before Dad had let them touch a hammer. "My father's a smith."

"Ah!" Gerard said. "Then you can work a hammer too, eh?"

Robert shrugged, being modest. "Pretty well," he said.

"Is that what you came here for, then? To give me a hand?"

It hadn't been—Robert wasn't sure why he'd knocked, only that the sound had drawn him—but now that Gerard said it... Yes. Robert wanted to help.

"I've got a hand if you need one," said Robert.

"Sure do. Ever made a spearhead before?"

Robert shook his head.

"Of course not. The Huctans frown on that, don't they? Kill you for it?"

"Yeah," Robert said. "No weapons allowed. Not beyond belt knives and arrowheads."

"Well, now's your chance to give it a try," Gerard said, "I'm making as many as I can finish today."

Robert bit his lip. "If it's alright," he said, "I'd rather work on something else. Horse shoes, or buckles, or whatever else you need."

Gerard took the buckle from the fire again and glanced up at him. "Don't worry," he said. "It's not difficult. I'll show you."

"No," Robert said. "It's not that. I'm just... not sure how I feel about making weapons."

Gerard furrowed his brows, finished with the buckle, let it cool a little, and then quenched it. Wiping the anvil again, he eyed Robert.

"You're the other kid they got from the fort," he said. "The one that didn't want to join the Band."

"Yeah," said Robert, feeling his chance to get a hammer back in his hand slipping away.

Gerard shrugged.

"Well, that's alright," he said, "if you can get some of the shoeing and tools done for me, it'll sure help."

Robert let out a breath. "Thanks," he said. "I'd like that."

Gerard rummaged in a stack of iron and picked Robert a short bar.

"Start off with that," he said, showing Robert a rounded wooden handle with a slot in the end. "For an awl. Needs to be a sharp point on one side and a square end that fits into the handle here, see? I've got one finished around here somewhere..."

Gerard rummaged around, knocking over some metal, and found what he was looking for.

"Here's a finished one," he said. "OK?"

"Yeah, I can do that," Robert said. It was a child's project, one of the easiest things possible to make from iron, but that was alright. Gerard would test him, and he would do well, and Gerard would give him more difficult things to make.

"Alright then," Gerard said.

Robert was careful and methodical, as he always was. He made six awls out of the bar Gerard had given him, quenching the points hard and letting the shafts anneal on a stone Gerard had set out for cooling metal. He caught the tall man eyeing him once or twice, and tried not to let the scrutiny affect his work.

Gerard gave him more iron and showed him a harness buckle. Robert began drawing out a long wire, and soon the beat of hammers and the smell of hot iron and the sweat of a forge on an early summer day blurred into a feeling so familiar that Robert lost himself in it. He was surprised when Gerard said it was time to eat some lunch. Taking off the tool belt Gerard had given him, Robert realized that he was hungry.

He followed the smith out the door and over to the large building across the street.

Several dozen people were inside, sitting together at tables and eating. Gerard pointed to a counter set up in the back corner with food. A middle-aged woman with her hair up in a bun came bustling out of the back room with a steaming pot of what smelled like lentils. Gerard hurried to lift the almost empty pot out of her way so she could set the full one down.

"Thanks," she said, taking the emptier pot from him and scraping the rest of its contents into the new one. She eyed Robert. "Is this one of the new ones?"

"Robert," Robert said.

"Good to meet you, Robert," the woman said.

"Robert!" someone called, and Robert looked over his shoulder to see Selena waving and beckoning him to a table with several other people their age. He held up a hand and smiled, then got himself some soup and cornbread.

"Take your time," Gerard said, "If you want to do some more, I'll be starting up again in about half an hour."

"I'll be there," Robert said, and went to join Selena and her friends.

"Here," a guy a little older than Robert said, scooting over his bowl and making room.

"Thanks," Robert said.

"I think he'll make it," Selena was saying.

"I'm Nick," said the one who had moved over for Robert, offering a hand. Robert shook it.

"Robert," he said.

"Nope," someone down the table was saying. "He's too old. They'll put him taking care of horses or something."

"Who're we talking about?" Robert said to Nick.

"Your friend." Nick held up a finger while he finished chewing. "We're trying to decide if they'll train him."

"I thought that's what he was doing today?"

"Hey, you're his brother, Robert, right?" The one who had said Timothy was too old stood and leaned across the table to offer a hand. "I'm Cody."

"Nice to meet you," Robert said.

"Your friend did pretty good today," Cody said. "I thought he was gonna have a heart attack after the run, though."

A boy next to Cody laughed, and Nick smiled.

"Leon tried to give him one," said the boy who had put a pillow over Robert's head. Jesher. "That was the fastest we've run in a while."

"Where is he now?" Robert asked.

Jesher had just taken a bite. Selena answered for him.

"He's with Haberd, one of the trainers. I took him over there just a couple minutes ago."

"Haberd'll work him over," Cody said. "He's always going on about how they used to get people so much younger and train them so much longer, isn't he?"

"Yeah," Selena said.

"How'd he look after two hours with Farland?" asked Kialo. The boy who had driven their wagon raised his fingers to Robert, and Robert nodded back, trying to quell the resentment that rose in his throat. If it hadn't been for that wagon, he and Timothy might be home by now. Timothy might not have sworn himself to a cause that would probably get him killed.

Selena shrugged. "Tired."

"So wait," Robert said, holding a spoonful of lentil soup in front of his mouth, "if Timothy is training already, then what were you talking about a second ago, with him making it or something?"

"He's getting tested today," Cody said, knowingly. "He thinks he's training, but it's all a test to see if it's worth the effort."

Robert frowned, suddenly angry. "So last night," he said, "when he was up there swearing to serve Botan..."

"That's no matter what," Selena interrupted. "What he's testing for is whether he gets to be a *Thane*."

"A Thane."

"That's us," Cody interjected. "The big shots." He made a

flourishing gesture, and the boy with curly-hair—Tolede—laughed again.

"The Thanes are the ones training to go on missions," Selena said. "When they're done training, they become Marshals."

"Or if they were done training before the Invasion," Cody interrupted.

"So if you're not a Thane and you're not a Marshal..."

"Then you're a nothing!" Cody said, and laughed along with Tolede.

"No," Selena said, giving Cody an annoyed look. "Most of the Band isn't either one. If you're not a Thane or a Marshal, there's no name for you, you just help out with other stuff."

"Like Gerard," Robert said.

"Exactly."

"And," Jesher said, "being a Thane does *not* make you better than everyone else. Just look at Cody."

The Thanes around the table laughed. Jesher finished eating and left, and several minutes later the rest of them followed. Robert waved goodbye and wolfed down the rest of his soup, sopping up the juice with his cornbread. Then he went and joined Gerard in the smithy.

When he got back to the cabin, it was dark. He was tired, but it was a good tired. It felt right to hold a hammer again, and if it made him a little homesick, it was still worth it.

Timothy showed up a little after him, escorted again by Selena. She stuck around long enough to tell him to be ready to go at the same time the next morning, said hello to Robert, and then left them. Timothy collapsed on his straw mattress and groaned.

"I hurt everywhere," he said.

"So whiny," said Robert.

"Look at this." Timothy rolled over and showed Robert his hand. His pinky was swollen and purple.

"Nice," Robert said. "How'd you do that?"

"A guy named Farland," Timothy said. "He hit me with a stick."

Robert waited for the rest of the story, but Timothy didn't say anything. Robert realized suddenly that Timothy was trying not to upset him, trying not to remind him that he had chosen to take the oath that Robert refused, and wanted to growl in frustration. When had they started worrying about each other's feelings?

"Well, are you going to tell me about it," Robert said, leaning over and punching Timothy in the arm, "or am I going to have to beat it out of you?"

Timothy looked up, grinned, and began to talk.

Farland was the fighting trainer, he said. He had had Timothy try to fight with him with all kinds of wooden weapons. That was how he got the bruise on his hand. And how he had been flipped over Farland's shoulder onto his back.

"Wow," Robert said, laughing at how excited Timothy was about it.

"And this morning, oh the run this morning was *terrible*," Timothy said. "Leon—he's one of the Thanes, but pretty much a jerk—the one that kept hitting me the other night..."

"I remember him."

"Yeah. He was in charge of the exercise this morning. He made everyone introduce themselves, and then told me to repeat everyone's names. I said, 'Um...', before I started, and he interrupted me and was like, 'Um is incorrect,'" Timothy made his voice deep and pompous as he imitated Leon, "And then he made me sprint across the field and back."

"Aw, poor little Timothy had to run across the field," Robert said.

"And *then*," Timothy went on, sitting up and holding up a finger, "as soon as I got back, he goes, 'Again, and this time follow instructions.'" This time Timothy accompanied his pompous Leon voice with a little head bobble and eye roll, and Robert laughed. "And then I ran it again, and he said the same thing again, and finally I figured out that he didn't think I was sprinting fast enough. So when I practically fell over trying to run faster, he finally decided that it was good enough."

"You're not making me like Leon any more than I already did," Robert said.

"Yeah. But that was the easy part. Then we all went on this long run up the hill. I thought I was going to die. It was at least three miles straight up the hill, and then back down. I fell a couple times and had to use a tree to pull myself back up. I was so tired."

"Mm," Robert said.

"And then there was the Ropes—that's what they call it, it's like a bunch of ropes tied at all these weird angles between trees—and right after the run, when I could barely stand up, Leon told me to climb this rope that was like thirty feet high." Timothy looked at Robert then, and got an embarrassed look, and shrugged. "Anyway, it was hard."

Robert pushed him.

"You make it up?"

"Yeah. I don't know how, but I made it up."

"Was that all the exercise?"

"No, there was an obstacle course, too. I finished like five minutes behind everyone."

"So," Robert said, trying to keep Timothy going, trying to keep the awkwardness that should not be possible between brothers at bay, "there was the exercise, then the fighting with Farland, then..."

"No, before Farland there were a couple hours with this guy named Comaro. He's a strategist or something. He just had me play this game called King's Table with all these carved pieces on a wooden board. It was confusing. You'd like it."

Robert sniffed a laugh.

"So exercise, then Comaro, then Farland, and then Haberd," Timothy said. "I don't even know how to explain Haberd, he's just... I don't know how to explain it."

"What's his thing?"

"*Eliniel.* It's a Botani word. Selena says there's not really a word for it in Common. It's sort of like spying, disguises, picking locks, forging letters... except there's a lot more to it, I think. Haberd kept asking me these questions, really fast, and then he told me to answer like I was a fisherman or a nobleman or a washerwoman. He gave me this code I was supposed to solve, but I couldn't figure it out. I don't know how to explain him," Timothy repeated finally, throwing up his hands.

"Sounds intense."

"Yeah." Timothy scratched the back of his neck. Robert rolled on his side and propped his head up on his elbow.

"So that was it?" Robert asked.

"No, then there was this lady named Aral that had me try to do a bunch of climbing and jumping and stuff and then spent half an hour throwing blunted javelins at me. I was supposed to practice dodging them, which I was bad at. I think she loved that." Robert could hear the distaste in Timothy's voice. "At the end there was Toman. He's an archer. He didn't say anything, though. We just shot. It was nice."

"You show him up?"

Timothy grinned and shook his head. "No. He was way, way better than me. They all were. At everything."

Well that was good. Timothy was competitive. If they let him train, he would work harder than anyone else until he was as good as they were. Robert was happy for him. He really was.

"So... how was *your* day?" Timothy asked after a minute. He was staring at the ceiling.

"Pretty good, actually," Robert said, wondering when they had started asking each other about their days, wondering how it had come to this so quickly. "I met up with Gerard, that guy that did your ceremony..."

"Thanks for coming, by the way."

"Sure," Robert said, though it felt all wrong. Timothy shouldn't have to thank him. Friends didn't thank friends, not for things like that.

"Anyway," Robert said, "he's a blacksmith, so he let me help him. I spent all day making awls and buckles."

Timothy turned and looked at him, looking surprised and pleased. "That's good," he said. Then he laughed. "Awls."

Robert laughed too. "It was good to get a hammer in my hands again," he said.

"I bet." After a minute, Timothy got up and snuffed out the lamp.

"Oh," Robert said, "I talked to a bunch of the Thanes at lunch today."

"Yeah?"

"Yeah. I don't think you were supposed to know, not today anyway, but they said all this stuff was like a test to see if you got to keep training."

Timothy froze.

"To see if I got to keep training? Selena said it was to see what my schedule would be."

"That's just what they told me," Robert replied.

Timothy turned over on his back, in the darkness, and was quiet for a long minute. Finally he let out a long sigh. "Well," he said, "I hope I passed."

Robert hoped so too. He honestly did. Timothy was going to be pretty mopey if he hadn't.

CHAPTER 10

Despite his nerves, Timothy was exhausted enough to sleep for several hours before he began to dream about what Robert had told him. He dreamt that the Marshals decided to let him train, came to his cabin to tell him the good news, found him asleep, and were so disgusted with his laziness that they rescinded their offer and set him to cleaning dishes.

When the cycle of dreaming nervous dreams, waking in a panic, and falling back asleep grew to be too much, Timothy got up. His body was stiff. His muscles felt cracked and inelastic, like bowstrings left stretched in the rain, and it was cold outside of his blankets. He sat on the stool by the table, in the dark, and pulled his cloak around him to wait. A part of him—a tiny, weak, disgusting part—almost hoped that he hadn't passed the test, that he wouldn't be a Thane, that he wouldn't have to train anymore.

At last, Timothy heard Selena's footsteps on the gravel. Rising, he went to the door and opened it before she had had time to knock. He expected a pronouncement, and waited for one, but Selena said nothing. For a moment she stared at Timothy, dripping from the drizzling rain and looking a little confused. Her eyes had a blurry, tired look, and for some reason this surprised Timothy. He hadn't expected Thanes to have a hard time waking up in the morning.

It was strangely encouraging.

After a moment Selena jerked her head, and Timothy followed.

They ran again, in the mud and the rain. They worked on the Ropes again, and ran obstacles, Timothy slipping and falling and slogging through the deepening muck while the Thanes jumped and swung and vaulted. They ate breakfast, and the muscle tremors in Timothy's arms were so violent that he had to steady one hand with the other to get a full spoon to his mouth.

After breakfast, Selena led Timothy to Comaro to begin the same grueling schedule of training he had endured the day before. He tried and failed at everything from strategy and combat to bowmanship and horsemanship. The thought of sleep—of taking off his sodden clothes and slithering under dry blankets to close his eyes for a while—was a constant torment to him. When he reached his cabin at last, he fell asleep before Robert could ask him about his day.

The third day—and the fourth, and the fifth—were the same. No one would tell Timothy whether the testing was to decide his training schedule or to decide whether he would *have* a training schedule. Timothy told himself that every drill and exercise might be the margin by which he would either become a Thane or a gardener. Don't go to the garden, he said to himself, and when he found himself halfheartedly executing some drill, or when he wanted to lie down and cry, he repeated this phrase in his head or under his breath and somehow found the strength to stay the course.

Yet staying the course, neither excelling nor giving up, was all he could do. His dreams of impressing everyone with his talent were flown and gone. He had no talent. Talent was what the Thanes had, beautiful and humiliating to watch and so far above Timothy that his best efforts were hardly recognizable beside them. If he became a Thane at all, it would be on the weight of his effort alone. Even then it would be a kindness, a mercy, a gesture of pity.

On the sixth day, Timothy rallied his strength and nearly kept up. On the seventh, Robert had to kick him awake.

Timothy ran dead-legged on that seventh day, head hung, eyes slitted open just enough to see the ground ahead of him. Someone—he thought it was Jesher—had to nudge him awake twice during breakfast. When Selena told him to skip strategy and go straight to Haberd's cabin, where they were waiting for him, Timothy was so exhausted that he nearly refused. Haberd's cabin was too far. He was too tired.

Then what Selena had said sunk in, and Timothy's dragging pulse quickened.

This was it. The pronouncement.

Selena left him to make the walk alone. Sniffing a deep breath of dry mountain air, Timothy straightened his back and prepared himself to take the news like a man.

As he walked, his mind went back to times he could have tried harder and done better. There were many such times, and he knew that they were going to haunt him in the garden.

Reaching Haberd's cabin, Timothy walked up the steps and knocked. Footsteps sounded inside. The latch moved. The door swung outwards, and Haberd bowed with a flourish that was probably characteristic of some ancient court he had infiltrated long ago.

"Come in," Haberd said.

Timothy went in.

"Sit down," Haberd said. Timothy took the stool and faced Farland, Comaro, and the empty chair that would soon hold Haberd. His hands felt as if they should be trembling, but they were strangely still on his knees.

"Well," Haberd said, using a little towel to draw a tea kettle off of the hook above the fireplace. "You know by now that we've been testing you."

Timothy checked his voice, making sure it wouldn't tremble when he spoke, and nodded. "Yes, sir," he said.

Haberd offered Comaro and Farland tea, then poured himself a small cup and took the empty chair in front of Timothy.

"I'll be blunt," he said. "The other Marshals tell me that you have abnormally slow reflexes, a tendency to rush strategy, and a tendency to hesitate in everything else. Toman finds you average, and Aral, to be quite honest, thinks you completely useless."

Timothy nodded. He had expected this, prepared himself for this. From the moment Robert had mentioned a test, he had known in his heart that he would never be a Thane.

So why did hearing the words, from Haberd's mouth, make him want to cry?

"In *my* opinion," Haberd continued, looking at the window as if the curtains were not drawn and something interesting was going on outside, "you're too old. It's one thing to bring in twelve-year-olds, like we've done here from time to time, when..."

"Yes, yes," Comaro interrupted, his tone holding a little

annoyance. "We've heard it a thousand times. It's better to have them start young, but the days of picking and choosing are over. We have to do the best we can, now."

Haberd nodded, lifting his cup of tea as if in a toast. "As you say," he said, "we have to do the best we can."

"Enough of the suspense," Farland said. "Tell him."

Haberd glanced at Comaro, who bowed his head and gestured back towards Haberd, giving the older man the prerogative of breaking the news.

"Well," said Haberd, "against my better judgment, we've decided to train you as a Thane."

Timothy, who had been staring into the fire without focusing, looked up sharply.

"Yes," said Haberd, holding up a palm as if to stop Timothy from protesting, "I know. It's a surprise to us all, really, but Farland said you worked hard, and he wants to prove to everyone that someone without the reflexes can still learn to fight."

Timothy would be training. In combat. With Farland. A grin tugged hard at the corners of his mouth, and he did not succeed in hiding it.

"We've decided to try something a little different," Farland said. "We're still working out the details, but the main thing is that you'll be getting more of my attention—and Haberd's—than we've given to any Thane before."

The hair on the back of Timothy's neck prickled. He would be training with Farland *and* with Haberd.

Farland had called him a *Thane*.

"This means," Haberd said sternly, "That you'll work *harder* than any Thane has before. You'll spend four hours with Farland in the morning, then four more with me. Alone. Those will be hard hours."

Timothy nodded, trying to convey grave determination.

"Aral will then have an hour with you," Haberd said, "after which Jesher has agreed to spend three hours supervising you in the practice drills that Aral and Farland assign."

That was twelve hours, Timothy thought.

"The last four hours," Haberd went on, "you'll spend with Selena. She will teach you the Botani and Huctan languages. Once you begin getting some basic proficiency—which had better happen pretty quickly—she'll work in some practice on the drills that *I* assign you."

The trembling feeling was back in Timothy's hands, but now it had more to do with giddiness than dread. Haberd pursed his lips and looked at Timothy as if searching for an excuse to retract his offer.

"As Farland noted," he said after a long pause, "we have not done this before. We are making a significant sacrifice, of time and resources, and we are taking a grave risk. Our hope is that you will, despite your age, reach a level of acceptable competency. Our hope is that you may yet be of some use to the Band. If you should find the training too difficult, or if it begins to look like our hope is misplaced..."

"We'll cross that bridge when we come to it," Farland said, slapping his thigh and standing. "I think that's about everything, is it not?"

Farland glanced at Comaro, who nodded, and then at Haberd, who shrugged. All three pairs of eyes looked at Timothy, as if waiting for him to make some response to all of this. Timothy cleared his throat.

"I'll do my very best," he said, and was surprised that his voice did not tremble.

Haberd sighed. "Well then," he said, "I suppose that's all we'll get."

Outside, a wind was picking up. The currents of air, carrying the smell of sage and the sound of aspen leaves clapping together, felt good on Timothy's face. His body was still exhausted, but he ran easily to the clearing Farland had sent him to.

The clearing where *he*, a *Thane*, would be learning combat from Farland every day.

Timothy checked to make sure no one was watching, then laughed out loud.

CHAPTER 11

HABERD

Farland, Comaro and Haberd stayed in the cabin for a minute after Timothy left.

"Do you think it was a little much?" Farland asked.

Haberd shook his head. "He can take it. He's the kind that'll try harder for it."

Comaro smiled under his mustache. "Aw, Haberd, don't get all mushy on us."

Haberd barked a laugh and got up, going to the window and drawing the curtain a little to peer outside. Something was alive, deep in his gut. Something that had been dead these fifteen years. Something he was afraid to acknowledge.

"I was fool enough to tell Ricera how good *he* was," he said. "Look where that got us."

CHAPTER 12

The king of Botan entered his apartments from the back door, shouting to wake his wife. He found her on the floor by the bed. Her nightgown exposed her knee, and the white fabric at her breast was stained crimson. For a moment, the king's tears could not overcome his shock.

The sound of steel rang in the hallway, and the king went to the front door with sword drawn. He flung it open just in time to see one of his most faithful friends gasp as a sword slid into his chest.

The murderer's back was to the king, but he heard the king's cry and turned in time to stay the king's first blow. The king attacked again, and felt his grief turn to rage as he saw that the murderer wore the colors of a Duest.

"Wait," the traitor cried, and as he retreated past a torch on the wall, light fell across his face.

"Ricera," the king said, and the tears began to come. They were hot on his cheeks: the tears of a king for friend and queen and country.

"Ricera!" the king said again, and he threw himself at the man he had shared his childhood with.

Ricera tried to speak, at first, but he and the king had studied under the same masters. Ricera was perhaps the better swordsman, but the king was strengthened with wrath. Ricera fell silent as the king pressed him hard down the stairs.

It happened in an instant. The king lunged. Ricera parried and riposted, and though he appeared to pull back his blow, steel bit deep and mortal through the king's silk shirt. The falling king swung once more, and his sword clattered on the stairs as he fell.

Ricera's blade fell beside the king's. He knelt. His hands reached for the king's head, then withdrew as if from fire. For a moment the living man stooped by the dead, trembling. Then fists rose to face, face sank to floor, and both men were still for a long moment.

At last Ricera rose, turned as one unsure of himself, bent to pick up his sword, and ran down the hallway.

Timothy took out one of the wooden swords and practiced a few swings while he waited for Farland. The bruises that ran in splotches across his hands and forearms flared in pain, but he found it easier to ignore them today. Today he wasn't testing, he was *training*.

Farland arrived a minute later, striding purposefully across the gravel. There was less gentleness in his eyes than there had been the past week. Less gentleness, and more determination. He did not bid Timothy a good morning.

"You won't need that," he said, taking the sword from Timothy as he walked by. Ducking into the shed that held his training materials, he rummaged around on one of the shelves. A moment later he emerged with a ball of string. Biting off about a yard and tossing it to Timothy—who dropped it and then scrambled to pick it up—Farland began untangling several more yard-long sections as he gave Timothy instructions.

"Tie that around your ankles," he said. "Leave about a shoulder-width of slack."

Timothy bent to obey, and Farland tossed the ball of string back into the shed.

"You won't be touching any of the weapons for a long while, now," Farland said. "You've demonstrated that you can't use them, so we're going to set up a good foundation of footwork. Some of these kids can get away with sloppy footwork and improvising because they're fast. You're not, so you're going to have to think. I'm going to teach you to plan your movements ahead, to *lead* the fight. That's the only way you'll have a chance. Have you got that string tied yet?"

"Almost," Timothy said.

"Well, when you're finished fiddling with yourself, stand up and give me your best balanced stance."

Timothy stood up. Farland pushed him, and he had to step back. The string broke. Farland took one of the lengths he had draped across his arm and tossed it to Timothy.

"It doesn't matter how good your stance is if you just stand dead on your feet like that. If you're dead on your feet, you're going to fall when you get pushed. Stance is about *readiness.* A balanced stance is one where you can move in any direction you need to without wasting time shifting your weight around first. There won't *be* time, when someone swings a sword at you. Do you have that tied yet? Do you need me to come down there and tie them for you?"

Timothy finished the knot and stood.

"Readiness," Farland repeated. "Not leaning back on your heels. Get up on your toes a little bit. A *little* bit, I said, not tip-toeing around like a princess. There. Now unlock your knees and get ready to move. Are you ready? Here I come. Don't let me touch you."

Farland came forward, hand raised, and Timothy shuffled backward, trying not to break the string. Farland caught up with him easily and gave him a ringing smack on the side of the head.

"Don't let me *touch* you," he repeated, and came again. This time Timothy broke the string, and Farland took another one from his arm.

"I won't say there's anything special about taking short steps," he said, "but this string will force you to take them for now. Big steps, the way people usually take them, tend to involve a lot of vertical motion. You jump your body up and then crash it down. Here's a riddle for you; is jumping and crashing a good way to be balanced?"

"No," Timothy said, trying to tie his knot faster this time.

"Very good," Farland said. "There's hope. Dare I ask why not?"

Timothy stood and rubbed the back of his neck. "Because someone might attack you while you're in the air," he said, repeating what Farland had told him on one of his first days testing. "Or while you're landing. And you won't be able to change direction until your weight is settled and you can plant your foot."

"And he listens!" Farland said. "I don't care what they say about you, Timothy. We're going to make a fighter out of you yet."

It was the only praise Timothy got that day, from anyone, and although it was sarcastic, it was enough to carry him through.

When he was finished breaking all the strings Farland had bitten off for him, Timothy began the drills. Farland made him walk in slow steps, advancing with his right foot turned forward and his left foot placed sideways behind it. He corrected the balance of Timothy's weight, the forward and backward lean of his torso, the pace of his steps.

When Timothy's knees were trembling with the effort of staying bent, Farland set him to carrying around a narrow rain barrel on his shoulders. The barrel was only partially filled with water, which meant that any slight tip in Timothy's shoulders sent all the water sloshing to one end and made it very difficult to keep the barrel balanced.

When Timothy dropped the barrel for the twentieth or thirtieth time, it was back to steps. They continued until Timothy's feet dragged in the gravel and his knees trembled even when he stood still.

Finally, Farland assigned the drill that Timothy was to practice with Jesher later that day. It was a simple one. Farland stood behind Timothy with a rag, and Timothy focused his eyes straight forward. Then Farland threw the rag over Timothy's head, without warning, so that it fluttered to the ground a few feet in front of Timothy's face. All Timothy had to do was lunge forward and catch the rag before it struck the ground.

Simple, but impossible. When Timothy hadn't caught the rag once after half an hour of trying, Farland handed it to him and said to spend an hour at it with Jesher that afternoon. Timothy nearly protested—the weariness and his hunger were beginning to get to him—but he wisely kept his mouth shut and nodded that he would.

Then he went to lunch, and tried to recover enough to be ready for four hours with Haberd.

When Timothy knocked on Haberd's door, it was not Haberd that answered. It was another old man. It was the old man who had questioned Timothy as he lay naked on the bench, that first night after his arrival.

But he spoke with Haberd's voice.

"Come in," the man said.

Timothy did not come in. He froze in the doorway, and it was a tribute to his weariness that it took him several long seconds to understand what was happening, to see the similarities between the Haberd he knew and the face he remembered from his first night at the Band.

"You're..." he began

"Haberd, yes," the old man said. "Come in, please."

Timothy took one step into the cabin. It was beginning already. He hadn't even gotten in the door yet, and he was already confused beyond bewilderment. He was beginning to think that *Eliniel* was just another word for Haberd making Timothy feel stupid.

"But you're also the one who..." Timothy began. Then it clicked, and he felt some relief. "Oh," he said. "You're in disguise. And you were also in disguise when you questioned me."

Haberd raised his eyebrows, as if this had been obvious.

"Or?" he said. "And please shut the door."

Timothy shut the door and tried to think. "Or..." he said, "Or you're you now. And you were you when you questioned me. And all last week, when you were testing me, you were in disguise."

"Excellent," Haberd said. "Genius. My shock is uncontainable. Which is it?"

Timothy looked at Haberd closely. He did not see any obvious signs of disguise. Then again, he wasn't sure what an obvious sign of disguise would be. He hadn't been able to see the signs of Lutho's disguise, either.

"I would guess..." he began, then hesitated.

"Spit it out."

"I would guess that you're in disguise now," Timothy said.

"Why?"

"Because otherwise you'd have had to wear a disguise all week, instead of just twice."

"So you're counting on my laziness."

Timothy shrugged. Haberd continued looking at him, as if he should be realizing something now. Timothy tried to think.

"Unless..." he said.

"Don't make me keep prodding you. Take this as a perpetual command: spit it out."

"Unless you knew that I'd think you would take the easier option, so you went to the effort of wearing the disguise all week just so you could fool me."

"OK," said Haberd. "Fine. And then I could also have known that you'd know that I'd know, so I might have just disguised myself today and last week anyway. How far down that road do you want to go?"

Timothy shrugged, and Haberd waved the question away.

"What else?"

Timothy was at a loss. He thought, then shook his head and shrugged. When Haberd continued to wait, he thought some more.

"Actually," he said. "You probably did wear the disguise all last week."

Haberd raised his eyebrows. Twirled his hand.

"Because if you were disguised when you were questioning me, then you'd have had to plan all this out ahead of time. Before you even knew you were going to keep me here. Before you knew I was going to join the Band."

"Counting on my laziness again?" Haberd asked.

"Not laziness. You just wouldn't have had a reason to wear a disguise, before you knew I was going to join."

"And I couldn't have disguised myself just in case?" Timothy cocked his head, but Haberd waved him off. "I know," he said, "it's not likely. That's called 'motivation'. We'll spend a lot of time on the subject. What else?"

And so, for the next half-hour, Timothy tried to puzzle out whether the Haberd he saw was the real Haberd or the disguised Haberd. At last, with help, he decided that Haberd had indeed worn the disguise during the week of testing, and was now himself. Haberd then showed Timothy what he'd done to make himself a different person. It had taken surprisingly little.

"Some disguises are elaborate," Haberd said, "with layers of makeup and resin and wax and hair. Go to Verinald if you want to learn that art. It is something of an obsession for him, and he is very, very good at it.

"But sometimes, *most* times, Verinald's art is unnecessary. Sometimes all it takes is a different slant of the shoulders, or an inflection, or a squint. It all depends on how long and how *much* your subject is going to be looking at you. You'd be very surprised at what people won't notice. Of course, if you keep eyeing them to make sure they're not noticing, they will. It's about *poise*, boy. Do you know the meaning of the word?"

"Yes," said Timothy.

"Good!" Haberd said, rummaging under his short desk and

withdrawing a large clay pitcher filled with water. "Your first assignment of the day, then. Carry this pitcher across the room without my noticing it."

Timothy almost asked how he was supposed to keep Haberd from noticing when Haberd had given Timothy the pitcher in the first place, but by now he knew better. This was the way of all Haberd's assignments. Pretend you're a nobleman. Fake a gimp leg. Act as if you're afraid of something. Convince me that you know where the gold is but don't want me to know that you know. All tasks aimed at deception, and all impossible since the lies were assigned by the very person they were supposed to fool.

Timothy went out the cabin door and closed it. Then, taking a deep breath, he went back inside and began walking across the room, holding the pitcher at his side where it would be shielded from Haberd's view.

"That looks very natural," Haberd said. "You don't look stiff at all. I'm not even curious as to why someone is walking across my house in the first place, let alone staring straight ahead with their arms at their sides like a marching soldier."

Timothy was used to the sarcasm. Without pausing he turned, left the room, shut the door, and then entered again. This time he walked more naturally. He even made eye contact with Haberd on his way across the room, nodding as one would when passing an old acquaintance.

"Oh," said Haberd. "You're greeting me. Nice to see you. How have you been? Why is your hand behind your back? Never mind. I can't physically see what you're holding, so there must not be anything there. In fact, here!" Haberd wadded up the ink-rag on his desk and flung it at Timothy. "Just cover it with that, and I won't even notice."

Timothy retreated and tried again. He tried balancing the pitcher in his tunic, and Haberd asked whether he was pregnant. He tried rolling up his cloak with the pitcher inside and carrying the whole bundle, and Haberd politely offered the hook on the wall to hang his burden.

Finally, not knowing whether he was trying to be funny or was simply frustrated enough to be reckless, Timothy snatched the ink-rag from where it had fallen on the floor, went outside, shut the door, and then threw it back open. With eyes wide, he flung the ink rag into the corner and pointed in exaggerated surprise.

"Look! What's *that?*" he said, and sprinted across the room with the pitcher under his shoulder.

Haberd was not amused. He laughed, but there was definite and real annoyance under his sarcasm now.

"Perfect," he said. "If I were four years old, that would have been perfect. Now go and try again."

Timothy was suddenly angry—angry and frustrated—and he slammed the door when he went outside. He paused for a moment on the step, trying to gather himself. What was this teaching him? How was Haberd's constant sarcasm and Timothy's constant failure helping things?

You're feeling sorry for yourself, he thought. Just do what you're told, and do it better. But he didn't want to try, right now. He knew this was self-pity, and he despised it, but that didn't stop the feeling. He was angry, but knowing that the anger was unhelpful did nothing to make it go away.

Then Haberd flung open the door behind him, and Timothy forgot his self-contemplation.

"Do you think my door is invincible?" the old man said, snatching the pitcher from Timothy and pointing at the hinges. There was fire behind his eyes, and the breeze played with the wisps of silver hair still clinging to his head. "Is your pouting worth ripping the hinges out of my wall?"

Timothy's own anger evaporated. Became fear.

"No," he said. "I..."

"Come here," Haberd said, marching across the room. "Put your ear here."

Timothy put his ear to the wall, and Haberd went to the door. He opened it, and then flung it shut with all his might. The wall reverberated in Timothy's ear.

"Does that sound like it's good for my cabin?" Haberd said. "Is it a *pleasant* sound?"

"No," Timothy said, "I'm sorry, I didn't..."

"Sit down," Haberd said, gesturing toward the chair at the desk in the center of the room. Timothy sat, feeling his face going hot, wishing he hadn't let a second of frustration get the best of him, wondering whether he had already ruined the chance he had been given.

"Now close your eyes," Haberd said. "Immediately."

Timothy closed them. He heard Haberd coming closer, leaning on the desk, looking at Timothy's face.

"No peeking," Haberd said, and his voice was suddenly much less angry than it had been. "Now," he said, "*without* opening your eyes; which side of the room is the pitcher on?"

Timothy frowned, and tried to remember. Haberd had snatched the pitcher from him at the door. Had he carried it across the room when he told Timothy to put his ear to the wall? Had he carried it back again when he went to slam the door?

"A-*ha*..." Haberd said, and Timothy opened his eyes. Haberd was taking a bow. The pitcher was sitting by the far wall, away from the door, in plain sight.

"You can get out of my chair now," Haberd said. "And I apologize for the rudeness. The door is fine. Slam it all day, if you feel like it."

Timothy got up. He looked at the pitcher, and at Haberd.

"Distraction," he said.

"That's right," Haberd said. "Now, pull up a stool—I think there's one in the cabinet—and let me explain Eliniel to you."

Timothy had thought he'd had a basic idea of what Eliniel was—the deceit, the manipulation—but Haberd took several hours to explain it in detail. He said it would be useful for Timothy to have some perspective, because in the next weeks and months Haberd was going to make him do things that he didn't understand, and he had to trust that Haberd knew what he was doing.

Eliniel was a Botani word, with no direct translation in Common. It involved espionage—picking locks, forging letters, coding messages, telling lies, ballroom dancing, court etiquette, disguise—but it was not *just* espionage. Haberd said that espionage was to Eliniel as a hammer was to blacksmithing. It was the tool most often used, and a vital one, but it was not everything.

Haberd promised that he would repeat this, over and over, while he taught Timothy the "low skills" like throwing his voice and changing his accent and opening a sealed letter without breaking the wax. He reiterated that true Eliniel was so far beyond Timothy's reach that it might as well be sorcery. True Eliniel was judgment, he said, judging situations and people with enough accuracy to then manipulate them to fit your purpose. If Timothy could learn good judgment, Haberd said, the rest would be easy.

Timothy almost asked how he had been supposed to *judge* himself across the room without Haberd noticing the pitcher of water. Haberd seemed to hear the unspoken question.

"For instance," he said. "How did I get the pitcher across the room without your knowing?"

"Distraction," said Timothy.

"Not the one-word summary," Haberd said. "The mechanics. How did I do it?"

"You pretended to be angry. You distracted me with that while you got the pitcher across."

"And how did I know to pretend to be angry?"

Timothy shrugged. Haberd widened his eyes, as if shocked by Timothy's audacity.

"Well," Timothy protested, "you could have pretended something else just as well. To be sad, or... distracted, or in a hurry."

"No," Haberd said, "I could not have. I could have pretended those things, but they wouldn't have worked as well as anger. Anger worked because you were angry yourself. It also worked because you are insecure about your new position as a Thane, so any disapproval on my part is going to cut you to the bone. You have a deep, predictable emotional response, and nothing distracts like an emotional response. Do you disagree?"

Slowly, Timothy shook his head. It was a little insulting, and more than a little embarrassing, to have been read so easily. But it also made perfect sense, suddenly.

"Nod that you understand," Haberd said.

Timothy nodded.

"Good. Because now I've just ruined a good tool by telling you about it. Now, if I tried to play your insecurity again, you'd immediately feel suspicious. In fact, you'd use it against me, pretending to be played so that you could see what my purpose was. Right?"

Timothy nodded, uncertain that he had enough room in his head at the moment to even feel suspicion, let alone use it.

"Good," Haberd said. "And now the point. How did I know about your insecurity, and your anger, so that I could manipulate your strong and predictable emotional response?"

Timothy paused, and then it clicked.

"Judgment," he said.

"Eliniel," said Haberd.

While Timothy's head didn't exactly *hurt* when he left Haberd's cabin, it didn't feel normal. The constant pretending, like a dream that he wasn't quite sure was untrue, felt jumbled with reality. He found himself pausing in the middle of the gravel path that led to Aral's clearing, standing and thinking, and had to shake his head until his lips jiggled to snap out of the stupor.

It was strange, how he could feel so incompetent and so excited at the same time.

Aral had a nastiness that went beyond Haberd's cutting sarcasm, and she clearly thought training Timothy a complete waste. But she was the reason that the Thanes could dive over, climb up, swing through or slide under just about anything, and Timothy was determined to learn from her.

Her training area, the Ropes, was near the obstacle course the Thanes ran in the mornings. It consisted mainly of trees, walls, stumps, ditches, poles, and (of course) ropes. Jesher was apparently going to accompany Timothy as a training partner, since many of the moves Aral taught required two people to execute. Timothy was glad of the help, but it didn't help the insecurity Haberd had identified in him to work with someone who could do everything Aral asked better than she could do it herself.

Yet, while it was embarrassing to work with Jesher, it was also an honor. Timothy hadn't met all of the other Thanes—many of them were out on missions, and Timothy had never been good at meeting people anyway—but he had absorbed some of the talk. He had seen Jesher drilling off to the side while Timothy endured the tests of the last week. On a few occasions he had spoken with Jesher, briefly, and it hadn't taken long to understand that Jesher was different from the other Thanes.

It wasn't that Jesher was more skilled, though Timothy had already heard enough talk to know that Jesher was one of the best fighters in the Band. It was something else, something behind Jesher's jokes and banter, that indicated a seriousness and depth of purpose that the other Thanes didn't have. Over the next few months, as Timothy spent an increasing amount of time with Jesher, he would find out exactly how deep his purpose went.

But right now Aral was trying to teach Timothy the loop-jump, and he was failing miserably.

"You're going to break your wrists," Aral said. "Your hands don't do anything to make you jump farther. All they do is start your body rotating the other way, so you land on your feet. You don't *have* to land on your feet. Jesher, show him."

Jesher jogged away a short distance. Turning, he ran toward the wide, flat table they were practicing on and took a flying leap. As he flew over the table, nearly horizontal to the ground, he slapped his hands on the top surface and pulled his knees between his arms. He landed on the other side running.

"No," Aral said, "I said show him *without* landing on your feet. Don't touch your hands."

Jesher obeyed. This time he sailed over the table at a full dive. When he reached the ground on the other side, where he should have crashed headlong, he tucked and rolled, turning a quick somersault before spooling up to his feet.

"The roll you'll learn later," Aral said. "The point is the jump. Did his hands touch the table?"

Timothy shook his head. Aral waited.

"No ma'am," Timothy said.

"No is right. And did he make it over the table just the same?"

"Yes ma'am."

"Yes is right. You have to jump far enough to make it over *without* your hands. Your hands only touch to spin your body, not to give you more distance. Now you do it."

Timothy tried to do what she said—he really did—but he could tell before he left the ground that he was doing it wrong. He slapped his hands hard and tripped over the far edge of the table, and when he fell, he fell hard.

"Listen to me when I speak," Aral said. "What did I say? You have to jump far enough to make it over, and that means you have to *dive*. The whole point of the loop jump is to jump over something you couldn't get over without diving. Jesher, help him move the table over to the pit."

'The pit' was a pool of water. It was deep and muddy, fed from the stream through a narrow, hand-dug ditch. Aral had Timothy and Jesher place the table at the water's edge. It wasn't hard to figure out what would happen next.

After a couple of stutter-stepped failed failures, Timothy was cold and wet and angry enough to jump at a full, horizontal dive. He cleared the table and slapped into the water hard. The blow stung his face and chest, and the water took his breath away, but he clambered out of the mud and began jogging back for another try.

"Good," Aral said, "Let's see it again."

Timothy did it again. The water stung worse.

"One more," Aral said.

Timothy did one more.

"Alright then. That's exactly the jump you have to make. I want you to do ten more of those—no hands—and then try doing the hand touch. If you still give a little bunny-hop and plant your palms, we'll go back to doing it without your hands. Go!"

While Aral was watching Timothy flop into the cold water, Jesher practiced one-man vaults on a board fence. The fence was at least twelve feet high, but Jesher ran up to it, jumped, planted his foot on the wall like he was going to run straight up the wooden planks, and caught the top edge. In one motion he pulled himself to the top, stood, and then jumped off the other side.

He was an artist.

When Timothy finished his ten no-handed jumps and then failed his regular jump, twice, Aral set him to practicing rolls. To demonstrate, she had Jesher climb to a tree branch some fifteen feet off the ground and jump off. Timothy winced as he watched Jesher fall, but when Jesher hit the ground he crumpled, rolled, and came up on his feet without so much as bruising a heel.

Timothy tried the same roll off of a two foot stump and almost broke his shoulder. Aral spent the rest of the hour showing him exactly how many mistakes it was possible to make while trying to do a forward tumble.

Aral's portion of the training concluded, as always, with her daily javelin practice. The darts she threw were padded, so they wouldn't really injure a person permanently unless they hit him in the eye or the face or a bone, but they hurt. Dodging them was supposed to help reflexes, but Timothy suspected that the exercise was more for Aral's enjoyment than anything else.

Timothy got hit four times, while Jesher caught ten out of twelve javelins with his bare hands. Three of the other Thanes showed up, then, and Aral waved Timothy off to start drilling with Jesher while she worked with the new arrivals.

"She's a pain, isn't she?" Jesher said.

Timothy scratched the back of his neck, remembered that he always scratched the back of his neck when he was nervous, and put his hand down firmly at his side.

"Yeah," he said, "literally."

Jesher was kind enough to give a little sniff of a laugh, and Timothy felt heat rise to his cheeks. His hand tried to return to the back of his neck. He refused to let it.

"One thing I noticed on your rolls," Jesher said, "is that you're hitting your shoulder hard and pretty much skipping your feet. Your feet are still supposed to absorb *some* of the impact, just not all of it. You want to roll out, but you want to give your feet a little time to absorb some of the shock."

"OK," Timothy said, stepping up onto the stump and trying to add Jesher's advice to the stack of things he was supposed to remember.

"Also, instead of holding your hands down at your waist, plant them like this, just barely, and then roll."

"Aral was telling me no hands..."

"Yeah I know, 'because you can break your wrists'. But I think it'll help you get your form down here at first. Here, watch me once."

Jesher got up on the stump and gave an exaggerated roll, planting his hands with his fingertips together and gliding smoothly through the motion until he came up standing. Timothy couldn't even hear the thump when Jesher hit the ground.

"OK?"

Timothy sniffed a laugh. "OK."

"Don't worry about it, it takes a while."

Timothy tried, put too much weight on his hands, and hit his heel when he rolled over. After twenty more tries and eighteen more corrections, Jesher told him to keep practicing and began doing a routine of his own.

Timothy spent half an hour on the rolls, stopping now and then when his head started spinning. Bruises were already forming on his shoulder, palms, the back of his head, and his heel. Finally Jesher swung down from a rope not far away and said that it was time to start working on loop-jumps.

"Sorry," Jesher said, as they walked toward the pit. "Just when you were almost dry."

"No, that's OK..."

"It's cold, I know, but you've got to know that you're not going to break anything if you land wrong. The loop-jump is all about committing to the jump, which is hard to do when you don't know if you'll be able to land it. I'll try to get you out of the water as soon as I can."

By the end of the hour they had moved the table away from the water and Timothy was doing the jumps on the land. Jesher stood beside the table, slapping Timothy's shoulder to get him spinning back to his feet before he hit the ground. A few jumps went well enough that Timothy tried using his hands. His wrists didn't jar and Jesher didn't have to help him spin.

For the last hour and a half of their time together, Timothy and Jesher practiced the drill Farland had assigned. Timothy stood, trying to stay balanced on his feet, and waited. Jesher stood behind him with a cloth in his hand. When Jesher threw the cloth over Timothy's head, Timothy tried to lunge forward and catch it before it hit the ground.

The problem was that by the time he saw the cloth and started lunging, it had usually reached the ground already. Farland said reflexes could be trained, but Timothy's were inexcusably slow, and they were not getting better. After twenty minutes, Timothy rolled his eyes and apologized to Jesher that they had to spend so much time on such a meaningless drill.

Jesher gave a polite smile, but did not laugh.

It clicked, then, that this was not a game to Jesher. Of course he'd *known* that it wasn't a game, but seeing his peer taking a drill seriously, while *he* instinctively bowed to the pretend-to-be-lazy, hide-your-enthusiasm mantra that he had despised for his whole life, put things suddenly into perspective.

Something changed, in that moment. Timothy found himself suddenly determined to catch the rag, even if it took him all year. Suddenly determined to do everything Farland or Haberd or Aral taught him, even if he had to skip sleep and drill through the night to learn it. Suddenly glad, because he had finally found someone that he did not have to pretend around.

When they were finished, Jesher and Timothy walked to dinner together, and Timothy didn't scratch the back of his neck once.

That night Selena came to work with Timothy on languages. Robert, who was back from another day in the smithy with Gerard, let her into their cabin with a deep, exaggerated bow. After a brief discussion, the three of them agreed that Robert would learn the languages along with Timothy. Selena said this would help Timothy learn faster, and Timothy was glad to spend some extra time with Robert.

And he suspected that Robert was glad to spend some extra time with Selena.

They started with Botani, which had of course been banned by the Huctans after the Invasion. Both Timothy and Robert caught on quickly, and at times Timothy felt that he almost recognized words before Selena told them the meanings. He liked to think that this meant he was a true Botaño, that the ancient language of his fathers was in his blood.

A ridiculous thought, he knew, but he harbored it anyway.

As the window darkened and they had to light the lamp to continue, Timothy's weariness started to come back. His excitement at passing the test had shoved his exhaustion to the back of his mind for most of the day, but now it was starting to catch up with him. He felt dull, and he ached.

But he did not feel the same despair as he had for the last seven days. He did not dread tomorrow. He might be tired, but he was tired for a reason. He was tired because he was training, as a Thane, and that was as good a reason as you could ask for.

CHAPTER 13

Months passed. Long months. Months of training hard for over sixteen hours a day. None of the other Thanes were pushed as hard as Timothy, but then again, none of the other Thanes had started as late as Timothy.

"We are taking a grave risk," Haberd had said, on that fateful eighth day. "We have not poured this much effort into a single student before. We are making a significant sacrifice, of time and resources. Our hope is that you will honor them."

Haberd's words became Timothy's mantra. The other Marshals and half of the Thanes complained that he was too old, that it was too late to make him useful, that he would be a liability to any mission. Timothy turned their complaints into fuel for his efforts. He strove to prove them wrong, to succeed in spite of their doubt, to keep their kindness from being wasted.

And, with Jesher's help, he improved.

Jesher. One of the better fighters. Often chosen to lead missions, and often mocked as a fanatic by the other Thanes. Jesher, who used only ten of the thirty minutes allotted for each meal for eating so that the other twenty minutes would be free for practicing drills. Jesher, who learned what he was taught and then practiced it until he could do it better than the person who taught him. Jesher, whose passion and love for Botan exceeded everyone else's the way the trees exceeded the grass.

The other Thanes rolled their eyes at him and called him obsessive, but Timothy saw the jealousy behind their scorn. Jesher was in the river deep while the rest of them paddled along the surface, and it made them uncomfortable to see their own shallowness.

Timothy understood being laughed at for trying too hard. He followed Jesher, and Jesher recognized his efforts. They found camaraderie in their otherness. It wasn't long before Timothy talked more easily with Jesher than he did anymore with Robert. With Jesher he didn't have to hide his enthusiasm, didn't have to hang back when he wanted to try something harder or practice something longer. Jesher was what he had always wanted to be, and thus, around Jesher, Timothy could be himself.

It was of course many months before he could keep up with Jesher to any degree. He consoled himself with the fact that some people never would.

"Go," Timothy said.

Jesher sprinted across the open ground, and Timothy followed, hands cutting the air as his feet parted and crushed the grass. The wind blew in his ears.

Jesher was making for the boulders. He reached them and

jumped without pausing from his sprint, touching one foot to a rock face and pushing with both hands to keep his momentum rolling up the face of the granite.

Timothy didn't have time to watch. The rock was in front of him, and he leapt without hesitation. His foot struck at the correct angle—not so steep that his foot slipped down the rock face, but not so shallow that he lost momentum—and he gained the top of the boulder. Instinctively he corrected a slight imbalance with a push from his left hand, and then he was chasing Jesher across the boulder tops.

The stones were huge, some close together and almost as low as the thorny brush, others rising ten feet above the ground with considerable gaps between them. There was a field of them, as if a giant had kicked the mountain and dislodged a spray of granite. A misstep would mean a nasty bruise, a turned or broken ankle, and a painful fall into the briars. But Timothy was skilled enough now to avoid that.

Hopefully he was, anyway.

There wasn't time for thought. A boulder in front of Timothy was within leaping distance, followed by another to the left that slanted downwards into the bushes. Taking a quick step, Timothy leapt for the first stone, landed running, and threw his weight into the almost vertical face of the slanted boulder to the left. It felt, for a few steps, as if he were running sideways. Momentum glued him to the rock long enough to cross the gap and jump. After a moment of flight, Timothy caught hold of the next chunk of granite and scrambled his way to the top.

Jesher was still ahead of him, floating across the rock-field at a full run. Timothy followed.

The shifts of balance, split-second decisions, and last-second corrections blurred together as Timothy skipped and scrabbled and leapt across islands of stone in a sea of thorns. It felt good to move like this. His eyes flickered constantly. When a foothold appeared, he took it and used it to gain height or distance before his mind had even registered that he was going to jump. There was no room for hesitation. A cracked ledge that gave him an instant of support in mid-leap would be impossible to balance on if he stopped. Momentum gave him stability, and hesitation broke momentum.

He and instinct and physical coordination were in harmony.

Jesher was veering to the left, up the embankment. There was a ten-foot cliff of eroded loam straight ahead, broken by small stones lodged in the side and a thin pine hanging from the top by its roots. Jesher's route avoided the cliff, but it also wasted valuable distance.

Timothy made for the cliff.

He ran up the thin, bouncing length of the pine with his arms held wide for balance. Dead branches cracked and fell before him. He glanced sideways as he reached the roots of the tree and saw that Jesher had gained the cliff-top. Timothy jumped, kicking the side of the cliff, and caught the uppermost roots of the fallen pine. Planting his hands, he used his upward momentum to roll over the ledge and onto his feet. He was running before the dust fell from his body.

The undergrowth was lower and less thorny than it had been around the boulders, but it was still enough to ensnare feet. Jesher had swung down from the boulders into the branches of a tree, and from there onto a log lying half-hidden under the tips of the bushes. He was running along the log, now, and Timothy was already on an interception course, jumping from rocks and swinging from low branches to clear the worst of the brush.

The gap was closing, Timothy realized. Jesher saw it too, and put on an extra burst of speed. He cleared the thick undergrowth a moment before Timothy did and went sprinting into the trees.

For a moment Timothy couldn't see Jesher, and something told him that Jesher would take this opportunity to duck down and double back. It was an old trick, but it was a good one, and Jesher had done it before. Timothy decided to risk a brief pause to listen.

His ears, sharper now than they had been a few months ago, picked up a single footstep to the left. He ran. Jesher's brown trousers appeared through the branches, and the pursuit became a close one.

If Timothy was suddenly invigorated by the scent of victory after months of frustration, Jesher's burst of speed meant that he was just as desperate not to break his perfect record. Deer would have been shamed to see them pounding through the woods, ducking branches, leaping fallen trees, skirting hollows and dodging clinging bushes so quickly that the wind filled Timothy's ears and the beat of his heart was almost as fast as that of his footsteps.

A small gully with a trickle of water crossed their path. Jesher planted a foot on a slightly protruding rock and made a fantastic leap, landing on the other side of the slope just as Timothy's feet left the ground. Timothy saw where he would land, saw Jesher slip as he scrambled up the embankment. He reached out a hand, and missed Jesher's heel by bare inches.

Clambering up behind Jesher and feeling his temples throb with his pounding pulse, Timothy reached deep.

He was two steps behind Jesher. Both of them were running a flat-out, jelly-legged sprint. A brush-filled hollow appeared. Jesher leapt, using a hanging branch to swing himself all the way over.

Timothy gathered himself and jumped across without the branch, a millisecond closer but now on the verge of collapse.

Jesher's hand caught a dead branch and flung it back at Timothy. Without thinking—and surprising himself when he did it—Timothy caught the branch and threw it right back at Jesher's feet. It hit Jesher in the back of the ankle, and though Jesher would never have let the pain of the blow slow him, the force of the impact was enough to make him half-miss a step.

Timothy took a chance that would end the game one way or another. He jumped, body parallel to the ground, arms outstretched. If he missed, he would fall on his face and Jesher would be ten steps ahead before Timothy could get up. But if he did not miss...

Jesher heard the change in the rhythm of Timothy's steps, turned his head, and tried to dodge out of the way. Timothy's hand touched Jesher's hip, slid down to his foot, and caught. Jesher stumbled and fell as Timothy hit the loamy ground on his elbows and toes.

The game was over.

Timothy had caught Jesher.

Nothing was impossible.

"You got me," Jesher said, panting and rising to his knees. Timothy rolled over on his back, chest heaving, and stared up at the leaves while euphoria spread through his body like a flood of warm water. They were both still for a moment, quiet except for their breathing, and a slight breeze ruffled the leaves. The air felt as good as anything could feel, wicking at the slick sweat on Timothy's skin and drying the dust in little streams on his forehead.

"Yeah," Timothy said after a moment. Jesher laughed, a sort of sharp exhalation between gasps. Timothy sat up.

"You know what this means," Timothy said, panting.

"That you're lucky," said Jesher.

"It means your time is over."

Jesher threw a stick at him. Timothy grinned through the sweat and swatted at a fly that was buzzing around his eyes.

"What this means," Jesher said, rising to his feet, "Is that I'm going to have to stop taking it easy on you."

"Yeah," Timothy said. "Not so much yawning, next time."

Jesher gave Timothy a nudge in the ribs with his foot.

"Get up. You're not tired, are you?"

Timothy made a grab for Jesher's foot, but Jesher twisted away. Timothy got to his feet. Stretching his arms, he looked back the way they had come, and then at the sinking sun. In the chase, he had not paid much attention to which direction they were going.

"What's the shortest way back?" he said.

"I dunno," said Jesher, backing up against a tree and cupping his hands. "Why don't you..."

But Timothy had understood him immediately. He took three running steps and sprung upward off of Jesher's cupped hands, catching the lowest branch of the aspen easily. Quickly he climbed until he could see through the tops of the other trees.

"Looks like there's a giant hill in the way if we go straight back from here," he called down. "We can loop around to the right."

After looking at the view and feeling the breeze a moment longer, Timothy descended. Then, as he dropped to the earth, he realized that Jesher was already gone.

Of course he was. Jesher would have paid attention to where they were, even in the middle of a game of Tag. He never lost his concentration, never made mistakes. And now he was rubbing it in a little, twitting Timothy back for winning today.

Timothy rolled his eyes and began to jog. When he had the wind for it, he went from a jog to a run. No doubt Jesher would be waiting for him at dinner with a smug little smile. The farther behind Timothy was, the smugger the smile would be.

He was starving. Most of the Thanes would have eaten by now. Robert would be finishing up his ironwork for the day, or maybe talking to Gerard again. Timothy had the vague impression that the smith was beginning to break through Robert's hostility towards the Band. After four months of living in the rebel camp while refusing to join the rebel cause, it was about time.

But Timothy tried not to think about that too much. He didn't want to get excited over what was probably nothing.

He didn't exactly *hear* Jesher behind him, but somehow he knew. He broke his run immediately, dropping to the ground and rolling to face his attacker as he did.

Most people would probably have fallen right over Timothy, tripping on his outstretched body. Jesher, of course, did not. He jumped, evading Timothy's kick as he passed. Landing just past Timothy's head, he plunged an imaginary dagger towards Timothy's chest.

Timothy managed to parry the blow with a sloppy twist of his forearm. Then he swung his left hand at Jesher's stomach, hoping to buy himself some time. Jesher slapped Timothy's blow aside and dropped his dagger-wielding hand to Timothy's throat.

Timothy sighed. Jesher stood up, twirled his imaginary dagger, sheathed it, and then offered a hand to help Timothy up.

“Tsk tsk,” Jesher said, “taken by ambush.”

“Too bad the only way you can take me is by ambush,” Timothy said, and he jerked Jesher’s proffered hand to begin a throw Farland had taught him.

But of course Jesher had helped Timothy learn the throw, and knew exactly how to stop it.

This time Timothy lasted almost thirty seconds. Dust rose around them as they fought, and then Jesher had him pinned on the ground with a leg across his throat and one of Timothy’s arms at an angle where Jesher could break it with a squeeze. Timothy tapped Jesher’s arm with his free hand, and laughed when they got up and realized how completely the dust had covered their sweaty clothing and faces.

Timothy’s victory in Tag that day would lead to many such contests, all of which Timothy would lose. He didn’t mind, though. He knew he was getting better. His pride was not easily wounded, because he hadn’t earned any pride to bother defending. He was surrounded by his betters—not just Jesher, but every Thane and Marshal in the Band—and he knew it. That knowledge pushed him.

And he was getting better. Catching Jesher proved that. It was a milestone. A victory. The first of many.

Or it *would* have been the first of many, if there had been more time.

That evening Selena and Robert arrived at the cabin together, which was unusual. Robert was usually first, and then Timothy, and then Selena. Apparently Robert had run late at the smithy today. Or he'd waited for Selena.

It wasn't that Timothy was jealous of Robert and Selena. Selena was pretty, true, and despite her occasionally brainless demeanor, she was also as sharp as a razor. She was the only Thane that had received a long-term assignment, stationed at the Huctan fort where Timothy and Robert had been imprisoned. While her rescue—without permission from her superiors—had earned her the new and much less exciting assignment of facilitating Timothy's training, she was still Haberd's favorite pupil.

Selena had been learning Eliniel from the old man since she was a toddler, and she was good at it. Timothy was beginning to appreciate *how* good she was, as Haberd had started assigning her as the target of some of Timothy's drills.

So Selena was beautiful and intelligent, but Timothy wasn't *jealous*. Sure, he had had thoughts at first, when she had gotten him and Robert out of Northelm and he had realized that she was not Huctan and did not want to kill him and was female. But that had only lasted a week or two. Then Timothy's training had kicked in, and he hadn't had time to think about her.

But it had become increasingly obvious, in the past several weeks, that she and Robert had been thinking about one another quite a bit. Timothy might be the one Selena had first met at Northelm, but Robert was the one she had fallen for. It had been easier and easier, as Haberd taught Timothy to judge people, to see the way Selena's eyes sometimes avoided Robert's until she realized what she was doing and made it a point to look him square in the face. It had become glaringly obvious that Robert never looked at Selena at all when he thought Timothy was watching.

Not that you needed Eliniel to see the signs now. The two of them were practically holding hands.

"Hey buddy," Robert said to Timothy, entering the cabin and holding the door open for Selena.

"Hey," Timothy answered, returning the smile and yawning, not because he was tired, but because yawning was a reflex, because at some point in his youth he had decided that it made him look casual.

He was so pathetic, sometimes.

"How was the hammering today?" he asked.

"Decent."

"*Botani or Huctan*," Selena said in Huctan, "*It is language time, as of now.*"

"*Yes, master*," Robert said, and Selena punched him in the arm. Robert looked shocked, and gave Timothy a look of mock affront. Timothy shook his head, as if disgusted with Selena's abusiveness.

A vivid memory of childhood came rushing back to him, in dream-like clarity. He was ten again, or possibly twelve. Fenae was still alive. She, he, and Robert were by the creek back home. He could almost smell the water.

"You're dumb," Fenae said to Robert, pushing his shoulder and turning to Timothy to roll her eyes. Timothy grinned. He knew what she was doing, but he didn't care.

"You're *dumb," Robert said, snatching the pewter comb out of Fenae's hair and putting it behind his back.*

"Hey! Give it back!" Fenae cried. Timothy was old enough to know that a girl's hair was very important to her, but he also saw the delighted smile on Fenae's face even as she pretended to be angry with Robert. She reached for him, and Robert danced around her, maneuvering until his back was to

Timothy. He held the comb behind him, and wiggled it. Timothy took it, palmed it, and resumed his amused spectator pose.

Fenae made a grab for Robert's wrist, and Robert let her catch him. He let her pry at his clenched fingers for a minute, and then he opened his empty hand.

"It's gone," he said, acting surprised.

Fenae looked confounded for a second. Then she whirled on Timothy.

"Timothy..." she said. The smile on her face was markedly less genuine–she really did *care that her hair was starting to come out of place–but she had said Timothy's name, was looking at him.*

"Yes?" Timothy said.

Fenae held out her hand, palm up. "Give me the comb," she said.

She wasn't going to try to grab Timothy's wrist. That hurt a little.

"What comb?" Timothy replied, starting to feel uncomfortable. Robert was laughing silently behind Fenae, and Timothy took the opportunity to distract Fenae by grinning at Robert. She whirled again to see what Robert was doing, and while her back was turned Timothy set the comb as far away from himself as he could reach.

Now he was free of responsibility. Now she couldn't get mad at him for hiding her stupid comb.

Not that she would get mad at Robert for keeping it from her all afternoon.

Timothy blinked, and came back to the present. Selena was rolling her eyes and telling them sternly to sit down and listen. Robert was making a deep, subservient bow and throwing Timothy a mischievous look. Timothy was shaking his head knowingly.

It was a strange feeling when every person in the room was pretending.

They studied grammar for a while. Timothy and Robert had both learned Botani quickly, so quickly that Selena had asked them repeatedly whether their parents had spoken it when they were children. Huctan was harder. They had learned enough by now to understand and speak it passably, but Selena said their accents were strong. Now, most nights, they studied grammar. Selena could no longer muddle them completely by talking quickly, so she had settled for criticizing their word order and occasional misuse of verb endings.

And their handwriting. After an hour of grammar, Selena drew the slates and chalk from her bag, and Robert groaned. He and Timothy could both write—though Robert was significantly behind Timothy, with all the code-writing and letter forging Timothy had been doing with Haberd lately—but apparently the neatness of Timothy's hand was vital to future missions. Over and over they formed characters, lines and lines of them, letter after letter for Selena to examine, criticize, and erase for them to write again.

But it was nice, in a way. Relaxing. They were learning quickly and studying hard, but compared to the rest of Timothy's day, language practice was slow-paced and relatively safe.

And tonight it melted easily into the drill Haberd had assigned Timothy, which was to tell Selena a given time and location without Robert realizing that he had told her anything. Timothy decided to try using the eye-signals he had been practicing lately. To cover himself, he struck up a verbal conversation in Botani as he did so.

Robert noticed anyway. "Wait," he said, when Timothy was halfway into his fake Botani conversation and his real eye-signal conversation. "Is this one of your Eliniel things?"

Selena laughed, effortlessly turning to Robert even as she

responded with her hands to ask Timothy who she would be meeting at the time and location he had given her.

"Maybe it is, maybe it isn't," she said to Robert.

"How could you tell?" Timothy asked. Had he been too deliberate with the blinks and pupil-shifts? Or had Robert simply noticed the way Timothy had to constantly pause, remember what he wanted to say with his eyes, say it, and then return to the verbal cover conversation?

Robert laughed. "Because you're only talkative when there's some drill. You act like a different person. It's like you suddenly trade quiet Timothy for conversationalist Timothy."

Timothy smiled and raised his eyebrows, and Robert pointed. "See?" he said. "Now it's not a drill anymore, and you're back to you."

Selena was sitting forward on her knees, eyes wide, looking fascinated.

"Yes!" she said, "That's exactly right! He's so shy, usually, but I've seen him be eloquent when he wants to. And it's always when he has an assignment."

Timothy was turning red now. And he was still silent. Robert laughed, but not unkindly.

"It just goes to show that it's not really shyness," he said. "Timothy just doesn't bother with small talk unless he has a good reason."

It was a gracious thing to say, and it dialed down the pressure of scrutiny enough for Timothy to stop blushing and squirming, but they all knew it wasn't true. Timothy didn't *choose* not to make small talk. He would have liked nothing more than to be able to banter easily with the other Thanes the way Robert did, to know them and be known by them and not have to stifle his false yawns and neck scratching while his mind raced for things to say.

But he couldn't. Not with anyone except Jesher.

Unless it was a drill, that was true. When it was a drill—a game, an assignment—he suddenly knew exactly what to say, and how. His tongue suddenly moved the way he wanted it to. He was suddenly quick on his feet, able to steer the conversation the way he wanted it to go, able to seem confident or nervous or whatever else the situation called for.

What kind of sick disorder was that, that Timothy could be friendly if it was an act, but not if it was genuine?

But Robert was talking with Selena now, about something someone had said at lunch today, and Selena was listening attentively while she signaled with her hands to ask Timothy whether Haberd really needed to see her or not. Timothy shook himself, shrugged off the self-pity, and got back to it.

When Robert announced the next week that he was joining the Band, Timothy wasn't as shocked and exultant as he'd thought he would be. He clapped Robert on the back and congratulated him, trying not to be condescending or say 'I told you so' in any way. He watched the smith take Robert's vow. He felt a lump rise in his throat as he saluted Robert. He inquired anxiously to see how Robert was doing in his first week, sympathized when Robert was short-tempered and exhausted, teased him about his bruises, and felt relief when he found out that the Marshals were going to let Robert learn strategy from Comaro.

This was what he had wanted—for both of them to be Thanes—but it all seemed *less*, somehow. Less than he'd thought it would be. Timothy was deep in the river while his old friend was still on the banks, and it was too late to bridge the distance between them.

CHAPTER 14

The smoke was thick when the wind blew from the west. The western gates were askew and charring on their great hinges. The western homes creaked and tumbled and sent up great gouts of sparks. The western streets were thick with the dead and the smell of blood and the shimmering night-light of blazing fire.

Ricera stood before Yansut, the young lieutenant commander of the Huctan army of Karkukto. Yansut kept his narrow eyes on Ricera and his hand on his sword. His guards did the same. Ricera stood still and kept his hands at his sides while they waited for the general.

The general came on his horse, with almost thirty guards streaming behind him in the body-strewn streets. The wind picked up again and blew a cloud of smoke low, obscuring the general and his men for a moment. When the smoke cleared, they were reining up close. Yansut saluted the general and spoke to him in Huctan.

The general looked at Ricera. His face was smooth, but there was distaste in his eyes.

"You are the one?" he asked.

Ricera inclined his head. "Yes, General."

"You have the thanks of the Emperor."

Ricera closed his eyes slowly and opened them. The general, apparently finished with Ricera, turned back to his Second and spoke in Huctan again. Ricera, of course, understood.

"*Yansut, what news in the Keep?*" said the general. "*How many yet live?*"

"*General, none. We broke through the last doors almost an hour ago. There were very few within. I suspect many have escaped.*"

"*How?*"

"*General, I know not. Men are searching for escape passages. They are well hidden.*"

"*Have you asked the traitor?*"

Yansut's eyes flickered toward Ricera, and there was more than distaste in them. "*General, I have not asked him.*"

"Traitor," the general said loudly, switching to Botani. Ricera looked up.

"Ricera, General."

"Ricera, then. Botani have escaped from the Keep. Do you know the passages through which they have done so?"

"Yes, General."

"Will you tell us where they are?"

"Better," Ricera said, "I will take you to where they lead."

The general looked pleased. Yansut did not.

"You need not take us, only tell us where they lead," Yansut said.

"I will take you," Ricera said. "I will need a horse."

Yansut looked as though he would strike Ricera, but the general held up a hand. He beckoned to one of his guards.

"*Give him a horse,*" he said. The guard glanced around, realized that the general meant for him to give up his own horse, and dismounted with a flat look on his face. He handed the reins to Ricera.

"And a sword," Ricera said.

Yansut's eyes narrowed. "*General,*" he said in Huctan. "*He wants to escape.*"

"*I think not,*" the general said. He gestured toward the dismounted guard. "*Your sword,*" he said.

The guard unbuckled his sword and brought it forward. The flat look on his face faltered, and hatred shone through.

Ricera inclined his head to the general and swung up onto the horse.

"Gather your men, Yansut," he said, buckling on the sword. "And follow me."

Timothy watched from horseback, in the shadows of the trees, as Jesher and Diane made for the road. Their horses were glad to be out in the open, after two days of winding through the forest. Jesher's gelding pranced across the meadow, trampling the drooping grass before him. Diane's mare trotted steadily behind.

According to Jesher, they were only eight or nine miles south of Suiton. The town was a small one, but the Band had contacts there, and it made a good starting point for the northwestern loop. The four of them—Jesher, Timothy, Diane and Selena—would check in, memorize any news the contact had, help with anything the contact needed, and then continue north. After ten or twelve days of travel, they would return to the Band with information from the outside world.

It was Timothy's first mission. The mission Haberd hadn't thought him ready for. The mission Farland had insisted he *was* ready for. Timothy was nervous, so much so that last night, when he had been on watch, he had woken everyone up in a panic before realizing that the 'intruder' he had heard was a grazing deer.

He shouldn't have been nervous. It was his first mission, after all, and the northwestern loop wasn't known for its danger. But it made him a little edgy to be out in the real world again. He had spent close to a year doing nothing but training, eating, and sleeping. He hadn't seen a Huctan since his escape from Northelm.

Jesher and Diane reached the road, and Selena yawned. She had done this before, probably dozens of times. Her hair, like Diane's, was pulled up and done in such a way that, with her hood on, she looked like a boy, albeit a very pretty one. It was a necessary precaution, Jesher had explained. Road travel was dangerous. Huctan patrols could come around any corner, and when they did, pretty young women like Selena and Diane had about a one in two chance of being left alone.

Timothy's spear was disassembled. The belt knife, with a removable pommel that revealed the hollow handle, was stuck in a small leather sheath at his waist. His walking stick, with a tip that just happened to be the perfect size to jam into the hollow handle of his knife, was strapped to his saddlebags.

He was just a Botani traveler, well within his rights to be carrying a belt knife, just as Diane was well within her rights to be carrying a hunting bow. It was swords and spears that the Huctans cared about. Swords and spears that would get a traveler tortured and killed if he was even suspected of carrying them.

Diane and Jesher reached the road and began riding north.

When they were about a quarter mile ahead, Timothy followed with Selena.

There was no reason to be nervous. This was the northwestern loop. This was his first mission. Nothing was going to happen.

On hearing hoof beats behind them, Timothy's first reaction was to ride on and pretend that he didn't hear. But that would have been a mistake. Haberd had warned him dozens of times that it often attracted more attention to be nonchalant than it did to be jumpy. Huctan soldiers expected jumpiness. It was a casual attitude that made them suspicious.

So when Timothy heard the hoof beats, he turned his head abruptly, raised a hand to his eyes, and looked at the riders behind them.

Two crimson cloaks marred the gray-green, late-winter landscape. The soldiers were approaching quickly. Selena and Timothy directed their horses to the side of the road and slowed to a walk.

"You'll have to do the talking," Selena said in a low voice. Timothy nodded. Selena had a pretty good teenage boy's voice when she wanted to, but she had told him that a patrol soldier would pick it out nine times out of ten. Patrol soldiers had spent more than fifteen years learning to pick out and exploit weakness in the Botani people. They were good at it.

Timothy hoped with all his heart that the soldiers would ignore them and ride by. He didn't feel ready to talk. Haberd was right. He should still be training.

But he also hoped with all his heart that they *would* stop. As contradictory as that was, it was true. He was afraid, and so he wanted them to pass on by, but he also despised himself for being afraid, and so he wanted the chance to overcome that fear. This was his first test. He had been training for this.

Quickly he ran some calculations. Jesher and Diane were around the bend in the road, out of sight, and would not miss the 'everything's OK' whistle for another thirty seconds. According to the plan, they would wait another sixty seconds to be sure something was wrong before they doubled back.

There were thick woods on the eastern side of the road. They would probably tie their horses and come back through the pines on foot. It would be a good five or six minutes before they arrived.

If there was any trouble, Timothy was going to have to stall it as long as he could.

He glanced back again. The soldiers saw him turn, of course, but any traveler would turn and look if there were Huctans behind him. The soldiers were very close now. They seemed to be slowing. Timothy's fear rose, and he momentarily considered wheeling his horse and making for the woods. Surely they could make it into the trees before the Huctans could aim crossbows at their backs.

No. Even if the soldiers didn't follow them into the woods, running now would ruin their mission. The Huctans would see them when they got to Suiton, and would recognize the travelers that had bolted.

One of the soldiers said something that Timothy couldn't quite catch. There was a laugh. Timothy turned forward again and nudged the belt knife at his side. Selena saw him eyeing his spear shaft and gave him a tiny shake of her head. Selena's strength was Eliniel, not combat. If it came to a fight, it would be better if Jesher were here.

It had been one minute. Jesher and Diane would have missed the first whistle.

One of the Huctans called out in Common.

"Halt!"

Timothy winced, glanced back, and reigned in his horse. As the soldiers approached, he kept his head bowed and eyes down. As with dogs, it was best not to make direct eye contact with Huctans. They saw it as a challenge.

"G-good day, officers," he stammered.

"Where are you going?" said the soldier in front, an athletically built man with long hair tied behind his helmet.

"Suiton, sir," Timothy said.

"What for?"

"I'm on my way home, sir," Timothy said, telling himself to ignore the soldier's rudeness, to forget everything the Huctans had done, to concentrate dispassionately on the situation at hand.

"You live in Suiton?"

"N-no sir, up past it about a day's ride. We've got a farm, just a little farm. Up that way." Timothy pointed, chewing his lip and glancing up a little with a nervous bob of his head. "Sir," he added.

The long-haired man seemed satisfied, but the one behind him, the older one with the stubbled second chin and the straining chain mail, was eyeing Selena shrewdly. His pupils glinted beneath the smooth, slanted fold of his eyelid.

"Why does your friend not talk?" he said. His accent was strong. Either he was new to Botan, or he hated the Botani so much that he had not deigned to learn any more Common than he had to. Timothy felt his loathing for the soldier increase.

No. He was dispassionate.

"Oh, uh, that's just my little brother," Timothy said. "He's a little shy, I guess. He doesn't say much. And that's a blessing, if you ask me." He faked an attempted laugh, then dropped his eyes and swallowed again when neither soldier smiled.

"Tell him to take off his hood," the fat soldier said.

This was going badly. There was a burning look in the soldier's eyes.

"Pardon?" Timothy said.

The fat soldier looked hard at Timothy. "Tell," the soldier made a speaking gesture with his hand, "him," he pointed to Selena, "to take off," he pretended to be pulling something away from his face, "his hood!"

As the soldier finished his sentence, he brought his spear haft around and struck hard at Timothy's head. Timothy had seen the blow coming, had seen the soldier's grip tighten in time to fit his own knife to his own haft and thrust the blade into the soldier's chest, but he had waited. When the blow came, he squealed as if surprised and brought his arm up just enough to absorb the blow with the meaty part of his shoulder.

It still hurt. Badly.

"Ah-YAH!" Timothy yelled, hunkering down in the saddle. "Sorry, sir, please! Please, I didn't mean anything by it, it's just I didn't hear you..."

Another blow, this time across his upturned forearm, made a sharp noise against the bone and almost blinded Timothy with pain. He screamed, and it wasn't much for show.

"Shut up!" the fat man shouted. "Do what I told you. Tell your little 'brother' to take off her hood."

The soldier knew, then. The pain in Timothy's arm was sharp and throbbing, but his anger made it distant. His hand trembled as he tried to keep it away from his belt knife.

"Eggar," Timothy said to Selena, cradling his arm and speaking between feigned sobs, "do what he says."

At that moment, the long-haired soldier spoke in Huctan. "*Someone is coming,*" he said.

Timothy's eyes darted. A single horseman was riding down the path from the direction of Suiton. No, there were two on the horse, one riding behind the other. They were approaching at a steady trot.

"*What do I care?*" the fat man said, slurping up the saliva that had collected on his lower lip. He glared at Timothy and raised the spear again. Timothy hunkered down farther, backing his horse away with his knees, and yelled this time.

"Eggar! Do what he says!" he said.

Selena didn't move. Timothy hadn't expected her to. Her shoulders quivered in a very, very good imitation of terror.

The Huctan dug a heel into the flank of his horse and walked it up to Selena in the same slow way he had walked it up to Timothy. His grip on his spear was still club-like. He was going to hit her.

That was good. At least he wasn't going to kill her.

Timothy recognized Jesher on the approaching horse, with Diane riding behind him. Jesher's walking stick was nowhere to be seen. Neither was his right hand. He had his spear, then. The long-haired soldier rode forward at a walk to meet them.

Timothy, drawing up his cloak to free his knife and kicking the end of his walking stick closer to his hand, yelled at Selena again. "Didn't you hear what the man said?" he shouted. "Take off your *hood*, Eggar!"

Selena's whole body was shaking, now, enough that Timothy almost wondered if she really *were* paralyzed with fear. But he knew better than that. This was Selena. She had done this before.

"What's your business?" the long-haired soldier was demanding, farther up the road. Jesher said something about getting down to Shadil. He wasn't slackening his pace.

The fat Huctan, who had apparently decided to take Selena's hood off himself, rode in close. Selena caught Timothy's eye and flickered her eyelids, still maintaining her almost convulsive trembling. Timothy fitted his knife to his walking stick without making a sound.

"I said, stop there!" the long-haired man shouted at Jesher.

Jesher slowed. The fat Huctan reached for Selena's hood suddenly, grabbing it in his fist with what looked like a handful of her hair.

It happened all at once.

With the fat man's arm lifted and his spear in the other hand, Selena drew her knife and struck upwards and inwards at his exposed armpit. The blade was slowed by the mail and didn't penetrate far, but the Huctan cried out. Slapping down, he caught Selena's arm with a blow from his gauntleted fist. She dropped her knife with a cry.

The long-haired soldier turned his head at the noise. Before his head had stopped turning, Jesher was off of his horse and running forward with his spear. Timothy saw, from the corner of his eye, as Jesher thrust upward.

The fat Huctan had caught hold of Selena's arm in his left hand and was wheeling his horse now, yanking her half off of the saddle and trying to bring his spear point around. His horse whinnied and reared just as Diane loosed an arrow.

The point struck the Huctan's thigh where his chest had been a moment before. The arrow passed through the flesh and stuck in the saddle. The Huctan yelled, and his horse let out a blood-curdling scream. Selena was yanked from her saddle completely. She fell hard and just managed to roll out of the way before the rearing horse's hooves descended.

The Huctan, with an arrow in his thigh and a wound under his arm, glanced toward his comrade. When he saw that the long-haired man was down, he yanked on his reins and wheeled his horse to flee.

Timothy had already drawn back his spear, had already spurred his horse forward. The Huctan faced him as his horse turned. His cursing mouth stopped moving as his sharp, lid-hooded eyes met Timothy's.

Thinking of Fenae, Timothy struck.

The blade went in easily, like a butter knife in a bowl of cream. Timothy withdrew his spear from the soft, folded skin of the Huctan's throat, and blood came. The soldier clutched at the flashing blood, and a panic rose in Timothy. He thrust again, this time all the way through, and kept pushing until he had toppled the Huctan soldier from his horse.

The arrow pinning the soldier's leg pulled out of the saddle as he fell, and the horse screamed again. More blood sprayed, when the soldier struck the ground, far enough to mist and float in the wind. The Huctan scrabbled at his throat, arched his back hard, and then slowly relaxed. Timothy looked away.

The next five minutes passed in a blur. Selena threw a rope to Timothy, told him to tie it around his saddle horn, pointed for the trees. She gave simple instructions, and Timothy followed them. He dragged the body of the soldier away from the road while Selena tried to clean up the blood.

Reaching a stone about two hundred yards into the trees, Timothy dismounted. Steeling himself, he began working on the rope around the Huctan's ankles. He felt his breath growing faster as he struggled with the knots. He was alone now in the woods. The smell of blood was in his nostrils and on his hands. The soldier's still-open eye was covered in dirt and blood. Timothy couldn't get the knots untied.

Finally he stood up, walked a step away, and took a deep breath. Shaking his head, he turned again to squat at the Huctan's ankles. He held his breath, worked deliberately, and finally got the rope free. He stood and coiled it slowly, resisting the urge to sprint back towards the road where the sun and the others were and the smell of blood was not.

Leaves crunched and Timothy saw Selena enter the trees at a run. She had two horses trotting beside her. She slowed the horses and held a finger to her lips as she approached Timothy.

"Someone's coming down the road," she whispered.

The fat soldier's horse whinnied, and Selena shushed it, stroking its neck and making little clucking noises in her throat. Then it was quiet.

Timothy closed his eyes to listen. He thought he heard hoof beats, but the road was obscured by trees, and sound was muffled by a blanket of needles. He couldn't be sure.

The smell of blood grew in his nostrils, and with it a clammy panic. With effort, Timothy stood still. He felt cold, even though the day was mild and his cloak was warm.

Presently Jesher came loping through the woods from farther up the road.

"They've passed," he said. "They didn't seem to notice anything."

"Good," Selena said, "I thought I got it all, but there wasn't time..."

"Go make sure it's all clean," Jesher said. "And keep an eye out."

As Selena ran back out to the road, Jesher turned to Timothy. He looked down at the face of the dead soldier and then up at Timothy. Timothy looked at the blood on his hands. They had been bloody before, bloodier, when he had cleaned fish or chickens or deer. But he had never been more repulsed by his own hands.

Jesher reached up to touch Timothy's shoulder, and Timothy started.

"You did good," Jesher said.

Timothy hesitated, then nodded.

CHAPTER 15

Stripping the stiffening bodies of their cloaks and armor was terrible work. Timothy hardened his stomach against the sticky, corrosive smell of blood and went about it roughly. He told himself it was like your first time cleaning a squirrel. You just had to fight through the revulsion until you got used to it, and then it wasn't so bad.

But it didn't get better.

They carried the bodies between the four of them, one at a time, and buried them another half mile into the woods. Selena cleared the road of blood and smoothed out the drag marks the bodies had left. Diane took the cloaks half a mile to the other side of the road and buried them deep, so that if the Huctan corpses were found, and they had rotted a little, they might not be immediately identifiable. Timothy helped pack the mail shirts, helmets, daggers and swords into a bundle on one of the Huctan horse's backs.

By the time they were finished, it was nearly sun-down.

Timothy was glad when they moved deeper into the forest, away from the corpses of the men they had killed, before making camp. They ate, and Timothy found it hard to put the food he had touched with his hands into his mouth. Telling himself that his hands were clean, that he had scrubbed them raw already, he forced himself to eat roughly and heartily. When he had eaten enough to prove to himself that he wasn't being squeamish, he huddled under his cloak and squatted next to the low fire they had built in the hollow.

"Timothy, you get the first watch tonight," Jesher said around a mouthful of bread. "The deer shouldn't be out and about for another couple hours."

Selena laughed, and Timothy forced a smile. He wasn't going to live down last night's scare. After lingering a moment more by the fire, he again forced his body to obey his will. Trying not to drag his feet, he left the fire's warmth and the comfort of being with other living people.

Finding a fallen, mossy log some forty yards from camp, he sat on it. After a moment he fitted his knife, which he had cleaned until it shone, onto his spear haft. Sitting with his legs crossed and his spear across his lap, he scrunched his cloak around his shoulders.

It was cold—unreasonably so, for how mild the day had been—and very dark. The fire was almost invisible in the hollow, and the glow it threw up on the trees was more eerie than comforting. A fear Timothy hadn't felt since childhood—a mindless fear of darkness and things watching him from the shadows—gripped him so that it was hard to keep from checking over his shoulder. He hummed a song that used to comfort him, when he was young, but it did not help.

Footsteps announced someone coming from the fire. Timothy turned and saw Jesher, already much closer than the sound of his footsteps had sounded. Timothy felt relief loosen his shoulders and warm him as if Jesher had brought the fire with him.

"Not very sleepy," Jesher said, climbing up onto the log beside Timothy and wrapping his cloak around him. "And the girls are boring."

Timothy sniffed a laugh. Jesher had come to comfort him, and they both knew it. But it was nice of Jesher not to say so.

They sat in silence for several minutes. After a while, Jesher spoke.

"That's not a normal mission," he said.

Timothy sniffed another laugh. He knew it hadn't been a normal mission. Hadn't he been told not to expect any action on his first mission, or second, or third?

"Yeah," he said. Then, "But I'm glad. Now I know that I can do it."

Jesher nodded, and took a deep breath. "It'll be harder the second time," he said. "But yeah. You can do it alright."

Timothy couldn't decide whether it was pride or sadness in Jesher's voice. He thought both.

After a while, Jesher spoke again. "That song you were humming," he said. "It's my favorite."

"Oh," Timothy said, embarrassed that Jesher had heard him. "Yeah, I don't even know the words. If there are any. But the tune is nice."

"The words are the best part," Jesher said.

"What are they?"

"What, you want me to sing for you? I can't sing."

"Say them, then."

Jesher was quiet, and for a moment Timothy thought that he wasn't going to answer. Then he recited, in Botani:

"Lokaren, thy love, has flown,
Like dew upon the mountain,
Like foam before the sea.
With Eldebar, the old, is she,
Beyond the horned climber,
Upon the upward way.
Lokaren, thy love, has flown,
Like dew upon the mountain,
Like foam before the sea."

Timothy and Jesher sat, for a moment, looking together at the darkness and rolling the words of the song over in their minds. The words didn't rhyme in Botani any better than they did in Common, but they had a rhythm to them, a similarity between the lines. Timothy imagined them with the tune of the song he had been humming, and they fit.

Maybe it was because Jesher liked the song so much, or because Mother had used to hum it to Timothy when he had nightmares, but Timothy suddenly felt that it might be his own favorite, too. It put a longing in him, a wistfulness for things that had been lost. Closing his eyes, he heard the words again, sung in haunting tones by a deep-throated bard in the hall of a forgotten castle. He imagined a great king, and his warriors, and his lady, reclining after a rich meal and listening with drooping eyes as the bard sang and the fire flickered and the hunting dogs curled and dozed before the warmth.

"How did you know the tune?" Jesher asked.

Timothy opened his eyes, then shrugged.

"My mother, I think. She used to hum it to us when she put us to bed, sometimes."

"That's rare," Jesher said. "I've only heard it once, and I had to beg Farland to sing it. He said it wasn't much known outside Eoriden, even before the Invasion."

"Outside what?"

"Eoriden."

Timothy gave Jesher a blank look. Jesher turned, and raised an eyebrow.

"Eoriden?" he said. "The Beloved City?"

Timothy shook his head. Jesher sighed, and looked away.

"Sorry," Timothy said, unsure of why Jesher suddenly seemed angry. "I'd... *like* to know about it..."

"Oh," Jesher said, hearing the hurt in Timothy's voice. "No, not..." He shook his head. "Sorry, it's not... it's just that *everyone* used to know about Eoriden. What Ricera did... sometimes it gets to me."

Timothy continued to stare blankly, and Jesher laughed.

"You don't know who Ricera is, either. I'm not helping very much, am I?"

"You're helping to confuse me."

"Good. That's the important thing."

Jesher got up, adjusted his cloak, and then climbed higher up on the log, where the end butted into a tree. Pulling his feet up onto the log and leaning back, he faced Timothy with his arms around his knees.

"Eoriden," he said, "was the name of the biggest, oldest city in Botan. It was built hundreds of years ago, maybe more; no one I've talked to really knows. It was huge. The outer walls were almost as high as the Great Trees, and some of the towers were even higher.

The Great Trees—which were as old as the city, some of them—were so big that the stump of one was used as a floor for weddings and dances. That was the only stump, actually, because no one was allowed to cut them down. That one supposedly had been struck by lightning and cut down so that it wouldn't fall against the walls. Farland said there were people who would come and cry for it. They called it *Gareldimar*, the Weeping Tree."

"*Gareldimar*," Timothy said, running the name over his tongue.

They stared into the darkness for a moment. The flicker of the fire in the hollow was dying down, almost invisible now. The forest was silent.

Finally Jesher sniffed, and shifted. "The king lived at Eoriden," he said. "During war time there were thousands of soldiers with him. There was a water spring in the center of the city. Almost an underground river. It poured out enough water for everyone there: the horses, the soldiers, the citizens, the crops... everything. Then it ran out, deep under the wall, and fed the moat, which overflowed down the cliffs on the northern side of the city and joined the river. That spring was the oldest part of the city, famous even before there *was* a city, before... well, before everything, I guess."

"You were about to say something else."

Jesher shifted and sniffed again. Although it was hard to see his face in the moon shadow, Timothy thought he saw a shy smile spread across Jesher's face.

"I was about to say "before the kings of old," Jesher said, "but I thought you'd laugh."

Timothy didn't laugh. He was thinking of the hall, and the bard singing, and the king listening before the hearth. *The kings of old.* That was exactly the way to describe those forgotten days he sometimes longed for, the days of yore, when mighty men had built cities and fought battles, when things were fair and ancient.

It wasn't that he actually knew anything about those days. But he believed in them. Maybe it was simply a desire, wishful thinking so strong he believed it to be true, but sometimes—now, when someone else mentioned what he had trouble expressing himself—he felt the proud dignity of the kings of old as palpably as he felt the cold night air on his face.

"The *noble* days," he said, seeing that Jesher still had an embarrassed smile, that Jesher didn't realize that Timothy knew *exactly* what he was talking about. "When all the stories happened." Timothy raised his hands, then dropped them, unable to explain.

Jesher looked back at Timothy, from across the log, and seemed to be trying to decide whether Timothy really understood. Timothy realized that it might sound like he was trying to humor Jesher, or to appease him, or to keep him from embarrassment. He needed to make Jesher see that he *understood*, that the two of them had the same wistful dream. He opened his mouth to explain, but Jesher beat him to it.

"Sometimes I... *yearn*, I guess, for those days." Jesher said. "I don't know how to describe it... it's like a sadness, for what has been lost. Do you know what I'm talking about?"

Timothy nodded, fervently. "I was about to try to describe it," he said. "It's what I was thinking about when you told me the words to that song."

"Exactly," Jesher said.

They were silent again, thinking, yearning, and then Timothy ventured a question.

"Where did you learn about Eoriden?" he said. "Farland?"

"Oh, no," Jesher sniffed a laugh. "I only got Farland to talk once, and he didn't tell me much. Most people in the Band—the ones that actually remember it, at least—don't like to talk about it. I've asked just about everyone. I'm sort of obsessed." He shrugged his shoulders and shifted again, and Timothy shook his head and held up his palms to say that he would have done the same, if he had thought to try.

"I bet Haberd knows all about it," Timothy said. "Have you asked him?"

Jesher sniffed another laugh. "Not all of us are Haberd's favorite student ever," he said.

"Me? More like his life's biggest disappointment."

"That's not what Selena says."

"Selena's not there when he tells me how dumb I am for four hours a day," Timothy said.

An owl hooted, low and soft, and Timothy searched the darkness of the trees for it. Something caught the corner of his eye, and for a moment, against the moonlight, he saw the dark form of the night hunter floating silently through the trees.

"Eoriden was the headquarters for the Duest, too," Jesher said. "They had all kinds of secret tunnels and stairways..."

"Wait, *Duest*?" Timothy interrupted. "What's that? Like *duist*?"

He had heard the second word, the Botani word for slave or servant, but he hadn't heard the one Jesher said. Maybe it was just a different pronunciation.

"Sort of," Jesher said, "but the stronger version of it. Not just servants... Vassals, maybe. *Duest*. Servants of Botan. It's High Botani, I think. People would send their kids from all over Botan to take the tests, and if they were smart enough and hard-working enough, they got to train. If they made it to their twentieth year, they became *Duest*. The best and smartest and bravest. They were spies and soldiers. The most trusted. The king's right hand."

Something clicked, and Timothy sat up straighter.

"That's what the Band was, before the Invasion," he said. "That's what all the Marshals are, isn't it?"

Jesher folded his arms. For a moment he didn't say anything.

"What?" Timothy said. "They are, aren't they?"

"Yes..." Jesher said slowly, "some of them. But that's something we don't ever talk about. If it got out to the Huctans that there were survivors of the Duest, they'd put a lot more effort into hunting us down."

Timothy nodded, trying to look solemn, but he could feel a grin playing at the corners of his mouth. The Band—the Band that he, Timothy, was a Thane in—was created by the *Duest*. Haberd himself, and Farland, and Comaro, and maybe even Aral, had been elite Servants of Botan in the ancient city of Eoriden.

A shudder ran down his ribs.

"We still make the same oath they did," Jesher said. "That oath is pretty much the definition of Duest. Back then it was... I don't know, *sacred*. More than it is now. And they were a lot better, back then. The leader was called the Crow—don't ask me why—and he was the best out of all of them. Like Haberd, Farland, and Comaro combined."

Timothy laughed, and shook his head.

"The only person with more power than the Crow," Jesher said, "was the king himself. The Crow almost had more power, in a different way. The king ran the armies, but the Crow ran the Duest. Not that it was ever a contest... the king and the Crow were the two great guardians of Botan. They worked together. The last king and Crow were actually *raised* together. Everyone thought they were the best of friends."

Jesher's voice didn't exactly crack, at the end of his last sentence, but he stopped abruptly. Timothy got the feeling that Jesher was about to tell him something terrible, something so sad and awful that it was almost too much to speak about. He waited several long seconds before venturing a small, innocuous question.

"What was the king's name?" he asked.

"Tromilian," said Jesher. "The Crow was Ricera."

Timothy started, at the name, and wasn't sure why, at first. Then he remembered that Jesher had mentioned the name a few moments before, had acted like Ricera had been at fault for Eoriden's forgottenness. Surely the Crow, the greatest Servant of all, hadn't been with the Huctans?

"People call it The Betrayal," Jesher said. "I think fifteen years ago, or maybe sixteen—when we were little kids, anyway—the Huctans started massing by our northern border. It was a big deal, but not huge. Our armies were quite a bit stronger than the Huctans', back then. And there was Eoriden. And Tromilian was a brilliant general; everybody always talks about how brilliant he was."

"Not brilliant enough," Timothy mumbled, but the way Jesher froze, the way Jesher's eyes looked at him through the darkness, made him suddenly ashamed of saying this. He hunched his shoulders in embarrassment. When Jesher continued, his voice was cold.

"He was betrayed," Jesher said, "by the one he trusted with his life."

"Ricera," Timothy said, feeling somehow sad for the Crow,

somehow disappointed.

Jesher nodded.

"One night he opened the gates and let the Huctans into Eoriden. Thousands of people died trying to escape with their families. The Huctans killed everyone. The story is that Ricera killed the king and queen with his own hands."

Timothy said nothing. Jesher shifted, sniffed, and was silent for several seconds. His voice was quieter when he continued.

"They pulled down every wall and tower," he said. "Tore up the streets. Scattered the stones. Salted the ground, so that not even grass would grow where the city had been."

Somehow this last detail—that they had salted the ground—brought everything together into a point that constricted Timothy's throat. It was hard to breathe.

"All of Botan fell within a month," said Jesher. "Armies were separated and leaderless. Ricera himself led the hunt for the remaining Duest. The Huctans slaughtered every soldier they found, taking no prisoners. Ricera's idea. He knew the only way to keep Botani quiet was to kill them."

Timothy's fist clenched. He hasn't killed them all, he thought.

"A group of Duest escaped and went south," said Jesher. "They slipped all the way to Jardon's border, riding through the night and dodging search parties, sacrificing themselves one by one to slow down their pursuers and deliver their message. There were only two survivors. One was Haberd, and one was Verinald."

Timothy started. He considered this—that his teacher had seen all that he loved fall around him, had seen his friends die, and had survived to go on alone—and suddenly felt his awe for the old man turn into something hard. Respect, maybe. Love, almost.

“Why?” Timothy asked. “What message?”

“The War Knot,” Jesher said.

“The what?”

Jesher frowned, then rummaged in his cloak.

“Do you have any string?” he asked.

Timothy checked, and shook his head.

“Well, I’ll show you later. It’s a knot, kind of like a square knot with the ends spliced together. If you trace one strand, it continues all the way. A never-ending knot, you know? That’s the War Knot. It symbolized the everlasting treaty between Jardon—that’s the kingdom to the south of us—and Botan. Two loops locked together, two countries locked together. An unbreakable bond. Whenever one was in trouble, they sent the War Knot, and the other came.”

Timothy imagined the knot, and the armies of the kings of old riding to the aid of their sister countries. Then he imagined a grim-eyed contingent of Duest, risking and losing their lives as they rode south for Jardon. He saw Haberd, his coat stained with the blood of his friends, his hands shaking with weariness, kneeling before Jardon’s king to present the War Knot.

Suddenly he felt unbearably sad.

“But this time Jardon didn’t come,” he said, not as a question but as condemnation.

“Nope,” Jesher said. “Some people say it happened too fast, or that there wasn’t enough time for them to do any good.” He sniffed, and sat farther back against the tree. “Maybe there wasn’t.”

They didn’t speak again for several minutes. The sadness and yearning in Timothy’s gut simmered slowly, but more than that, stronger than that, a black steam rose in his throat.

None of this had had to happen. The kings of old didn’t have to be lost. Eoriden didn't have to be scattered and destroyed. The ground didn't have to be salted. Fenae didn't have to be dead.

"I'll do it again," Timothy said. "I felt a little guilty before, to be honest—about killing that Huctan—but suddenly I don't anymore. I'll do it again. Gladly."

Jesher shifted, but did not answer. Timothy couldn't see his face, in the shadow, but he sensed that Jesher did not completely approve of this statement.

"When it's needed, of course," Timothy clarified. "I'm not saying I'll just go looking for a chance or something—you know I'm not saying that—I'm just saying I won't feel guilty anymore. They deserve it. After what they've done. After what's been lost."

Still Jesher was silent. He didn't say anything, but Timothy felt judgment instead of approval. He felt Jesher saying Robert's words, condemning him as a shallow, vengeful boy the way Robert did, and suddenly he was furious. It was difficult to remain sitting. It was difficult to keep his tone even when he spoke again.

"What's *your* reason?" he said to Jesher. He did not add, 'if you're so high and mighty', or 'you killed a Huctan too, and didn't seem worried about it'. He didn't shout.

"Reason for what?" Jesher said quietly.

"For fighting the Huctans! You care about the Band more than anyone else. You train harder, you care about the missions more, you do everything you can... *everything* you can, not just enough so you can say 'well, I did my best', like the rest of them do. They're candles, and you're a fire. What's your reason, if it isn't to pay the Huctans back for what they did? For what's *lost* because of them?"

Timothy knew he was doing it, knew he was setting himself up for a speech about how the real motive, the better motive, was to help people, to free Botan, not to get revenge on the Huctans. He knew that motive, knew that Robert felt that way and had finally joined the Band because Gerard had convinced him that doing so was righteous. But if Jesher said that, right now—if Jesher, who Timothy felt was almost an extension of himself, *preached* to him—Timothy was going to break.

Jesher was silent, for a long time. Timothy began to think that Jesher was going to ignore him, and he had to calm himself to keep from demanding an answer. He was angry, and guilty, standing on the edge of a knife blade waiting for Jesher to topple him or steady him. His hands were shaking, and he wasn't cold.

Jesher cleared his throat at last.

"When I was younger," he said. "Before I joined the Band—eight years old—I lived at a mill with my parents. You've seen a mill?"

Timothy shook his head.

"It was on a river, just below some short falls. There were a bunch of giant wheels, with paddles, that would catch the water pouring down and turn a giant wooden shaft. There were ropes wrapped around the shaft—we called them belts—that turned a few other shafts and ended up turning the millstones that ground the grain. That's what we did: people would bring us grain, and we would grind it into flour and sell it for them.

"Well, I was fascinated with the waterfall and the wheels. I would go out close to that big shaft, and look at everything turning, and see the power of it all. It was... beautiful. The weight of that water, especially in the spring when the snow was melting off in the mountains, would make that giant shaft flex, like a bow, even though it was thicker than I was.

"My dad would see me watching, and would explain how it

worked to me, but most of all he would tell me never to play on it or get too close to the belts. If my hand got caught, he said, I could be killed.

"I always said OK, that I would never get too close to the shafts and wheels and belts, but one day in the summer, when the water was lower and the shaft was turning slower, I couldn't help myself."

Jesher was frowning, and speaking in a very soft voice. Timothy hardly breathed.

"I started playing on the part of the shaft that hung over the mill," Jesher said. "Just standing on it and walking slowly so I would stay on top while it turned. Then I edged out toward the wheels. When I got to the first wheel, I timed it and stepped through the gap between spokes. On the other side I kept walking, slowly, and then I turned and started walking backward on top of the shaft so that I could watch the waterfall. That's when I slipped.

"It was a little slip, just one foot, but it was enough to make me drop to my knees. And the shaft just kept turning. I had to wrap my arms around it and hang on while it turned me upside down. I tried to get up, when I was right-side up again, but I couldn't time it right. I went upside down again, and tried to get up again, and almost fell. I got scared."

Jesher's voice was getting angrier now—not louder, but angrier—and Timothy was very still and quiet as he listened.

"I shouldn't have been scared," Jesher said. "It was only a ten or fifteen foot drop, into the water. At the worst I would have slapped the water hard or gone too deep and broken an arm or something. But I was scared, so I started yelling for my dad. I yelled, and he came running out, and when he saw me he didn't even yell at me for disobeying him. He just started walking out on that shaft."

Suddenly Jesher's voice went from angry to soft again. Small.

"I missed it, when it happened. He was about to try going through the wheel, and I was upside down. The gaps between spokes in the paddlewheel were easy for me to get through, but harder for him. He had to get on his hands and knees to get through. He could have done it, if he'd had time to think, but I was so busy yelling and screaming like I was going to die that he hurried it. He slipped. I heard something hit hard—it was his head, on the paddlewheel—and then I heard my mother scream.

Jesher stopped, took a deep breath, shifted, sniffed.

"That scream," he said finally. "I..."

Then he was silent again, for almost a full minute. Timothy's rage was gone, and the guilt was stronger now. He sat and waited, feeling miserable and hollow and alone.

"He had hit his head on the way down," Jesher said. "I think that's what must have happened. My mother screamed, and then she went in after him. She had a dress on, and she couldn't swim very well. The river was deep, there." Jesher coughed, and shook his head, and crossed his arms.

"Sorry," he said. "I haven't told this story before."

"No..." Timothy mumbled.

Jesher coughed again, cleared his throat, and went on in a slightly louder, more business-like voice.

"When neither one of them came up, I finally stopped bawling and started inching my way back toward the wheel. When I got into the hole in the wheel, I was able to stand up, even when it took me upside down, and then I was able to step back out on the shaft and get back to the mill.

"I expected them to be downriver, and angry at me, I think. For some reason I hid. When the neighbors found me, they took me to someone who cared for orphans. A Marshal came one day—I didn't know he was a Marshal at the time, of course—and watched us playing. He talked to me, and asked if I wanted to come with him. I asked him why, and he said to do good things, and I said yes. I wanted to do good things, to make up for the terrible thing I'd done."

Jesher looked up at Timothy, and the rising moon glinted on the whites of his eyes.

"I think that's my reason," he said. "It's all the rest, too. What they destroyed, the wonderful things that will never be again because of them. The stuff Robert talks about, too, about protecting the weak and everything. But basically, I think I'm still just that little kid, trying to do as much good as I can, hoping to make up for the bad."

Timothy nodded, and tried to control his constricting throat, and looked out at the darkness. Several long minutes passed in silence.

"I knew a girl," he said finally. His voice was hoarse, and he cleared his throat roughly. If Jesher could tell his story, so could Timothy.

"I knew a girl named Fenae," he said. "She lived in the canyon with us. She was nice to me, usually, though it was probably more for Robert's sake than for mine."

Jesher was watching him, listening intently, and Timothy felt strength come to him.

"Her father was a drunk," he said. "Their family ran the store in our town, and they should have been one of the richest families around, but her father spent his money buying liquor that none of the canyon people would touch, and then drank it himself.

"The taxes were hard on all of us, but with the money the store brought in, even more was expected of Fenae's family. The first year her father didn't have it, he took half his stores up to Watchton—that was the bigger town—and sold them there at a lower price. He lost money, but he got enough to pay the Huctans."

Some of the old rage was coming back, the old disgust. Timothy's mouth moved quickly, making the words before they had a chance to simmer in his mouth.

"He should have learned then, but he kept drinking. The next year he did it again, and lost more money, and we started having to go to Watchton for supplies because he hardly had anything left.

"The next year, even selling the stores wouldn't pay his taxes. He had a son, two years older than me and Robert. There were slavers coming through, offering good money for death-slaves. I don't know if it's the same down here, but up north, the Huctans allow slavers as long as the sales are consensual."

Jesher nodded. Timothy couldn't see his eyes, in the darkness.

"So Fenae's father sold her brother. He went willingly. The slavers took him away, and her father had money to pay another year's taxes."

The anger was making his hand tremble, and the grief he had suppressed for the past year and a half made his eyes tingle with the effort of not crying.

"Fenae hung herself," he said, spitting the words out like a person rips an arrow free. Quickly, cleanly, and painfully. "She couldn't bear the shame."

Timothy's voice broke, and he was silent for a long time, waiting for his throat to relax, waiting for the ability to speak without crying to return to him. Jesher was silent as well. The night swirled slowly around them.

"I swore, then," he said, "that the Huctans would never break me the way they broke Fenae. That I would never so much as cry because of them. That I would hurt *them*, if I could, but they would never hurt me."

Jesher was silent for a long time. Then he said, "I'm sorry."

Timothy nodded.

When his watch was up, Timothy offered to stay, but Jesher told him to get some rest. As Timothy padded back to the hollow and took his place by the glowing coals of the fire, he felt as close to Jesher as he ever had to anyone.

"I haven't told this story before," Jesher had said. Yet he had told it to Timothy. And Timothy had told his.

CHAPTER 16

ROBERT

Robert rested his chin on his fist and stared at the wooden board. With six people now watching over his shoulder, it was hard to concentrate on the game.

Nick had a good defensive position set up. Every time Robert made a move to break through, Nick anticipated his plan and cut him off. Robert's own position was starting to open up more than he would have liked. If he didn't keep the pressure on Nick, he was going to find himself on the defensive, and his open position would become his downfall. Nick still had both of his archers and had only lost one of his cavalrymen. If the game turned to an all-out grind, Robert would lose.

Losing to Nick would be no surprise. Robert was expected to lose. He had only been a Thane for a few months, while Nick had been training under Comaro since he was eleven years old. Nick was a master of strategy, and while there was more to strategy than a board game like King's Table, people tended to equate skill in the game with skill in the art it was supposed to teach.

And Nick was very good at the game. Robert had hundreds of losses under his belt, and over half of them were to Nick. Every day, when Robert was finished learning about supply trains or covered retreats or terrain utilization from Comaro, he played King's Table with Nick. The fact that Nick continued to play with such a boring opponent proved that he was a decent person. Every game made Robert feel more like a child challenging a sword-master, but Nick kept playing him, and Robert kept trying.

Nick's victories had taken longer in the past few weeks. In the last few days, they had only been able to get one game in over each meal. Today's game, played over dinner, had drawn the attention of some of the other Thanes. Even a few adults had joined the semicircle of silent onlookers.

Robert reached forward and moved his archer behind Nick's lieutenant.

It was a bold move, and a reckless one. Comaro would not have approved. Too much of Robert's plan depended on trickery, and Comaro always said that a win caused by your opponent's mistake was a win of luck. A real win, a solid victory, was one in which there were no right moves for your opponent to make. In a solid victory, you could lay all your cards face-up on the table and your opponent would still have no way of stopping you.

All Nick had to do, to stop Robert, was to attack that archer. Whether he did attack it depended on how far he thought Robert's skills had advanced.

At very first glance, the archer was obvious bait. The archer's new position did not threaten any of Nick's key pieces, and it was vulnerable to attack by Nick's lieutenant. Yet if Nick *did* attack with his lieutenant, he would open up a key point in his defenses, and Robert would probably be able to take several pawns before Nick could staunch the bleeding.

But the trap was so obvious, so blatant, that Nick would see it and immediately know that Robert was up to something else.

Thus Robert's own lieutenant. Previously penned in by his archer, it now had a clear path to take Nick's remaining cavalryman. If Nick fell for the first, most obvious trap, Robert would take his cavalryman. It would gain him an edge, but not enough to sway the game.

But even this was not Robert's true goal. His true goal—the outcome that would lead in four moves to Robert's victory—depended on Nick ignoring the first trap, seeing the second trap, and taking the most obvious move to avoid it. And that would only happen if Nick knew Robert well enough to realize that the first trap was a decoy, but not well enough to realize that the second trap was also a decoy.

Nick touched his cavalryman, and then hesitated. Robert worked hard not to betray any emotion. All he needed was for Nick to move the cavalryman one square to the left. All he needed was for Nick to think he was seeing through a semi-clever ploy, to feel no need to look for other traps. To ignore the fact that his cavalryman had been pinning one of Robert's pawns, which in turn kept Robert's pikeman from threatening Nick's general.

Click. Nick moved the cavalryman one square to the left. Still his finger rested on the carved wooden piece. Robert realized that he was being too still, staring at the wooden horseman too intently, and raised one hand to scratch under his eye. Someone coughed, and Robert let his eyes wander.

Nick withdrew his hand.

He had fallen for it.

Robert pretended to study the board for a long time, though he knew exactly what he would do next. Better not to let Nick know that Robert had wanted this to happen. If Nick realized that he was falling into a trap, he might see the single remaining way to escape.

Robert moved the pawn.

"Check," he said.

Nick's eyes traced the path between Robert's pikeman and his own general, then closed for a brief moment. For Nick, the gesture was as clear as a slap to his own forehead. He knew he had made a mistake. His only choices, now, were to move his general and leave the interior of his defenses open to Robert's pikeman, or to sacrifice his cavalryman to plug the gap for one move more.

Nick chose to move the general. Losing the cavalryman, at first and even second glance, would gain him nothing. And Nick still didn't know Robert well enough to bother with a third, long look at the board.

Robert felt his throat loosen. Now there was no room to wriggle. He moved his pikeman, knowing that his and Nick's next two moves were inevitable.

Nick raised his hand to move his general, and then froze. It was a tribute to his genius that he saw his mistake almost immediately.

His general was threatened again. He had to move it, and there was only one place to move it to. Then Robert would move his pikeman once more, and Nick would be forced to put his general in an unprotected corner.

A corner where Robert's archer could close the final gap.

A corner created by Nick's own unmoved cavalryman.

One of the onlookers made a sound of surprise in his throat. Nick gave the situation forty long seconds. Then he reached forward, placed a single finger on top of his own carved general, and toppled the piece.

"Good game," said Robert.

"Good game," said Nick.

They shook hands, and the talk among the onlookers began immediately. It was whispered, but Robert caught "genius" and "planned the whole time" and "only a few months". He did his best to ignore the others as he assured Nick that he had been lucky.

"Well played," Nick said, as graciously as could be expected.

"Thank you," Robert said.

Timothy returned from his mission the next day. Robert missed him at lunch and dinner both, but there was enough buzz among the other Thanes for him to gather most of what had happened.

Robert missed language practice. His own training didn't require him to speak Huctan as fluently as Timothy needed to, and Comaro thought those four hours were better spent on other things. Even so, Timothy was still awake when Robert finally returned to the cabin.

"You're back early," Robert said.

"Yeah," said Timothy. Then, "You heard what happened?"

"Yeah," said Robert. He tried to keep his tone neutral, to not betray sadness or judgment, but there was no hiding anything from Timothy anymore. Between Timothy and Selena, with their Eliniel, Robert's chances of keeping any emotion to himself were practically non-existent.

"Haberd says it's my fault." Timothy said. "He says I should have talked my way out of it."

"Haberd is full of salt," Robert said. Selena had told him about the way Timothy handled the soldiers, and he couldn't think of anything Timothy could have done differently. Even if Timothy still thought of himself as dirt beneath Haberd's shoes, Robert knew Timothy's reputation, and Selena's. If Timothy and Selena together hadn't been able to fool the soldiers, no one could have.

Timothy sighed. "No," he said. "He told me four different ways I could have gotten out of it, without us having to kill them. I should have kept my head."

He seemed almost apologetic, as if killing the Huctans had been a personal affront to Robert. Robert wanted to hit something. He wasn't judging Timothy, wasn't even sure that Timothy had had a choice in the matter. Why wasn't Timothy meeting his eyes?

What had happened to them?

"I don't understand why the council is so upset about it," Robert said.

And he didn't. It was true that Thanes had been risked. It was also true that Huctan soldiers had disappeared near the Band's secret location, and that attention might be drawn to the hill country if an investigation were made. But it wasn't as if Jesher's squad had made any egregious mistakes. They had been met with a difficult situation, and had handled it well. The outcome had been the best possible under such circumstances. There was no reason for Verinald to be as furious as Selena said he was.

"Jesher and Selena barely kept them from putting us all on probation," Timothy said.

"Why? What did they want you to do?"

Timothy shook his head and lay down. "Talk our way out of it," he said.

They were silent for a while. Robert undressed, snuffed the lamp, laid down. The two of them stared at the ceiling for a while, neither one sleeping, neither one speaking.

"Timothy," Robert said finally, hating how difficult it was to talk with his brother, hating how formal his voice sounded.

"Yeah."

"I'm glad you're alive," Robert said.

There was a long pause.

"Thanks," Timothy said.

CHAPTER 17

JESHER

Clarena escaped Eoriden because she was one of the first out of the tunnels. She kept running, though her arms were already cramping with the weight of the children, and did not stop when she heard the screams of those behind. She ran, and the boys did not cry out.

A country family had pity on her and let the boys ride in their wagon as they fled. Clarena walked behind, willing the farm horse to go faster, willing the Huctans to search elsewhere. Although she feared pursuit, she could not look back, for the column of smoke rising from the Beloved City tore at her heart.

In the months that followed, she heard word of the razing. Huctans rode in marauding bands over the land, quelling resistance and destroying all trace of the Old Kingdom. Clarena prepared to die when they came to her new village, but of course the Huctans were looking for soldiers and Duest, not women with small children.

She married a smith—more for the boys than for herself—and in time came to love him. Sometimes she thought of her first husband,

and his death at Eoriden, and her heart grew hollow. More often, with shame, she thought of her son's father.

Clarena gave the boys Common names, and taught them the Common tongue, and vowed that they would not follow their fathers in patriotism and death. She taught them to keep their heads down, to avoid the Huctans, to do their work, and to never speak of Botan.

It broke her heart to do so, and it was all for naught. The Huctans took them anyway.

Of course, Timothy's combat training went poorly for several weeks after his first mission. And, of course, Jesher volunteered to help. He remembered well how a wooden spear began to feel different after you had used a real one. He understood exactly why Timothy, who had been hard to beat only a week ago, now fought with alternating hesitation and haste.

Jesher knew that the only way Timothy could overcome his handicap was by training harder, so he showed no mercy in their bouts. Timothy began to walk stiffly from the bruises Jesher gave him. But in a few weeks his body started behaving again.

And when it did, he was better than he had been. Much better. That was the thing about real fighting. You could train with a wooden sword until the river ran dry, but actual combat taught you more in sixty seconds than training would teach you in a year.

"We should fight Huctans every day," Timothy said on one occasion, when he had managed to disarm Jesher with a particularly good twist of his spear, "We would be invincible."

"We'd be better," Jesher said. "And we'd probably be dead."

"Worth it," said Timothy.

Jesher laughed.

"Has Farland given you his Skill-Doesn't-Matter speech?" Jesher asked.

"No," said Timothy. "Sounds depressing."

"It is. He says that how good you are at fighting doesn't matter nearly as much as people think it does. It's not deterministic."

"Big words," said Timothy.

"If you have a heavy rock," Jesher said, ignoring Timothy, "and you have a light rock, and you weigh them, then the heavy rock will weigh more. Every time. That's deterministic."

"I know what deterministic means," said Timothy. "I was being sarcastic."

"I know that you know what it means," said Jesher. "But you wanted Farland's speech, so I'm trying to stick to the script."

"Very well," Timothy said, twirling his hand magnanimously. "You may continue."

"You're too kind," said Jesher. "Where was I?"

"Heavy rock, light rock, heavy rock always wins," said Timothy.

"Always," said Jesher. "But now say you take an amazing fighter—for example, myself—and an OK fighter. For example, *your*self."

"Hey."

"In that case, the amazing fighter doesn't always win. Not even most of the time. A majority of the time, maybe, but a small majority."

"*You* win nine times out of ten," Timothy said.

"Well, I may be more than amazing, and you may be less than OK."

"Was that in Farland's speech?" said Timothy.

"I may be improvising," said Jesher. "In bouts, it's different, though. When we both have the same weapon, and we're both ready, and there's a little circle that we have to stay inside of, then skill is more deterministic. But when it's real, when one person is on a horse and the other's not sure their opponent is really going to try to kill them, and one has a spear while the other has a sword or a crossbow or a pitchfork, then it's suddenly different. You can put your money on the good fighter, but you're not going to get rich doing it."

"So what you're telling me," Timothy said, "is that we're wasting our time. That we might as well go out with a pitchfork and see what happens."

"No," Jesher said. "I'm telling you not to get a big head."

Some of the playfulness vanished from Timothy's expression, and Jesher realized that his own tone had been a little sharp. Well, it was an important point.

Timothy cocked his head, and then nodded. "Point taken," he said, after a moment. "Real fights are serious, no matter how good I am, no matter how bad the enemy is."

"Yes," said Jesher. "Exactly."

Timothy nodded, to show that he understood. Then he offered a hand, with a half-smile.

"I promise that I won't get killed if you won't," he said.

"Done," Jesher said, taking Timothy's hand and shaking it. Then, with a smile of his own, "Non-deterministically, of course."

Spring overtook winter. The last snow fell. The time for another mission came. Timothy said he didn't feel ready. Jesher told him that no one ever felt ready, that you just had to go out when you were sent and do your best.

Their route, the southwestern loop, was a long one. They started on the same road as they had on their first mission, but this time they cut south and west, through the Pyrie valley and all the way to the coast. Then they turned south and began the meandering journey back east through sleek, budding farmland.

Timothy had never seen the ocean before. Jesher took him on a detour of about two miles to some low cliffs overlooking the waves. They sat atop their horses together—he, Timothy, and Selena—and watched the crests. Timothy's mouth hung open, and Jesher was glad.

They gathered reports from the Band's contacts along their loop. Sometimes Jesher left Selena and Timothy camped while he went to meet the contacts. Other times he and Timothy camped while Selena went to meet them. Jesher explained to Timothy that each Thane knew the locations of a few contacts, but not all. It was better if no one person knew everything.

When something finally happened, it happened all at once.

A farmer had given them permission to stay the night in his barn. Jesher left Selena and Timothy to rest while he went to meet their contact. Alonso, a hired farmhand who was loyal to the Band and kept an eye on several villages in the area, had word of a letter. Two Thanes were needed to access it.

Jesher knew that the prudent thing would be to have Selena help him. She was more experienced than Timothy, and this was

Timothy's second mission. The second real mission—the mission after a Thane had first seen death—was always the most dangerous. It was usually best to make sure that a Thane's second real mission was something that would not end up killing him if he choked.

But Jesher trusted Timothy, and nothing would re-clinch Timothy's confidence like successfully stealing a letter from a Huctan guard tower.

Alonso followed him to the barn, which was near the main road and only a little ways out of the town. When Jesher opened the latch, Selena and Timothy sat up from the hay with squinty-eyed looks, as if they had just woken up. Jesher almost believed that he had caught them off guard, but then they recognized him and dropped their sleepy looks like masks. Timothy sheathed the belt knife that Jesher hadn't seen in his hand.

"This is Alonso," Jesher said. "Alonso, Timothy and Selena."

"Let's get on with it," Alonso said. He was anxious, and rightly so. Sundown was swiftly approaching.

"Timothy, we need your help," Jesher said. "Leave your spear haft."

Timothy was already on his feet. Selena rose too.

"I'm supposed to observe..." she said.

"Fine, follow," Jesher said. "Fifty yards minimum. Don't be seen."

Selena nodded. They were at the door, ready to go. Jesher's fingers tingled.

"Alonso?" Jesher said.

"Let's go," said the long-limbed man, breaking into an easy, loping run. Jesher followed, hearing Timothy fall in beside him and Selena behind. Their feet made muffled noises in the grass, and after a while the sound of their breathing grew louder. Alonso set a fast pace.

It was a mile and a half to the village, and almost twilight when the walls came into view. Alonso came to a halt, and Jesher joined him. The tall man put a hand on Jesher's shoulder and pointed.

"On the left there?" Jesher said, puffing and pointing to the wooden structure just to the side of the village gates.

"Straight in the window," said Alonso.

"On your signal."

Alonso gave him a slap on the back and trotted away towards the road. Jesher dropped to a squat, and Timothy knelt beside him.

"Here's the deal," Jesher said, panting a little. "Some letters arrived today. They're in the guard shack on the left, supposedly, and we're going to find one of them.

"The guards are about to switch. Alonso's going to try to distract them while we go through the lookout window. We can't take the letter, so we'll have to speed-memorize."

Timothy nodded that he understood.

"Alright," Jesher said. "Let's go."

They crept closer, through the grass, using the slight rise in the field to cover a swift doubled-over run before dropping to the earth and slithering forward. It would have been a hard approach in daylight, but the lengthening shadow from the low wall was enough to obscure them in the shadows. They reached the stand of tall grass closest to the tower just before Alonso came ambling into sight on the wagon road.

There were still forty yards between where they lay and where the wall rose to the window, but they would wait. When the guards switched, there would be no one in the tower to see their approach.

"You jumping or standing?" Timothy whispered, just as Jesher opened his mouth to explain.

"Standing," Jesher said, suppressing a grin. Working with Timothy in the field was as easy as doing drills with him. They almost didn't need to speak.

They waited. Jesher raised his head just enough to see Alonso's advance. He held his hand up.

Alonso was at the gate, talking with one of the guards. The signal came: Alonso reaching over his head to scratch his back. Jesher took one more deep breath. He hoped Timothy was ready.

He dropped his hand. They bolted.

Jesher led a little as they approached the wall, and Timothy fell back. Some ten yards ahead of Timothy, Jesher turned and braced himself below the window. The sill was a good fifteen feet up. It was going to have to be a good jump.

Timothy slowed, measured his last steps, and leapt high enough to kick off of Jesher's cupped hands. Jesher pulled just as Timothy's weight settled, and he knew it was a good jump even before Timothy shot upwards from his hands like an arrow from a bow.

Jesher wanted to look, wanted to give Timothy advice on getting his elbows into position in the sill, but he forced himself to trust. Leaving the wall, he circled for a running start.

Timothy was ready, hanging in a perfect elbow grip. Jesher ran, scraped his foot on the wall, and caught Timothy's ankles. Hand over hand he climbed, using Timothy's hips and shoulders to gain the window before pushing aside the shutter and slithering into the dim light of the watchtower.

Timothy followed, and they descended the ladder softly. Jesher could hear Alonso, still talking with the Huctans outside. Any minute they would finish and two new guards would come inside to begin their watch.

He had to hurry.

A lamp was lit on a small desk beside an open flagon. Crumbs were scattered about. Weapons hung along one wall, and a shelf opposite held maps, papers, and a small chest. Jesher began rifling through the papers. In a moment he found what they were looking for and unfolded it on the table. He pointed to a section of the letter, and again he and Timothy communicated without words. Timothy began to memorize his part of the letter, and Jesher began his.

They were both still for a moment, leaning over the document with eyes flickering. Jesher found it difficult to ignore the door that might open at any second.

Timothy finished just before Jesher and straightened. Jesher scanned the lines one more time and set part of his consciousness to reviewing and repeating. Then he whisked the letter off the table and replaced it on the shelf before following Timothy up the ladder.

He heard the door open behind them just as he pulled his foot through the trap door. Quickly he tip-toed across the upper floor to the window. Timothy had lowered himself until he was hanging from the sill by his fingertips, and he now dropped down to land softly. Jesher followed suit, and together they sprinted for the cover of the tall grass.

This was how it was supposed to be, thought Jesher. This was perfection, teamwork. This was the work of Thanes.

The rule, when you speed-memorized, was that no one could talk to you until you had transcribed your message. They met Selena and jogged back to the barn in silence. Selena got them some rolled bark and a stick of charcoal. Timothy scribbled his half of the message and handed Jesher the charcoal. Jesher began writing.

Transcription was the hardest part for him. Reading his own words as he formed them made him forget the rest almost as bad as talking did. He still practiced almost every week, though he had done it enough times by now that he should have been able to do it in his sleep.

Timothy, of course, seemed to have no trouble. Speed-memorization was probably one of the easiest skills in Eliniel.

At last Jesher finished. He read the letter, then gave it to Selena. Her eyes widened as she scanned the lines. When she was finished, she caught Jesher's eye, and he gave a slight nod. Selena gave the letter to Timothy.

Timothy read the letter twice, then looked up at Selena and Jesher. Jesher nodded grimly, and Timothy read the letter once more. Then he rolled it, carefully and slowly, and gave it back to Jesher.

"It was sealed?" Selena asked Jesher.

"The seal was broken," Jesher said, "but yeah. Black wax."

"Black wax," Timothy muttered, as if trying to remember something.

"It's the royal seal," Selena said. "That letter came straight from Taras Abor."

They were up and riding before the farmer had come to milk his cows.

When dawn bloomed, an hour later, Jesher thought how strange it was that dawn was beautiful wherever he went. He had grown up thinking it was unique to the river country, that it had something to do with the way the fog flared and burned off and the distant mountains made soft silhouettes on dawn's edge. But he had seen beautiful dawns in the half-wooded hill country of the Band, in the bare foothills to the south, and on the flat plains to the northwest. Now, as he watched the sun splashing color through the gray fog and blue shadows moving across the low dunes, Jesher decided that dawn was beautiful for its own sake.

Timothy, riding beside him with the pink glow flushing his face, crowed. Jesher laughed aloud at the barnyard cry, and was glad. He didn't have to try to explain the magic of it all to Timothy. Timothy knew. He felt it himself.

Gradually the vibrancy faded to a wan, cold glow and the fog reluctantly began to burn off. Jesher waited, and at last Timothy spoke about the letter.

"So," he said.

Jesher looked at him. "So."

"When are you going to tell me about the Move?"

Jesher sniffed. "Still haven't decided if I'm supposed to."

"You wouldn't have let me see the end of that letter if you weren't," Timothy said.

"What, you think I never make mistakes?"

"I *know* you make mistakes. But that wasn't one of them."

Jesher sniffed another laugh, then glanced back. Selena was visible, about a quarter-mile back, but well out of hearing.

"How come you all know about it anyway, and I don't?" Timothy asked.

"Some of us socialize," Jesher said. "We hear things. Not everyone spends every second of their lives training."

"You do," Timothy said.

Jesher shrugged. There was a long silence. Finally, Timothy prompted Jesher.

"Well?" he said.

Jesher shrugged again. He didn't know why he was delaying. He had already decided to tell Timothy. The council might not think that new Thanes should know such things, but if Jesher was reading that letter correctly—and Selena thought he was—the council would have much bigger things to worry about.

"Well," he said, "you obviously know how the Huctans were rounding boys up last spring."

Timothy nodded, a little of the playfulness leaving his face. He had been one of those boys. Jesher realized, suddenly, that he had never asked Timothy about his captivity. He had never asked whether Timothy's parents had been hurt when they took him. He'd heard stories about families trying to protect their sons and being slaughtered for it.

Jesher promised himself that he would ask, someday.

"Well," Jesher repeated, "We don't have a ton of information about them. Most of the reports are of illegal slavers. Apparently the Huctans tried to keep their kidnapping a secret. Did it at night, or dressed in civilian clothes. Is that what they did with you?"

Timothy nodded. "At night," he said. "Secretly."

"We do know a lot from Selena," Jesher said. "And we have a few more reports since. About the training they've been giving the Botaños they kidnapped. The Huctans have been pretty brutal—I guess you know that—but it sounds like it's working."

"Working?"

"Yeah. They're making the Botaños into soldiers. The Huctans have armies stationed all over Botan, now, and quite a few of them are heavily padded with kidnapped Botani boys in Huctan uniforms.

Timothy scowled, but he did not seem surprised.

"They were turning already, when we escaped," he said. "Someone from my own village tried to raise the alarm." Then, "What do they need so many extra soldiers for?"

Jesher shrugged. "We're not sure, exactly. We intercepted a letter from a general, a few weeks ago, telling a colonel to get his troops ready. It's something big. We've been calling it the Plan. I guess now we know what *they* call it."

Timothy was silent again. Jesher glanced at him, from the corner of his eye, and remembered how it had felt after his own third or fourth mission. At some point he had realized how sheltered he was, how training and training and training had kept him from any knowledge of the real world.

Now he had been on dozens of missions, and knew a little of what was happening, but the feeling of smallness had never entirely left. He wondered if Timothy was feeling the same thing now.

"We have no idea what they're getting ready for?" Timothy asked finally.

Jesher sighed. "Not *no* idea," he said. "The popular theory is that they're going to attack Jardon."

Timothy squinted. "Jardon," he said. "The country that refused to answer the War Knot."

Jesher nodded. They rode for a minute, and then Timothy spoke again.

"I'll bet they've told all the kidnapped boys about the War Knot," he said. "To make them angry. It almost makes me angry enough to fight against Jardon myself."

"I'll bet they have," Jesher replied. His instinct told him that he should qualify, that he should make some excuse for Jardon, but he squelched the impulse. He wasn't Timothy's father. He was his friend. And he didn't exactly disagree, either. Jardon deserved whatever punishment came to them.

"The letter," Timothy said at last. "Does it mean that Ricera is looking for the Band? That they plan to wipe us out before they make "the Move"?"

Jesher winced at Timothy's bluntness, and shrugged.

"That's what it looked like to me," he said. "But I hope we're wrong. I hope we're wrong."

CHAPTER 18

Verinald, whose son was in the hands of the traitor, who had earned his freedom by a promise to help Ricera when the time came, found his old master near the Jardon border.

"Haberd," he said. "I thought you were dead. What happened? Did you deliver the knot?"

Haberd's face was haggard, his eyes hollow. He looked at Verinald almost without recognition.

"I delivered it," he said. "They ignored it."

Verinald took Haberd's shoulder and embraced him, hissing a little at the pain in his leg. The crossbow bolt he'd requested from Ricera's soldiers had only passed through the meat of his thigh, but the wound was more painful than he could have imagined.

"All is not lost," he said, hoping his tone was even, hoping the guilt in his chest did not spill over into his voice. "I know of a place. The hill country between Suiton and Shadil has always been wilderness. We can hide there. We can regroup."

For a moment, Haberd said nothing. Then he said, "All *is* lost." His voice was as hollow as his eyes.

Verinald felt a strange surge of relief at his old master's despair. Verinald was no stranger to lying, but in all his years he had rarely, if ever, been able to fool Haberd. When he had seen Haberd waiting at the rendezvous point, seen that his first act as a traitor would be to deceive the undeceivable, he had almost despaired himself.

But Haberd *was* deceivable, because Haberd was broken. Verinald grieved for what had been lost, but Haberd was beyond grieving. Haberd's slumped shoulders bore the weight of a country lost, but they also bore the heavier and sharper burden of guilt. It had been *Haberd's* pet student, Haberd's *favorite,* Haberd's beloved *Ricera* that had brought this disaster upon them.

How that must eat at him, thought Verinald. How it must sicken him. And shouldn't it? Shouldn't Haberd, of all people, have seen through Ricera's deception?

"Much is lost," said Verinald, "but not all. We will regroup. We will not give in."

Haberd did not reply, only stared and stood.

"Haberd," Verinald said. "I need you. Please come with me."

For a moment, it seemed that Haberd would refuse. Verinald wondered whether telling the old man his planned location had been a mistake. He wondered if he would have to kill Haberd, and the thought was not as horrifying as it should have been. His hands itched to do something, to make someone pay.

But then Haberd nodded. A slight movement of the head, a shrug of the shoulders that said, Why not? It can't be any more futile than standing here until I die.

"Thank you," Verinald said. "Thank you."

Timothy expected resistance when they brought news of the letter before the council. It was bad news, and no one likes to accept bad news. It was also coming from three Thanes who had been reprimanded harshly for risky behavior in their last mission.

And it was outrageous. Ricera, the archenemy of Botan, who had not been heard of since the Betrayal, was looking for the Band.

Yes, there would be resistance. But Selena and Jesher, at least, were reliable and tested Thanes. Their word was trustworthy, and the letter was unmistakable. The council would have to believe them.

Timothy expected resistance, but he didn't expect Verinald to actually laugh.

Verinald—hated by most of the Thanes, yet loved and respected by the adults of the council as the wisest and most dignified among them—heard Jesher explain the letter and laughed out loud as if a child had just told him about the moon-fairies.

"It's a long shot," Jesher said, though it wasn't a long shot at all, "but all three of us read the letter independently and came to the same interpretation. It seems like..."

"It seems like the Thanes are eager for adventure," Verinald said, with a smile that was meant to look kindly while simultaneously patronizing the three young Thanes. A few members of the council chuckled. Jesher was silent for a moment, almost in shock.

"Ricera is dead," said one of the council members, an old man with a thinning ring of hair around his ears. "Once he outlived his usefulness, the Huctans killed him. That is the payment that is always due a traitor."

Many of the others nodded agreement, and Timothy felt his eyebrows curl in incredulity. Had any of them *seen* Ricera killed?

Did any of them have evidence to base his death on? He would expect fools and children to let wishful thinking turn into belief, but not his elders and betters.

Then Timothy saw Haberd—who of all people knew better, who of all people should have trusted *Selena,* if not Timothy—nodding along with the rest. Suddenly his scorn turned to hurt. He felt betrayed.

"With respect," Selena ventured, "I have been in the Band from the beginning. I have trained in Eliniel under Haberd since I was a little girl. My sober opinion—based on my training alone, because I definitely don't *want* it to be true—is that the letter means what it says. Ricera is being given authority to root out the resistance and prepare the way for 'the Move'."

Verinald, who had been hiding a smile and giving Selena a patient look as she made her speech, nodded with the graveness one uses when trying not to upset a petulant child.

"None of us wishes to slight your training," he said, holding up a pacifying hand as if Selena had been shouting. "You have done very well, for your age. We would not have sent you to Northelm if we did not recognize your talent."

As Verinald's words sunk into Timothy's ears, many things became clear, suddenly and with certainty.

First, Verinald was not a fool. His response to Selena's challenge was perfect. Without addressing Selena's argument, he twisted her words to sound like a sulky defense of her own honor. In the same stroke he reminded everyone of her youth and inexperience. Then, the killing blow, he brought up Northelm.

He did it in such a way that no one could possibly accuse him of trying to slur her credibility—he made it a compliment, for pity's sake—but it had the desired effect all the same. Everyone thought immediately of the way she had rescued Timothy and Robert without permission, then of the excitability and recklessness that must have caused her to do this, then of her current status as a Thane on probation. In this light, the fact that she interpreted the letter one way suddenly became evidence that it meant the opposite.

The second thing Timothy realized was that Verinald was willfully and actively trying to squelch the letter. He *knew* that it said what it said, but he was trying to minimize it, conceal it, hide its implications. He was trying to keep the Band from doing anything about it.

Why?

"I think Selena's point was different," Jesher said innocently, as if he actually believed that Verinald was being obtuse rather than malicious. "What she meant was that..."

"Yes, yes," said the old man with the wispy ring of hair. "We know what you mean. You think Ricera is coming back. You think you saw this in a letter, in a little, poorly protected guard hut in some jerkwater, southwestern village."

The old man laughed, as if this were the most ridiculous part of the story, as if all significant things were to be found in castles and great cities. He shot a glance at Verinald during his laugh. The glance was subtle, but Timothy saw it, and he could tell by the shifting of Selena's feet that she saw it too. It was a glance for approval, a glance that a young bully gives an older one to make sure his belligerence is noticed and approved of.

Verinald did not smile approval. He knew, of course, that the council was watching him, and that many of them were a little disgusted by the old man with the wispy ring of hair. Instead,

Verinald looked grave and a little disappointed at the man's rudeness.

The old man, clearly hurt, stopped laughing and turned a nasty eye on Jesher. "Leave the interpretation of letters to those who understand such things," he said.

Jesher swallowed, and was unnaturally still.

"Ask Haberd," Timothy said suddenly, knowing that if he said anything, it would have to be something they could not interrupt, something simple, something that might disrupt this pattern of riding roughshod over the Thanes.

Yes, they were young. Yes, they had never lived in Eoriden or known the great struggles of the true Duest. And yes, they were right about the letter. Haberd would see it. He had nodded his head along with the rest, but Timothy still could not believe that Haberd was a fool. If they asked him, he would give a fair interpretation of the letter.

"He," Timothy said, "of all people, should have the training to recognize some subtlety or code that we poor, stupid Thanes have missed."

Selena gasped at this last, and Timothy knew he had gone too far, defeated his own statement, drawn the focus to his anger and disrespect instead of to Haberd and the question at hand. Verinald knew it too, and took full advantage.

"Yes, what does Haberd think?" said Gerard, but Verinald spoke at the same time, and in a louder voice.

"We are all quite capable of interpreting the words you have parroted to us from the letter," he said, again with a kindly smile that clashed harshly with the way his eyes set when he looked at Timothy. "I assure you that there is no need to worry. Even if you memorized the letter correctly—and I know it is easy to miss or add a word that might shift the apparent meaning, especially on your second mission—we have no reason to think that our position is compromised. We have been careful, scrupulously so, and we have always been ready to respond if true evidence showed that our location were discovered."

"What would "true evidence" be?" Timothy said, knowing that he should stop but finding himself unable to do so. "A personal confession from Ricera himself? The sound of cavalry coming over the hill? Huctan soldiers knocking on your..."

"Furthermore!" Verinald said, and his voice snapped like a whip. He paused, looked at Timothy, and interrupted himself to make an infuriatingly calm threat.

"By the way," he said, "If the Thanes cannot show proper respect, they will prove themselves unfit to serve Botan in their privileged capacity." Verinald gave Timothy a meaningful look, and Timothy widened his eyes and gave an exaggerated swallow of horror. Verinald ignored his mockery and returned to his speech.

"Furthermore," he said, "The council is correct; Ricera is long dead or imprisoned in Taras Abor. Even the Huctans would not trust someone like *him* to do their bidding."

Like they didn't trust him to round up and destroy Duest after the Invasion? Timothy wanted to shout, but Selena pressed her foot against his, hard, and with an effort he held his mouth rigidly shut.

The ring-haired man chuckled, at the idea of the Huctans trusting someone like *Ricera*, and Verinald turned to meet his gaze with a twinkle in his eye. Yes, Timothy thought, appeal to everyone's pride and hate for Ricera. Very subtle.

Verinald stood, brushing his hands together, and smiled down at

Timothy, Jesher, and Selena again.

"Even so," he said, as if offering condolence, "you were right to report the letter to us. The work to obtain it was no less valuable because it did not contain what you thought. The council thanks you."

Timothy opened his mouth again, but Selena ground her foot over his. Turning his flinch into a vaguely disrespectful yawn, Timothy turned to leave.

"Before you go," Verinald said, as if just remembering something. "And I assume the answer is no, but I'll ask anyway: have any of you spoken to anyone else about this matter?"

Timothy could not bring himself to speak civilly. Selena answered for them.

"We came to the council first," she said.

"Good," Verinald said. "I think we'd like to keep it that way. If the council agrees?" he spread his hands and swiveled, glancing at the others. Timothy glared at Haberd. The man who should have seen *exactly* what Verinald was doing was sitting on his hands and watching it happen.

"Yes, then," Verinald said, turning to face the Thanes once more. "With the authority of the council, I give you all strict orders to keep this letter a secret. You are not to tell anyone of its contents, and you are most assuredly not to tell anyone of your literal interpretation. We do not want a panic starting."

Selena and Jesher nodded, and Timothy felt his head move in a way that might resemble a nod. Then he was outside, and someone had enough sense to take the door from him before he could slam it.

They walked together, stiffly and with some dignity, until the window of the council's cabin was out of sight. Then Jesher, with a kick at the road, took off running for the woods. Timothy followed him.

"Wait..." he heard Selena say, but he did not wait.

When they reached the pines, Jesher's jog turned into a sprint, and for several minutes they ran up the hill, burning aggression into sweat until they broke through the dense pines to a widening near the top of the hill. Slowing to a walk, they caught their breath. Timothy picked up a dead branch and dashed it against a tree. Jesher sprang up onto a fallen log and sat down.

It was a warm day. Timothy's sweat sat heavy on his forehead and dampened the skin under his heavy cloak.

"Verinald's an idiot," Timothy said. "They all are."

Jesher didn't answer. Timothy picked up another branch and sat down on the ground against a tree. They were silent, for a while, Timothy breaking his branch into smaller and smaller pieces and Jesher idly tearing bark off of the fallen log he sat on.

Finally Jesher spoke, quietly, staring down at the log almost as if he were talking to himself.

"He was trying to hide it, wasn't he?" he said.

Timothy took a deep breath through his nose, flung away the pieces of his stick, and nodded. A small part of him felt honored that Jesher was asking *him*, that Jesher trusted *him* on such things now, but he pushed that pride to the back and kept focused on the situation.

"I think so," he said. "He was bald-faced about trying to make it look like we were unreliable. It was almost like he suspected that the letter was real, but didn't want to panic people or something."

Jesher's knee began bouncing. He stopped breaking bark,

brushed his hands together to get rid of the little flakes of wood, and looked back down the hill.

"We should be warning the others," he said.

"I know," said Timothy, picking up a handful of pine needles to crush. "We should be getting everyone ready, putting out more guards, maybe moving the whole Band. *Something.* But no, Verinald doesn't want people to get scared, so instead we're all going to just sit here and wait to see what happens."

"No," Jesher said, turning to look at Timothy. There was something burning in his eyes, something rebellious and reckless that Timothy had not seen there before. "No," he repeated, "*We* have to warn the others."

Timothy realized suddenly that Jesher wasn't talking about what the council should be doing.

"You mean *us*," he said. "Against Verinald's orders."

Jesher nodded.

"But you *never* go against orders."

"I'm about to," Jesher said, losing some of his calm and jumping down from the log. He began breaking off bark again, in big chunks that he crumbled down in his hands. "What are they going to do to me?"

"They'll put you on probation," Timothy said, still looking at Jesher out of the sides of his eyes, still not quite sure that Jesher was serious. "You'll end up like Selena. They'll have you run errands for the Marshals and help the other Thanes with their drills, and if you go on any missions at all it'll be 'to observe'. You won't get to do anything meaningful."

"Like we do now?" Jesher said. His voice was sharp, like a dry branch snapping, and he stopped pacing suddenly. His eyes were burning harder. Timothy wanted to shrink back from them.

"What is it we're doing, now?" Jesher demanded. "We run errands for the Marshals, and train, and go on 'missions'. What is that? What does that accomplish?"

Timothy did not answer. He did not comprehend. These words, coming from this mouth, were incoherent. Jesher loved Botan. Jesher was the fire next to the candles. Jesher would never say anything against the Band and its accomplishments.

"We're not doing *anything*," said Jesher, answering his own question. "The Band is paralyzed."

Timothy closed his mouth, and then his eyes. He wondered, for a moment, if he was dreaming, if this was even real.

"We're planning," he said to Jesher. His voice sounded small. "Waiting for the right..."

"The right time," Jesher interrupted, "Yes, the 'right time'! The right time is never, for them. They're *comfortable*," Jesher pointed a quivering finger down the hill in the direction of the cabins. "They love the way things are right now. They get to train Thanes and make big decisions and have solemn meetings like they did in the old days. They get to feel important. They've got a whole..."—Jesher held his hands together as if cupping something—"a whole *system*, set up around them, to make it seem real and valuable and for Botan. But it's *not* for Botan. It's not for anything. It's for *them*."

Timothy sat against the tree, and looked at Jesher, and said nothing. He was angry about Verinald, yes, but Jesher was talking about something else entirely. He was talking about something deeper, questioning things that had been clear and solid until five minutes ago.

Until five minutes ago, Timothy had had faith in the Band and faith in Jesher as the most vehement and zealous member. Now he was suddenly uncertain, and he didn't know if it was his faith in the Band or his faith in Jesher that was wavering.

Jesher began pacing again. Timothy swallowed, started to speak, and stopped. Then he gathered his courage and started again.

"I thought you believed in it," he said, and despite his efforts to be calm, his voice cracked a little. He cleared his throat roughly. "In Botan and everything."

Jesher stopped. His shoulders slumped a little. He spoke quietly, without the fire.

"I do," he said. "I do believe in it, with all my heart. But the *Band* isn't *Botan*. That's all."

They were quiet for several minutes. Jesher sat down against a tree a few feet away, and the two of them hugged their knees and watched the sunlight dying on the dust motes in the air. Breeze pawed at the branches. A jay flitted through the trees, landed, eyed them from a branch, and then took off again to disappear farther up the hill.

"I told you how obsessed I am with the old days," Jesher said finally. "I think you understand that part, the oldness and nobleness and everything."

"Yeah," Timothy said. "I do."

"It's like... it's like *that*'s the truth, you know? I have these doubts about the Band, and when you see someone like Verinald and realize how happy he is to be in charge of whatever it is he's in charge of—not Botan, not really anything—when you see him, you suddenly feel like all those doubts are real and everything around this place is fake, like a... like the things you and Selena do with Eliniel. Like the whole Band is pretending to be something it's not."

Timothy chewed his lip.

Jesher took a deep breath. "That's why I try to learn about the old days," he said. "I need to know that it's real, sometimes, that Botan is real and what we're fighting for is real and that people can really believe in something bigger than themselves. Not like Verinald, pretending to believe for control in his own little kingdom, but really *believe*."

Timothy swallowed and sat back. It was difficult to think.

One part of him—the former part—still saw the Band as the incarnation of everything good. Invincible. Incorruptible. A beacon of light, dedicated to Botan alone, synonymous with patriotism and loyalty and devotion. That part of him was angry with Verinald for squelching the letter, upset with the stupidity of not preparing, but not really afraid. That part of him never seriously thought that Ricera or anyone else had a chance of finding or destroying the Band. That part of him trusted, like a child, that things would be alright.

The other part—the new part that Jesher was creating—was deathly afraid. The new part felt as if the shutters had been thrown, the blanket pulled back. The new part felt like cold and dark seeping into a warm, well-lighted place.

The Band was not invincible. The Band was not omniscient. The Band was not incorruptible.

Timothy's hands were shaking. He told himself to stop being such a baby, but could not stop the constriction of his throat and chest. He was afraid. There was the obvious physical fear—if the Band were not invincible, then they were in real physical danger—but that was only a tiny part of it. What made Timothy tremble was the sudden realization that he had *responsibility* for Botan. Training and obeying and trusting the Band was no longer enough. The Band might not know best. Timothy might have to decide for himself what Botan needed, then do that thing whether it coincided with his orders or not.

His simple world had expanded suddenly and irreversibly, and the terrible magnitude of it made him sick to his stomach.

From this perspective, though, the thought that they would *not* warn the others was suddenly laughable.

Jesher gave a bitter sniff of a laugh. "None of this makes any sense, does it?" he said.

Timothy shifted, opened his mouth, but couldn't bring the warring parts of himself to agree on what to say.

Jesher slapped his knees and stood up.

"Anyway," he said. "None of that matters. Even if the Band and Verinald and everyone was perfect, I would still have to warn the others. I promised myself I would save people, not just kill them. I have to, and it doesn't matter what Verinald does to me."

He looked down at Timothy, and his eyes softened.

"But you don't have to come," he said. "This is all a little crazy to you, probably. I mean, I'd like it if you came, but you don't have to."

"I'm coming," Timothy said, suddenly feeling that at least one thing was certain. "If you're going, I'm coming."

Selena met them on their way out of the woods. She was sweating.

"Where have you been?" she hissed, shooing them farther back into the trees and coming close.

"Thinking," Jesher said, giving Selena a hard, wary look. "Where have *you* been?"

"Trying to *do* something about this! Don't you realize what's happening? Tell me you're not planning to just sit here and wait for it."

Jesher lost some of his defensiveness and looked at Selena sharply.

"You've started warning people?" he asked.

"What?" she said. "No. That would be stupid. We'd warn a few people, someone would tell Verinald, and we'd be locked up and under guard."

Jesher frowned.

"Maybe if enough people realize how stupid Verinald's being..." Timothy started.

"Timothy! Don't be an idiot. You *know* Verinald wasn't being stupid. Tell me you saw that."

"I saw him trying to hide what that letter said," Timothy said, stinging a little, "which is pretty stupid, if you ask..."

"Exactly," Selena interrupted. "Trying to *hide* it." She looked at both of them, back and forth, as if disbelieving.

"You're not actually saying he *knows*," Timothy said. "I mean, he knows what the letter says, obviously, but are you saying he..."

"Knew already," Selena said. "Yes. I'm saying that Verinald is a traitor."

CHAPTER 19

HABERD

Something in Haberd had suspected from the moment the council meeting was called. Maybe it was the convenient way that someone forgot to notify him of the meeting, or the twinkle of surprise in Verinald's eyes when Haberd arrived. Maybe it was the lack of tension in Verinald's shoulders, when there should have been some nervousness about what the Thanes had found out. Maybe it was a year of unconsciously noted clues, tiny turns of phrase or action that had built in the back of Haberd's mind until they spilled forward, manifesting as a nagging, sharp suspicion that something was very wrong.

Suspicion became certainty when Jesher read the transcription of the letter they had found and Verinald listened without flinching. He should have shown surprise, or doubt, but instead he sat and seemed to feel nothing.

He might as well have begun sweating. He knew what the letter said—had known already—and was cutting off all emotion while he considered how to hide what these Thanes had brought to light. His laughter was as hollow and emotionless as his eyes.

The immediacy of the danger struck Haberd only a moment later. Things were in readiness. Nearly all of the Thanes were back from recent missions. Even some of the spies posted throughout Botan had been called in to headquarters for various unrelated reasons.

The fruit was ripe for the plucking.

Haberd tried not to dwell on the fact that he had been fooled for fifteen years. He tried not to think about how numb he had been, how stupid, how caught up in his own misery. He tried not to wallow in the knowledge that only his recent awakening had allowed even his unconscious mind to notice enough to grow suspicious.

Instead, Haberd immediately began thinking of what to do. He nodded along with the council—he could not be seen disagreeing, could not draw suspicion from Verinald—and saw Timothy flinch visibly. Selena made her appeal, and Verinald handled it smoothly, scouring the last traces of doubt from Haberd's mind. Certain, now, of who and what Verinald was, Haberd settled on the only course of action available to him.

He signaled. Timothy was too busy glaring at Verinald to notice the eye-signs and guarded hand-signs, but Selena saw them. It was good that at least one of them paid attention. Haberd would not be able to meet with them in person, after this council meeting. Verinald would be watching. If Selena were to get anything done without eyes on her back, it had to be before Haberd had spoken with her.

Timothy suggested that they ask Haberd for his interpretation of the letter, and the look of hurt in his eyes when Haberd did not respond was almost too much to bear. Haberd had the sudden and insane urge to explain himself, to tell Timothy that he was being quiet because argument was useless, to explain that even if he *could* persuade the council to take caution—to set more guards or make preparations for a quick escape—caution would not help them now. Verinald had betrayed them. Ricera was coming. Caution was a sandcastle wall against the tide.

But he did not explain himself. He signaled to Selena, and watched Timothy leave with a stiff back and rigid shoulders.

By now, if all was well, Selena would have explained what Haberd could not. She would be almost finished with the simple instructions Haberd had been able to convey with his eyes and hands.

First, Farland, Comaro and Aral would have received his request to send the Thanes on a joint training exercise. If she had done well at inventing a purpose for the exercise, they would have agreed, each thinking that the others had already approved of it.

Second, Selena would have been to Toman, the horse-master. If Toman was to be trusted—and if anyone was to be trusted, it was Toman—two horses would be packed and ready for Timothy and Jesher's journey north, provisioned with food for a week and money for two weeks more.

All that remained was the packet and letter in Haberd's hand.

He was nearly finished. He had written what needed to be written and woven what needed to be woven. His hand was hovering over the blank space at the end of the letter.

Haberd hesitated again, closed his eyes, then opened them and continued writing.

And to Timothy, he wrote. *If I do not see you again—and I do not expect to–know that I am proud of you. What I have said and done, I have said and done to make you stronger. You are a better man than your*

Here Haberd made an exasperated noise, withdrew the pen from the paper, and used a small knife to cut this last bit of writing from the letter. Then he drizzled sand over the paper to dry the ink, placed what he had woven in the packet along with his message, and took a very old seal from a secret place in his desk drawer. While the wax melted, he looked at the seal, thumbing the symbol of burning torch and sunburst. After a moment he sniffed, rubbed one wrinkled eye with the back of his hand, drizzled wax across the packet's edge, and pressed the seal into the green pool.

Then Haberd burned the strip he had cut from the letter. When it had blackened and curled, he rubbed it between his palms and tossed the gray dust into the air.

Then he closed his eyes, took a deep, slow breath, and prepared himself for what had to be done.

CHAPTER 20

There was no way to know whether it was exactly midnight, but with some constructive reinforcement from Selena, Timothy had developed a pretty good internal clock. Haberd had sent her night after night to douse him with cold water if he wasn't awake on the hour Haberd had assigned him. After a week and a half of shivering in a wet bed, cursing Selena and Haberd and listening to Robert snore with a smile on his face, Timothy had learned to wake when he wanted to. He had only been doused twice since then.

When Timothy was certain that no one was watching his cabin, he made his way through the shadows to the stables.

"No one saw you?" Jesher whispered, and Timothy nearly jumped at the sudden voice coming from the moon-shadow of a gate post. Pretending that he had seen Jesher, he sank to his heels and shook his head.

"No one. You?"

"Nope."

They waited in silence. Several minutes passed, and Timothy wondered whether he should have woken Robert and risked the noise of their talking.

The last time Timothy had seen Robert awake had been earlier this evening, at these stables, when he and Jesher had casually walked by to see whether Toman had readied their horses. Robert had been in the middle of a drill, hanging off the side of a galloping horse to conceal himself from view. He had been doing a pretty good job of it until he tried waving to Timothy. Timothy had laughed as Robert almost fell, and waved back.

Timothy would remember that wave—and the cool air sharpened with the dry wind and softened a little by the smell of manure and leather—for a long time to come. He would regret not waking Robert to say goodbye. He would regret it from the bottom of his heart.

He and Jesher waited for Selena, and at last she came.

Timothy had to hand it to her; she was one of the sneakiest people he knew. By the time he heard her behind them, she was only three steps away.

"I thought you'd be waiting by the gear," she said. "Didn't know I had to search the whole pasture."

Timothy and Jesher swiveled at the sound of her voice, and Timothy thought they did a pretty good job of not jumping out of their skins.

"Didn't realize you'd come slinking out of the forest," Timothy whispered.

"I thought about hooking up a wagon and some lanterns and rolling right on down the path, but I figured it might attract attention," she replied.

It was strange, that they were exchanging banter when all of them were trembling inside. It was almost as if they were drunk, or giddy.

Selena cleared her throat and grew serious.

"Here's the deal," she said, "Haberd thinks Verinald is going to move soon, and there isn't much hope that he and I will be able to convince enough people of what is happening to make a difference. We're going to need help.

"Help?" Jesher asked, but Selena held up a hand that she wasn't finished.

"You two are supposed to go to Moure," she said. "Get gear there, then go up the mountain. Find the Mirresotas. Haberd thinks they may have escaped notice by the Huctans so far. Find one of their leaders, and give him this."

"What is it?" Jesher said, taking the packet Selena gave him.

"A packet," Selena replied. Jesher raised an eyebrow, then put the packet carefully into the inner pocket of his robes.

"Who are you supposed to find?" Selena asked.

"The Mirresotas."

"And where are you supposed to start?"

"Moure," they answered together.

"Good," she said. "Have a nice trip."

Before Timothy could press her for more information—what she and Haberd were going to do, or who the Mirresotas were, or what kind of help they were asking for—she had slunk away into the night.

Timothy and Jesher crouched for a moment, as if waiting for something.

"Well," Jesher said.

Timothy nodded. They made for the stable.

The Band had paths in the hill country. Some were used more

than others, but the paths farthest out were used the least, so that they would not form well-beaten tracks leading straight to the Band. Timothy barely knew the trails within a two or three mile radius of the camp, so when they reached the trees and mounted up, he followed Jesher without question.

The shadowy, moonlit forest was lovely. The air was brisk, and despite running on only a few hours of sleep, Timothy felt very alive.

He prepared a story with a semi-plausible reason for two Thanes to be leaving with provisions in the middle of the night, but he did not have to use it. Strangely, they were able to navigate the paths without coming across a single sentry.

At the time, this only struck Timothy as very lucky.

They followed the Path of Plains northward. Jesher explained—very quietly, when they were hunkered down in a well-hidden hollow for the night—that the torch and starburst on the green seal enclosing the packet were the same as those on the Botani flag. They took this to mean that the seal was a royal one, or maybe the seal of the Duest.

The lump in the packet, they could tell by carefully feeling through the vellum, had about the same shape and rigidity as a wadded sling, or a strip of leather, or a small glove. They took this to mean that they had no idea what was in the packet.

But they knew the packet's purpose. They were to find help, from the Mirresotas, and quickly. Verinald was a traitor, and the Band was in grave danger.

Moure was a long way away. Jesher had only been so far to the north once, and he thought it was almost a week-long journey. But the Path of Plains was an old road, and a good one, and the tribal drums of adventure and urgency throbbed beneath the rhythm of horse hooves and heart beats. They made the journey in four days.

The mountains loomed, first low and faded and then high and dark. In the morning they were misted reflections; at evening they were jagged shards of shadow biting at the fire of the dipping sun. The Path of Plains became a path of hills, and Timothy was reminded of his home country.

They caught their first glimpse of Moure from a bluff, but soon lost sight of it as the road dipped into a small valley. When they crested another hill they were much closer, and Timothy saw that many of the houses in Moure were made of stone. This meant that Moure was old, built in more prosperous times than these.

A Huctan stepped wearily from the guard tower as they drew near. Timothy got ready to explain that they were here to get some equipment his father's friend had borrowed, but the soldier merely prodded their saddle bags and waved them through the gates without questions.

They followed the frosted breath of their horses into the town. Once a sprawling city, according to Jesher, Moure now seemed to be a half-populated ruin. As they split up and began their search for clues about the Mirresotas, it became apparent that almost everyone living in the city was a craftsman or merchant making his living by selling to the mountain people.

Most people drew no difference between the mountain people and the Mirresotas, and it took Timothy a while to realize that the two terms were not quite synonymous. Both lived on the mountain, and both shepherded goats and wooly sheep, but the Mirresotas were rarely seen. Those who admitted a difference between them seemed to think of the Mirresotas as exaggerated mountain people, the elitists of an already snooty breed.

This snootiness—which almost every person Timothy questioned referred to in some manner—seemed to be the single defining characteristic of the upland people. Some spoke of the Mirresotas with respect bordering on reverence, but nobody spoke of them with affection.

Timothy met Jesher near nightfall to compare what they had learned. Jesher had gotten the same impression about the Mirresotas, and had also learned some more useful information about what types of provisions to buy. Apparently the roads were too treacherous for riding, especially at this time of the year, when the spring melt had muddied many of the upland paths. They would have to walk, using their horses to carry supplies.

As it turned out, supplies in Moure were expensive beyond reason. With the dregs of Jesher's purse and half the remainder of Timothy's, they managed to buy two pairs of warm mittens, a heavy blanket, and what they were told was a week's supply of *lushka*. The word meant something like 'life-blood' in High Botani, but for the price it cost to get the little bag of what looked like dirt, it might as well have been gold dust. Apparently it was a mixture of dried meat, berries, and nuts. Several merchants swore that a handful could keep a man walking for a day.

They had to trade one of the horses to get the heavy winter cloaks—lined with the thick white wool of the mountain goats—that were reportedly essential for traveling up the mountain. The cloaks were highly prized and finely made, but Jesher still grumbled that the horse was worth a dozen coats.

The merchant who had taken their horse, apparently feeling a little indebted to them, allowed them to share his small fireplace for the night. Stowing their gear safely by their heads, Jesher and Timothy huddled on the straw floor and fell asleep. The next morning they set out early.

The most difficult thing about walking up a steep hill in such bitter cold—besides the steepness and the coldness—was deciding whether to wear a coat.

On cracking the merchant's door open that morning and feeling the icy mountain air, Timothy had immediately decided to try out his new goat-hair cloak. After an hour of pushing up the first little hill, however, he had begun to sweat. Removing the fur coat, he had felt his skin immediately with goose bumps under his thick woolen cloak. Thinking that his body would adjust in a few minutes, he had continued on. When he found that his elbows and knees were having trouble bending, he had to put the heavy cloak back on.

Two days passed, and the air grew cooler. When they woke in the morning, the ground shimmered with the frost of a mountain so cold that it leaches fine mist from dry air. Opening his cloak enough to stand made Timothy gasp, and he ate quickly. Drinking the icy water in their skins made his head hurt and set him shivering, but he forced himself to swallow enough to keep his body going.

They came to a village of hard-eyed mountain people. The hardness in their eyes—the utter lack of warmth—struck Timothy. It wasn't that the desperately poor and hard-backed farmers of Botan's flatlands were soft. But the mountain people were harder, in the way that granite is harder than limestone. The rocky slopes under the mountain people's homes were hard, the stinging wind that whistled down through the canyons was hard, the razor peaks of the Qeralski above were hard, and the mountain people were hard.

After three days, the trembling sensation in Timothy's legs and the burning in his thighs and calves began to fade a little. He was adjusting to the altitude, adapting to the mountain. Jesher seemed to be feeling better as well. They began to talk a little, when words seemed appropriate. Mostly they looked upward, breathing deep of the fresh, frigid air and pushing their booted feet to take step after step after step. The slowness of their pace was excruciating, and worry about the Band made Timothy push himself harder. His head began to ache constantly.

On the evening of the fourth day they met their first Mirresota.

Timothy and Jesher had been walking steadily, talking between icy breaths about the poem that went with the song Timothy had been humming that day in the woods. Jesher had been repeating it almost every day, letting his tongue roll over the Botani words. He said something about this mountain reminded him of the song. Timothy said that he was right.

Then they rounded the corner of a switchback and saw the boy.

Timothy felt a fondness for him immediately. It was not because the boy was a Mirresota, or because he was the proud son of a village chieftain, or because his older brother had been killed by the Huctans. Timothy knew none of these things, couldn't even see the boy's face yet. What he *could* see was that the boy was jogging straight up the mountainside, ignoring the switchbacks, and that a Huctan soldier was pursuing him.

This alone was enough for immediate friendship.

They watched for a moment in curious silence as the figures

below inched up the frozen rock. Timothy expected the boy to collapse any minute, or at least to stop for breath. The road had switchbacks for a reason, and even the path itself was too steep for running.

Yet the boy ran, and he did not stop. Timothy realized, as the two figures came closer, that he and Jesher were witnessing the climax of the chase. The Huctan was riding his horse, urging his mount dangerously up the switchbacks, passing back and forth across the stony grade it had taken Timothy and Jesher all afternoon to climb. Even at a fast walk, the horse wouldn't be able to keep the pace for long.

Neither would the boy.

"I wonder what he did," Timothy said.

They stood staring a moment longer. It all seemed a little unreal, from their vantage point. Things seemed to be happening so slowly. Timothy had to remind himself that it was *very* real for the boy, who was tearing frozen air into his lungs with the ragged, bleeding gasps of two miles past utter exhaustion.

Thinking he was being high-minded and focused on the mission at hand by resisting the urge to take action, Timothy said, "It's probably best not to get involved."

Jesher looked at him, then, and that look—the look Jesher gave him when he suggested they abandon the boy—would haunt Timothy for the rest of his life.

"No," Jesher said, looking back down the mountain. "We're Thanes."

"You're right," Timothy said quickly.

Putting belt-knives to spear-hafts, they pulled the horse back from the ledge and began creeping down the switchbacks.

CHAPTER 21

VERINALD

Verinald had long ago stopped hoping for the life of his son. His son was gone. His son was dead. Verinald had no son. A father cannot remain a father without seeing his son.

No, Verinald was not selling his soul in hope of a happy reunion. He was not sitting in the privacy of his cabin now, applying the first layer of his disguise with permanent resins and dyes, because he trusted Ricera's word. Who would trust a man whose name had become synonymous with treachery? Who would betray hundreds for the sake of a boy who would not even recognize him?

Verinald was selling his soul, yes, but not for his son. He was selling it for revenge.

But first, he had a chance to do a small bit of good. Not enough good to cover the evil, but good nonetheless.

A knock came at the door. Verinald straightened from the polished mirror on his desk.

"Haberd?" he asked.

"Yes," came the reply.

"Come in," Verinald said, and then raised the blow-pipe to his mouth.

Haberd's reflexes were still sharp. He opened the door, saw the disguise that Verinald was wearing and the weapon aimed at his chest, registered what this meant, and began backing out of the cabin almost before the dart had reached him. Verinald dropped the blow-pipe and sprang up from his chair. He was at the old man's side in an instant, propping him up, shutting the door behind him, dragging him to the desk.

He almost didn't see the knife in Haberd's hand. Only the glint of light, shining through the window and reflected off of the no-doubt poisoned blade, gave him warning. Luckily Haberd's hand was slow, already going limp from the liquid that had coated the dart's tip, and Verinald was able to chop down and deflect the blow. Haberd's knife clattered to the floor, and the old man's eyes rolled back in his head.

In a moment Verinald had laid his one-time master down, poured a liquid into his mouth, and stroked his throat until he swallowed. In a moment more he had opened the trap door hidden under his rug and dragged Haberd's sleeping body into the stone-lined space within.

Verinald did not lock the trap door, though he placed the rug carefully over the seam line. Taking a deep breath, he picked up Haberd's blade, placed it in a drawer, and sat down again at his desk.

Pulling his mirror close, Verinald looked into his own eyes for a moment. Eyes that were, by happy coincidence, the same shade of brown as Haberd's.

The first layer of his disguise was complete. Verinald felt at the modifications he had made to his nose and cheekbones. They were harder than real flesh, but only slightly. He had experimented for many years to find the right blend of materials for such a disguise. They would suffice.

Verinald's own hair was shorn from his head, which was dyed and stained with the mottled splotches of old age. The hair he had removed was carefully sewn into a wig, which was lying on the desk next to the mirror.

Verinald closed his eyes for a moment and took a deep breath from his nose. Haberd was safe now. The Huctans were on their way. Time was short.

As calmly as he was able, Verinald began donning the second layer of disguise. The delicate layer, made of oil and clay, which would come off easily when Verinald took his final revenge.

CHAPTER 22

ROBERT

The canyon was silent. At least, for Robert it was silent. Probably the other Thanes, who had been training for their whole lives instead of a few months, could hear the caterpillars spinning their silk in the sagebrush. For them, shifting concentration to sound alone and hearing more than should be possible was a refined and automatic skill.

Robert couldn't seem to manage it even with his eyes closed, his breath held, and his hands cupped to his ears.

It was ridiculous for him to be leading this exercise. Even if Comaro thought him a natural leader, even if the other Thanes were still buzzing about him beating Nick in King's Table the other day, putting Robert in charge of other Thanes was like putting a duck in charge of the horses. Even in a game, it was a little humiliating.

Robert heard something, deep and low—almost a vibration in the ground—and knew suddenly that someone was close. No one should have been able to come so close without Robert hearing, not here in the canyon where the ground was littered with cheat grass and dry twigs and crackling rabbit brush. Yet someone *had* come close, and that single, low thud was the only sound that warned him.

A blue jay called, loudly, and Robert almost jumped. He thought the blue jay was real, for a second, until his mind connected the thud with the quick intake of breath he had heard just before the blue jay called.

A hundred yards away, on the other side of the canyon, another blue jay call came. Robert shook his head.

They were very good calls—there was no denying that—but it was stupid to use them in this situation. Bird calls were fine when your enemy wasn't looking for you, or when your enemy wasn't aware that you could make good bird calls. But they were all Thanes here. They all knew that the Thanes on the other team were somewhere in this canyon and were capable of making perfect bird calls. It was obvious to everyone what was happening. The two blue jay callers had just given away their positions to Robert's team as well as their own.

This was why Robert had gathered a few items before they left for the hills. Hopefully, his new method of signaling would be better.

Very carefully, knowing that even the rustle of his fingers against his coat might alert whoever it was just below him, Robert withdrew the small brass mirror he had brought from his room. Positioning it carefully, he flashed the reflection twice across the large tree nearest his position. Watching over his shoulder, between the sage branches, he caught the barest hint of movement as Diane relayed the signal to the other side of the canyon. He waited, and then Diane flashed him back.

Two flashes. Everyone was ready.

Replacing the mirror, Robert steeled himself to do what he'd been trying not to do for several minutes. Gripping his wooden sword—though it would do him little good against any one of the Thanes—he stood up and prepared to step on a twig.

He didn't have to. His standing had made enough noise to draw the attention of whoever was right below him, and the crackling of cheat grass announced a quick attack. Robert stepped back and held his guard.

Leon himself sprung up from below onto a boulder at Robert's level. Grinning to see Robert—and Robert knew that he looked comical to someone like Leon, standing as if he were ready to defend himself—Leon relaxed. Approaching Robert, he attacked.

One hit, stick against stick, was all Robert needed. The noise would attract the attention of every Thane in the canyon, draw them out of hiding to look, and then Robert's archers would do their work.

Robert managed to block one hit because Leon was obviously enjoying the look of concentration and nerves on Robert's face. This was why Leon was stupid. This was why overconfidence led to mistakes. If Leon had just killed Robert immediately, as he surely could have, there would have been no noise to draw everyone's attention.

As it was, there *was* a noise, and no sooner had the swords clashed than Diane let loose her arrow.

It struck true, of course—Diane rarely missed—and Leon grunted as the blunted and slightly padded shaft struck him hard in the ribs. As the grin slid from his face and appeared on Robert's, Leon lowered his sword and sat down. He had been eliminated.

Robert ran back the direction Leon had come from, hoping to flush out more of Leon's team for Diane and Selena to shoot down. He heard someone yell in frustration, across the canyon, probably at an arrow in their back. Then more swords clacked as a fight between equals broke out below him.

Then he heard the screaming.

It was distant, so distant that it could have been something else, if anything else had the sound of humans in pain and terror. Robert stopped, cupping his hand to his ears, and ignored Lutho when he emerged from the brush and touched his sword to Robert's chest.

Lutho paused then, too, and cupped his own hands to his own ears. The other Thanes across the canyon stopped fighting. The clacking of swords ceased. The canyon was silent again.

The screams, which had been clear, had gone quiet. There was something, a buzz, a tinkling, but it was so quiet that Robert was not sure he heard it.

Then there was another scream, clear and terrible. It was a woman's scream, and it was not a squeal of delight or a shriek of fright. It was a full-throated scream, long and agonizing and terrible.

"Oh no," Robert heard Selena say, as clearly in the silent canyon as if she had been right next to him. Then there was noise, people running in the sage, and Robert had to shout to make sure he was heard.

"Get high!" he yelled. "Someone get a look!"

Diane was already climbing; he could see her scrambling up the tall pine with her bow slung across her back. Several Thanes were farther up the canyon, running for the boulders that were piled around the top of the hill. Those on the far side of the canyon were rushing down and climbing up to this side.

“Robert,” Selena said, climbing down from her tree, beckoning fiercely for Robert to come to her. Robert started towards her, and when he saw the tears running down her cheeks, he began to run.

“What is it?” he asked, putting his hands on her shoulders as she trembled and tried to blink away her tears. “Did you see? What’s happening?”

“Verinald, that bastard,” she said. “Haberd was right. I knew I shouldn’t have left him...”

“Selena,” Robert said, shaking her arms, but then Diane yelled from the top of her tree.

“I see red!” she shouted. Then she gasped, and in the sudden stillness of every single Thane in the canyon freezing to listen, the sob that escaped her lips was clearly audible.

More screams were now floating up to them on the warm spring breeze.

“What is it?” someone—Leon—shouted, when Diane was silent for a moment.

“It’s the Huctans,” Diane replied, her voice choking. “They’re...”

But she couldn’t finish, and she didn’t have to. They didn’t need the screams to know exactly what the Huctans would do if they ever found the Band.

CHAPTER 23

With spears ready, Timothy and Jesher hugged the inside track of the path and descended as fast as they could.

They were working, now, together, and Timothy's body adjusted. Everything felt smoother, more crisp. His eyes opened a little wider. His lungs drew a little deeper. A rock banged his elbow as they ran around the corner of a switchback and slid down the rocks, but the urgency flowing in his tendons dulled the pain.

They were close. The spot was good. They crawled on their bellies to the edge of the path to look over and downward.

Timothy heard the boy before he saw him. He had imagined the agonized steps the youth was taking to be something like his own on his first day running with the Thanes. He expected to hear ragged breathing coming in little groans and heaving gasps.

The actual sound that reached his ears frightened him. It was hollow, dry, and cavernous. A little longer, and the boy would die.

The boy's head appeared suddenly behind the lip of the switchback below them. Even at thirty yards distance, the steam rising from his exposed skin was visible. He did not pause to rest on the path—*could* not pause, Timothy realized, or he would break stride and fall—but came up the steep grade below, taking tiny steps and grabbing at the earth and stones with gloved, trembling hands.

Timothy watched, feeling sick, until the boy was almost upon them. Looking for a handhold, the boy saw them at last, but neither recognition nor surprise registered on his face. He kept climbing.

"Keep going until the next path," Jesher whispered. "We're friends. We'll take care of the soldier."

The boy kept climbing, and Timothy wondered if he'd heard.

A red cloak caught the corner of Timothy's eye, and he pulled his head back, peering just over the edge to watch the Huctan's approach. The soldier had dismounted, leaving his horse steaming and trembling, and was jogging at a steady pace up the switchbacks. He looked up, and Timothy held perfectly still, slitting his eyes to keep light from reflecting off of his pupils.

The soldier was moving to the right. In a moment he would reach the bend and come back to the left on the track immediately below Timothy and Jesher.

When the soldier looked down, Jesher slithered closer to Timothy's ear.

"It'd be best if it looked like an accident," Jesher said.

Timothy nodded. If anyone came looking for the Huctan and found him speared, they might take vengeance on the nearest village.

"What, push him down?" Timothy asked.

"Might not die from just a push. Better to hit him with a rock first, to make sure. Think you could hit him with your sling?"

"I can try," Timothy said.

"Yes or no."

"Yes," Timothy said.

This, too, Timothy would remember in his nightmares.

"If you miss, we'll have to spear him."

Timothy took a deep breath. "I'll meet him at the corner. He'll be looking at me. If I miss, you can get him from the side."

"Don't miss. Go!"

Crouching and hugging the inside of the path, Timothy ran down the road to the bend, shrugging off his sheep-skin coat and pulling the sling from his inner wool. Stooping for a rock, he found that it was half-buried and too big. Finding another, he crawled into position at the bend in the switchback, took off his mittens, and fitted the sling around his fingers. He clasped his left hand over his right, trying to keep the fingers warm while he waited.

Jesher was moving silently to the edge of the track twenty yards back, looking catlike as he peered over the edge. Timothy felt a shiver of violent pride as he waited. Jesher and he were the perfect team.

The Huctan was rounding the corner below. He would reach them in less than a minute.

Timothy glanced upward. The boy was sprawled out on the rocks, heaving, one leg pushing spasmodically at the rock but only succeeding in dislodging some shale. Timothy hoped he was alright.

The top of the Huctan's head appeared below, and Timothy lay down completely.

The soldier had taken his helmet off. That was good. Timothy waited, with an ear to the ground, hearing the steady drumbeat of the soldier's footsteps coming closer. Finally Jesher turned his head and made eye contact with Timothy. It was time.

Standing up, Timothy took a step forward, whirled his sling once, and let fly with the stone.

He had hoped to catch the Huctan with his head down, but at the moment he stood, the soldier saw him, and some reflex made him duck. The stone clipped the soldier's ear, tearing a piece of cartilage from the cold tip.

The Huctan hissed, face wrinkling in agony. Timothy was already bending to pick up another rock, the cool, smooth feeling fast giving way to panic. The Huctan took a gloved hand from his bleeding ear to grip his spear in both hands. He rushed Timothy.

Timothy's hands fumbled with the stone. Every instinct told him to get out of the way, to run, but Jesher had leapt over the edge of the hill above and was hurtling down towards the soldier. If Timothy ran, he would draw the soldier's eyes to Jesher.

The soldier was almost within striking distance. Timothy got the stone loaded.

Jesher's foot slipped on some loose dirt, and the Huctan turned. Recovering, he raised the large stone he was carrying above his head and leapt forward. Timothy whirled the sling.

CHAPTER 24

With a crack, the Huctan's spear pierced Jesher's sternum.

CHAPTER 25

Jesher's face went white. The stone dropped from his hands. It bounced off of his shoulder as his body slumped. The Huctan leaned into the spear thrust and twisted as Jesher fell.

Timothy screamed, releasing the rock in his sling.

The rock struck the soldier in the back of the skull. Still screaming, Timothy dropped the sling and rushed forward. He jumped, landing a brutal kick to the Huctan's spine as the man's knees struck the earth. The soldier's body flew forward, face striking the ground like the end of a whip. Timothy kicked the soldier's head, felt a toe break, and kicked again with his heel. The smell of blood was everywhere, blood from the soldier's ear, head, face.

Blood from Jesher.

Nauseated, trembling, Timothy fell down at Jesher's side. He tried to prop his friend's head up, to ease the awkward angle of the spear jutting out of his chest.

But Jesher's face was cold. Blood from his wound glared red on his cheek, which was quickly losing color. Timothy patted the cheek, tried to cup his hands around the wound to keep in the blood, tried to move the spear. When the hot blood stopped squirting between his fingers—when Timothy realized that Jesher was not screaming or even wincing—he knew.

Yelling so that something in his throat tore, Timothy crashed a fist into the Huctan's back, bodily rolling him over. Lifeless eyes and a lacerated face met his gaze. Timothy picked up the stone Jesher had dropped and raised it above his head. He screamed again as he brought it down.

Jesher was dead. Jesher was dead.

Jesher was dead.

CHAPTER 26

RICERA

Ricera strode down the gravel street between the cabins of the Band. Behind and beside him strode a Huctan officer and a young Huctan soldier, both clothed in crimson. To either side, bodies lay where they had fallen, their blood clothing the ground in scarlet.

A straight-backed man with silver hair pulled back in a ponytail stood in the center of the gravel street. He held no sword. His hands were still at his sides, his face carved from stone. Only his hair moved, in the breeze, as Ricera approached.

"Verinald," Ricera said. "You have done well."

The straight-backed man inclined his head. His features did not change. He did not look at the woman two paces to his left, body lying head-down on the stairs to the eating-hall. He did not look at the slightly curved Huctan sword at Ricera's hip.

"Where is Haberd?" Ricera asked, coming to a stop. His brown eyes were hard.

"Dead," said the straight-backed man. "I killed him."

The change in Ricera's gaze, at this statement, was slight, but there was a weight to it that was almost more frightening than a shout of rage or grief would have been. The straight-backed man shifted and stepped back, as if from a blow, but he said nothing.

"You were to keep him alive," Ricera said, slowly and quietly. "I was very specific."

Still the straight-backed man said nothing.

"T'shira," Ricera said.

The young Huctan soldier—also an officer, by the pin at his breast—stepped forward. Drawing a knife from his belt, he took the straight-backed man by the shoulder and thrust the dagger into his abdomen.

As T'shira stepped back, Ricera stepped forward, propping the now-bleeding man up by his shoulders.

"Your life was always meaningless to me, Verinald," said Ricera, in a voice that no one else could hear. "But for the sake of our master, I might have spared you."

A shimmer of emotion fluttered across Ricera's face as he said this last, and for a moment his features were almost brittle. Like hardened glass forced, under great stress, to bend and flex.

"I even kept my promise to you," Ricera said, turning and gesturing to T'shira. "Behold, I have your son."

The man's eyes flicked upward, met those of T'shira, and then closed. His head began to fall forward.

Suddenly Ricera's control was gone. Gathering the neck of the man's cloak in one fist, he clasped the man's throat viciously with his other hand, forcing him to raise his head and stare Ricera in the eyes. He squeezed, and blood from the man's mouth trickled down Ricera's arm.

“Haberd was the only one who ever loved me,” he said, in a voice that was more hiss than whisper, more emotion than reason. “Haberd was the only one who ever believed in me. In killing him, you have damned yourself.”

Here two things happened at once.

First, Ricera’s voice slowed, as something smeared and shifted under the flow of blood from the man’s mouth and nose. He looked closely into the man’s face, and something in his own eyes focused.

Second, the man twisted, and the knife in his hand flashed upward and inward, aimed at the soft flesh below Ricera’s ribcage, poised to pierce lung and heart.

Ricera’s reaction was immediate. He pushed the man away, with both hands, while simultaneously thrusting his own hips back to change the position of his torso. The silver-haired man cried out, but his hand still drove upward, tearing through cloth and piercing skin.

But Ricera’s hand dropped to the knife even as he twisted, slowing, stopping, and then reversing the blow. Turning the twist into a whirl, Ricera drew his own knife, turned the blade, and drove it deep into the silver-haired man’s side.

The man’s ponytail shifted. The wig slid and then fell from his head, striking the ground at the same time as the knife that had failed to kill Ricera. The man’s knees struck the gravel a moment later. For a moment his body was still, like a propped-up toy, like a tree about to fall. Blood flowed in slowing spurts from side and abdomen and mouth and nose. Then his stained and weathered skull slumped forward.

Suddenly Ricera was throwing away his own knife, kneeling,

grasping the old man's face in his hands, tearing at the oil and clay that had disguised him.

"Haberd," Ricera said, in a voice that did not belong to him. "I..."

The old man coughed, and blood came from his mouth in a froth. He began to fall, and Ricera lowered him gently.

The old man tried to speak, choked, and then closed his eyes. Ricera leaned close, putting his ear to the old man's mouth.

The bloody lips did not move for several seconds. Then, slowly and softly, they formed four words.

"I have *your* son," the old man said. And then he died.

CHAPTER 27

Night was falling when someone put a goatskin coat around Timothy's shoulders. He'd heard the steps and a voice, but it took the cloak to still his shivering and bring him back to reality.

He turned his head. The boy was standing next to him. His gaze was turned outward, as Timothy's had been, at the dusk-graying plains and low hills below. The boy's knee was trembling. After a moment he sat down, folding his arms together for warmth. His cloak was damp with sweat.

"I thank you for my life," the boy said, after a few moments. It was good of him to say it, but it made Timothy think again of Jesher's cold body lying next to him. He buried his face in his stiff, numb hands.

The sun dropped further, and Timothy took a deep breath, opening his eyes again. It was dark, but the hillside was illuminated by a nearly full moon. The very rock seemed dead.

He stood up to keep himself from lapsing into semi-consciousness again. Things needed to be done. They could freeze to death, just sitting there.

The boy was shivering. His damp cloak wasn't doing him much good. Timothy saw Jesher's coat lying carefully folded next to his body. The boy must have found it and brought it near, but he hadn't put it on. Part of Timothy was fiercely glad that the boy hadn't presumed to wear Jesher's cloak. That part of him might have killed the boy if he had. The other part, the rational part, knew better.

Timothy bent for the coat, but couldn't make his numb fingers pick it up. He rubbed his hands together and weaseled them beneath the fur and wool until he felt the warm skin of his armpits. He caught his breath and waited. After a moment he bent again and took up Jesher's coat.

"Here," he said to the boy, who was a few years younger than he. The boy looked up at the coat in Timothy's outstretched hand, then at Jesher's body, and stood.

"You honor me," he said.

"Just take it," Timothy said.

The Huctan's mutilated body was lying in the road, twisted and hideous. Timothy didn't feel much fury for it anymore. He didn't feel much of anything except cold. Bending down, he tried to grip the body, but his hands were going numb again. He found his mittens in the pockets of his woolen cloak and put them on. His toe hurt.

Bending once more, Timothy heaved at the Huctan's body. Here at the turn of the switchback, the mountain dropped sharply off to the east. The body was heavy and stiff. Remembering what the man had done, Timothy took the corpse by the belt and one arm. Shuffling toward the edge, he spun once and threw the body with a yell that echoed against the stone. The Huctan fell a short way, cracked, rolled, and slid to a stop forty or fifty yards down. Timothy kicked some of the bloody earth and rocks off the path with his left foot.

Summoning his courage, he turned to Jesher. His friend was lying where he had fallen. The spear that had killed him was next to his body, broken. The bloodied point and six inches of the shaft had been thrust into the ground. Timothy vaguely remembered that he had done this.

The boy, who was standing now, was still shaky. Timothy handed him the spear haft to use as a walking stick. The point he placed reverently in the pocket of his cloak.

"You didn't use your spears so that it would seem like an accident," the boy said.

What a dumb idea, Timothy thought. What a stupid, arrogant idea.

"The horse is at the top of the ridge," he said. "We can get some food and camp there."

The boy nodded.

Timothy looked down at Jesher's body and took a deep breath. Then he knelt. He tried to be gentle, but the body was heavy and stiff. Lying down on his back below Jesher, Timothy settled the weight on his shoulders, then stood up. A low exhalation escaped Jesher's frozen lips as his chest settled on Timothy's shoulders. A brief flash of hope sparked in Timothy's muddled consciousness.

Then he realized the truth, that the breath had been pushed from Jesher's dead lungs by the compression of his chest on Timothy's shoulders. Timothy's throat constricted.

"You carry the spears," he said to the boy. Without waiting, he turned and began trudging up the road.

His joints were stiff, but he was fresh; he'd been sitting around for the past couple hours doing nothing. Even so, Jesher's dead weight on his shoulders was oppressive. He knew the weight well from the jumping drills, from wrestling matches, from the time they'd read the letter in the guardhouse. But Jesher was heavier, now. He would never spring lightly off of Timothy's cupped hands again.

He was dead.

Rounding the first switchback, Timothy glanced back. The boy was struggling doggedly to keep up. It was a wonder that he was able to walk at all, after the climb he'd made.

By the time they rounded the second bend, Timothy's heart was pounding. He trudged on with weak legs, thinking now of Robert and the night he had carried his beaten and bloodied brother out of Northelm. It seemed long ago, impossibly so. A gust of bone-gnawing loneliness tore at him.

The last switchbacks were well past the limit of his endurance. He sank to the ground, lowering Jesher gently against the slope behind him, and rested. Then, angry, he got up again and pushed on.

When he reached the top and tried to lower Jesher to the ground beside the horse, he fell. His palms struck hard and bruised against the gravel, even through the thick wool and sheep-skin of his mittens. Jesher's body began rolling off his back, and Timothy just managed to catch Jesher's head before it struck the shale. He knelt there for a moment, panting, and then stood and sniffed hard to stop the tears from coming. Then he grabbed Jesher under the armpits and dragged him to the edge of the rock, sheltered.

The boy was not far behind, and not in much better shape, but he bore his weariness well. He stumbled all the way to the horse before falling on his knees next to Timothy. He sounded as if his throat had been stripped with wire.

When Timothy was able, he got some water and *lushka* from the saddlebag. After filling their cooking pot twice with water for the horse and putting a couple handfuls of grain in its nosebag, he sat next to the boy and offered him food and drink. The boy drank gratefully, slowly at first and then in great gulps. They both ate a full handful of *lushka*, then huddled together next to Jesher's body. The full moon shone on their cold, pale faces.

"I'm Timothy," Timothy said.

"I am called Ashka," the boy said.

Timothy tightened the straps on his cloak legs and pulled the blanket over both of them, cinching his hood up until only his eyes were exposed to the night sky. For the third time he fought back tears, because it was a boy named Ashka sharing the warmth of the blanket with him while Jesher lay in the cold.

In the morning Jesher's body was frozen stiff. Timothy had put off loading it as long as he could, but the sun was getting ready to rise and everything was ready. He squatted next to Jesher's body and slid an arm around his waist. Wrapping his friend in a bear-hug, he lifted, almost dropping the body as he straightened. Somehow he got his shoulder under Jesher's weight, heaved him onto the horse's back, and did his best to tie him down. The cold and death made the body stick out awkwardly from the saddle.

Timothy told himself that Jesher would have laughed.

"My village is there," Ashka was saying, pointing up ahead to where the narrow road disappeared between two hills. "We can be there in half a day."

Timothy noticed for the first time that Ashka had an accent and a formal tone.

"You are a Mirresota?" Timothy asked, glancing around to make sure everything was in order.

"Yes," said Ashka. Timothy nodded, and took the horse's reins. Ashka, who had now recovered some of his strength, fell into step behind them.

By midmorning the stiff breeze had slackened. Timothy opened his mouth twice to break the silence, but didn't. Finally, in a tone that sounded angrier than he had intended, he spoke.

"Why was the soldier chasing you?" he asked.

"I ask pardon," said Ashka, taking a few quick steps to catch up. "What did you say?"

"Why was he chasing you?"

"The Huctan soldier?"

"Yes."

The boy was quiet. "The Common words are hard for me," he said finally.

"What words do you speak?"

Again the boy was quiet. Then he said, "I speak Botani words."

"*Speak them, then,*" said Timothy in Botani. He felt the boy pause, and squint, then hurry to catch up. There was a brief silence. At last the boy spoke.

"*My brother,*" he said, "*was a great man. He did not love the Huctans.*"

Ashka paused, waiting to see if Timothy would warn him about speaking against the Huctans. Timothy said nothing.

"*He left to trade skins for grain, a month of days past. He should have been back in a week of days, but he was not. My father worried, but he would send no one to look for him. It is dangerous for my people to go down the mountain.*"

Timothy could see why, if they spoke Botani and didn't love the Huctans.

"*But you went anyway,*" he said.

"Yes," said Ashka. "*I did not wear the Mirresota headband. No one knew that I was Mirresota.*"

Timothy doubted that.

"*In Moure I asked about my brother. I called him* 'that Mirresota'. *Some people knew about him. The Huctans*"—again Ashka pronounced the word the same way Timothy felt it—"*the Huctans made trouble with my brother. They said he was too proud. They told him to kiss their boots. They killed him when he would not.*"

The boy said the last in a rush, but his voice did not tremble. Timothy wasn't sure he could have told Jesher's story as bravely. Not yet, at least.

"*I found the Huctan that killed him,*" Ashka said. "*He was drunk. It was night. I waited until he was alone, near the latrine. I took his sword and killed him and pushed him in.*"

Timothy looked back, realizing for the second time that Ashka was not much younger than he.

"*I got away. A friend, one of the mountain people, let me stay with his sheep two nights ago. He woke me before dawn and told me that a Huctan was looking for me. I went. At midday I saw him behind me. I left my pack and ran until I saw you and... your friend.*"

"Jesher," said Timothy, and almost couldn't get the word out of his mouth. He closed his eyes, then said it again. "*His name was Jesher.*"

"*I will remember his name,*" said Ashka. Timothy nodded, then stopped walking and turned to look into Ashka's eyes.

"*What was your brother's name?*" he asked.

"*His name was Eliasayed,*" said Ashka, and his voice broke at last.

"*I will remember his name,*" said Timothy.

A small crowd gathered when they arrived at the Mirresota village. A tall man stepped forward to meet them, but did not offer a hand in greeting. Icy gray eyes the same shade as Ashka's flicked from Timothy to Jesher's corpse, then settled on Ashka.

"Ashka, where is your brother?" the tall man said.

"*Father, he is dead,*" said Ashka in Botani.

The tall man flinched visibly, and a middle-aged woman that had once been beautiful let out a small cry. The rest of the dozen or so Mirresotas wearing the thin, powder-blue bands across their foreheads seemed similarly stricken with grief, but many of their lips were set, as if they had expected the news.

"Why do you speak those words around a stranger?" the tall man said sternly, still in Common.

Ashka stepped forward. "*He is no stranger,*" he said. Murmurs that had been passing between the Mirresotas hushed.

"*A Huctan soldier killed my brother Eliasayed because he would not bend to kiss the soldier's feet,*" Ashka said. "*He died well. I have returned death on the murderer's head.*"

The woman that had cried out put her hands to her mouth, and the tall man blinked.

"*Father,*" said Ashka, "*This is Timothy. Timothy, this is my father,*

Harashor."

Haberd had told Timothy, once, that in Botani courts it had been customary to introduce the more honored of two people first. Judging from the cloud that crossed Harashor's face, Timothy thought that Ashka's introducing him before his own father had some of the same implications. He frowned.

"*Yesterday,*" said Ashka, and his voice rang out, "*I was pursued by a Huctan up the mountain. He intended to take my life, and I could not prevent him. These two men attacked the soldier. Although they had spears, they used stones, to spare the village blame.*"

The small crowd was silent. Ashka was a good talker. Timothy stared at Jesher's now drooping form and clenched his fists inside his mittens.

"*The man on the horse is named Jesher, may-his-name-never-be-forgotten,*" said Ashka. A few in the crowd closed their eyes and mumbled briefly, repeating the phrase Ashka had used: 'may his name never be forgotten'.

"*These men saved me from death,*" said Ashka, striding forward and taking Timothy by the forearm. "*Before the village, I acknowledge my life-debt to Timothy.*" He said the last loudly, as if expecting to be argued with, and knelt, grasping Timothy's right foot. Timothy resisted the urge to pull his foot away.

No one spoke. Ashka rose again and held an open hand, palm forward, towards Timothy. "*Will you accept my life debt?*" he asked.

Unsure of what he was doing, Timothy held his own hand up, taking off his mitten. "*I will accept your life debt,*" he said. Ashka pressed their palms together, then squeezed firmly and leaned toward Timothy's ear.

"*Will you allow my people to honor Jesher's body?*" he asked.

Timothy hesitated, then nodded.

Ashka went to his father. They spoke softly, and the Mirresotas with powder-blue headbands were silent. Harashor nodded, and turned to face the people.

"*Let us prepare to honor the body of Jesher, may-he-never-be-forgotten,*" he said.

Obedience was immediate, though Timothy saw one or two eyebrows rise in surprise. Harashor approached Timothy swiftly, holding out his open right hand. Timothy reached to grasp it, but the tall man took his wrist instead, reaching around Timothy's shoulder and pulling him close in a formal embrace. They stood for a moment, forearms locked together and left arms encircling sheepskin cloaks. Harashor broke the embrace and looked Timothy in the eyes.

"*I thank you for my son's life,*" he said.

Timothy thought of the look Jesher had given him, when Timothy had suggested they mind their own business, and did not know what to say. He nodded, and Harashor seemed satisfied.

The Mirresota did not bury the bodies of their dead. The cold did not make for efficient decay, and graves were difficult to dig and easily disturbed by the summer melt and roaming wolves. They burned the dead, and the ashes were left to scatter in the wind.

Wood, though not precisely scarce, was not plentiful. Still, the people piled Jesher's pier high with dry pine. Timothy helped lift Jesher's stiff, bent form from the horse. Women removed the woolen cloak and boots and covered Jesher's face with a thin cloth before setting him in his tunic on the sap-smelling bed. Timothy felt cold when they handed him the torch, cold when he stepped forward, and cold as he pushed the oily flame into the thirsty wood. Flame lapped at the pitch, then at the pine, and finally began to devour Jesher's flesh.

They stood back at a distance, watching the flames rise on the stone hilltop. Timothy almost ran back up the hill when the flame reached the body. He felt that it was at last destroying Jesher, that when his form was reduced to ash he would be truly gone. He felt anger at the flames, anger at himself, anger with Jesher for letting himself be killed. He fought back tears again, mightily. It had never been so hard to keep his oath.

He kept the spear point, washing the blood from its blade and carving away the splinters on the short piece of shaft before thrusting it in his belt like a knife.

Timothy's hand hesitated when he knelt to gather Jesher's ashes. The Mirresotas left the ashes of their dead where they had been burned, but he could not bring himself to let Jesher be scattered across the mountains.

The embers had died and the ashes were cold. Some had already been blown off of the slate-colored mound, leaving a feather trail of silver dust. Timothy reached down carefully and scooped up some of the ash, pouring it from his hand into a small pouch. A little of the gray stuck to his palm. He put his hand to his leg, as if to wipe the ash off, then closed his hand and put his fist to his face. Keeping the tears in by the pressure of his squeezed eyelids and clenched jaw, he sat and trembled for several minutes.

At last he stood and tied the pouch. Some of the ash had gotten onto his face from his clenched hand. He licked his lips, and tasted the lye. It was sharp, and bitter.

Timothy met with Harashor, Ashka's father, the Mirresota chieftain. He expected the man to ask him how he knew Botani and why he had killed a Huctan and what he was doing on the mountain. Instead Harashor said, "*You do not love the Huctans.*"

"*No,*" said Timothy. "*I love Botan.*"

"*That is good,*" said Harashor.

Timothy told the tall man why they had come. He gave Harashor the packet, which he had almost forgotten to retrieve from Jesher's tunic. He watched as Harashor looked at the seal, opened the packet, and withdrew the letter and the lump. The lump was a small knot, which Harashor held for a moment before setting on the table. Timothy looked at the knot—which was of course the War Knot—and suddenly realized how Haberd must have felt when he survived his friends and delivered the same knot to Jardon's king.

Harashor now took up the letter. His eyes moved slowly. He reached the bottom of the letter, frowned, and then looked at Timothy.

"*There is a part that I cannot read,*" he said. "*Perhaps it is for you.*"

Timothy took the letter. The first part—the part that Harashor had read—was written in simple Botani. It appealed to the Mirresotas to rise up to war, to take this last opportunity to fight the Huctans before they had taken Jardon and increased their strength beyond hope of defeat.

Timothy knew by the look on Harashor's face that the Mirresotas, like Jardon, would not accept the call. He would have known even without the look on Harashor's face. Timothy and Jesher had been sent on a fool's errand.

The last part of the letter was written in code. Timothy recognized the cipher and read it easily.

To both of you, it read, and for some reason this first phrase almost overcame Timothy. He closed his eyes briefly, swallowed so that it hurt his throat, and continued.

If the Mirresotas do not accept the War Knot–and I do not expect them to–do not return to the Band. We will be overrun before you are halfway to Moure. I am doing my best to make provision for the other Thanes, as I have for you. If there is time, I will do the same for as many here as I can.

Do not return to the Band. I cannot tell you where to go, or what to do. Even if I could, I would not, for if I am caught alive it is better that I do not know where you are. You–and the other Thanes–are on your own. Botan rests in your hands.

Timothy set down the letter and looked at Harashor. His trembling stopped and gave way to a cold, smoldering rage. With the rage came a strength, or a lack of caution. It was as if he were dreaming, and nothing he did had implications in the real world.

"*You will not answer the call,*" he said to Harashor. He did not hide his contempt.

Harashor heard Timothy's judgment, looked down, and then looked up.

"*No,*" he said. "*We will not.*"

"*I have come far, Harashor,*" said Timothy. "*I have lost much.*"

Harashor stared back at Timothy, and though his face did not move, Timothy saw a brief flicker of doubt in the hard man's eyes. Then Harashor blinked, and stood, and put a hand on Timothy's shoulder.

"*I am sorry for your loss,*" he said.

Timothy shrugged the hand off. Harashor stood still, for a moment, and then left the room.

Timothy took the pouch with Jesher's ashes and climbed up the rocks above the first Mirresota village. He found a cranny that seemed safe and placed the pouch inside. Searching briefly, he found a few large stones and piled them over the pouch. Then, in the fading light, he sat before the grave. He thought some, remembered some, but mostly he simply sat.

At last he opened his mouth.

"I'm sorry," he whispered. The tears almost came, but he kept them in with the palms of his hands. Then he picked up another stone and dashed it against the grave as hard as he could. Then he sat, and was still.

The poem came to him, and he spoke it without thinking, as if it were being channeled through him, spoken by someone else.

"*Lokaren, thy love, has flown,*
Like dew upon the mountain,
Like foam before the sea.
With Eldebar, the old, is she,
Beyond the horned climber,
Upon the upward way.
Lokaren, thy love, has flown,
Like dew upon the mountain,
Like foam before the sea."

The wind blew. Timothy sat. Then a voice profaned the silence.

"*That is an old poem,*" the voice, Ashka's, said. "*And a fair one.*"

Timothy twitched in surprise, then turned to face Ashka. He had the sudden urge to kill the boy—for surprising him, for listening to him, for being the reason Jesher was dead—and the urge was so real that his hand began moving toward the spear point in his belt.

"*We know of the halls of Eldebar,*" Ashka said. "*The way is on the mountain. I have seen the horned climber, once.*"

Timothy's hand closed around the handle of his spear-point knife. He waited. Ashka looked up and to the right, where the trail disappeared over a false peak some half-mile up.

"*There are three great peaks,*" he said. "*Irgata, Decada, and Encarn. The tallest is called Encarn—Despair—because the wind is always blowing, and the air is thin. On Encarn lies the way of the poem. I have seen it, once, but I have never followed it.*"

Timothy looked at Ashka, and stayed his hand, and remembered the way Jesher had spoken of the poem, how he had said that the poem seemed to belong to the mountain.

"*Take me to this place,*" said Timothy.

Ashka turned back to face him, and slumped.

"*It is impossible,*" he said, "*it can only be reached at the end of the summer, when the ice has melted from the northern face.*"

The urge for violence returned, in full strength. Timothy wanted to shake Ashka, to tell him that he *would* take Timothy up the mountain, that it *was* possible, that he hadn't come this far and watched his friend die so that the Mirresotas could ignore the War Knot and the boy he had saved could refuse to help him. But he said nothing. He looked at Ashka and trembled in the space between crying and killing.

After a moment, Ashka lowered his eyes and left.

Timothy crept away from the hearth in the early morning. Harashor's wolf-like dog watched him leave the village, but did not protest. The moon was still bright, and the air was bitterly cold.

Ashka overtook him before noon. He had no horse, but he carried a large pack. Timothy saw him above, but kept walking.

When Ashka overtook him, Timothy spoke without turning his head. "*Why do you follow me?*" he said.

"*I owe you the life debt,*" said Ashka. "*You have accepted it.*" There was anger in his voice, as if *he* were the one with a grievance.

Timothy stopped walking. The boy overtook him, stopped, faced him.

"*You owe me the life debt.*" Timothy said.

"*Yes.*"

"*I have accepted it.*"

"*Yes.*"

"*Then this is my command. Do not make Jesher's death a waste.*"

Timothy began walking again. Ashka stood as if stricken, and Timothy knew that all the venom and bitterness he had felt on speaking had reached the boy. Something told him to retract his words, but he held his lips sealed.

"*But I would serve you!*" Ashka called after him, desperately, as Timothy turned the corner of a switchback.

"*I will come back,*" Timothy said, still coldly, still without looking back. "*You will lead me up the mountain.*"

He continued walking, and the boy did not follow him.

CHAPTER 28

ROBERT

Many days away, beyond the plains, south of the snow, Robert squatted on his haunches and chewed on his lower lip. A low, leaf-pattering spring rain wet his exposed hand, but he didn't feel the cold.

"Robert," Selena said again, louder.

Robert realized suddenly that she had been trying to get his attention for several seconds. He looked up.

"You OK?" she asked.

Robert sniffed. None of them would be OK, not for a long time.

"Yeah, I'm OK," Robert said, smiling across the fire at Selena. "Just thinking."

It was all happening too fast. He hadn't had time to grieve, to think of Gerard and Comaro dead and gone. He hadn't had time to think of anything but the next immediate action.

"OK," Selena said. Concern showed in her eyes for a second, and he thought she might be coming back to him. Then she blinked, and when her eyes opened they were hard. It would be a long time before the mission-minded, country-first Thane let its guard down enough for the girl underneath to show her face again.

"They're starting to wonder what we're going to do," Selena said.

By 'they' she meant the other Thanes squatted by their fires in the damp forest wondering if everything they had known and loved was dead. By 'they' she meant a dozen young warriors with more experience, skill and knowledge than Robert, who had, for some unfathomable reason, chosen him as their leader.

Robert already knew that they were starting to wonder. They'd been trudging through the trees in a vague northerly direction for days. They were clear of immediate danger now. In many ways, *most* ways, that was good, but in one very important way it was bad. It meant that the Thanes now had time to muse, doubt, and smolder. The escape-with-their-lives mission was complete, and now they were neither training nor performing. Without purpose, Thanes would molder and die as quickly as flowers without sun. They needed direction, now more than ever.

"I know," Robert said. He wanted to tell Selena he'd been agonizing on it for days, that even now that he'd come to a decision, he doubted. Doubted the rightness of it as much as whether the Thanes would accept it.

A week ago he *would* have told her. A week ago, opening his heart to the woman that had become the only person he could really talk to would have been second nature. But that was before the Huctans had attacked the Band. That was before the Thanes had begun acting like children, as if part of them had died with the Band, as if their rationality and drive were so irrevocably intertwined with the village and Marshals and training that one could not live without the other.

Only Robert had kept his head, in that canyon, and he hadn't been able to stop Leon or Cody from going back.

And now, by the common consensus of eleven grieving, hollow-eyed, dangerous Thanes, Robert had been elected leader. He, the least experienced, the least trained, only recently converted to the cause, was expected to shoulder the responsibility for Botan.

And to top it all off, Selena had shut herself off from all human emotion.

Stop wallowing, Robert thought, with sudden self-disgust. Hundreds of people had been slaughtered in the mountains while they ran and escaped with their lives, and all he could think about was how hard it was to be Robert.

Selena was waiting for him to explain himself, waiting for an "I'll tell them soon" or an "I'm thinking about it". Robert didn't say anything. After a minute, Selena nodded and rose to a stoop under the half-fallen log that was protecting the fire from the rain. She gave Robert one last look as she adjusted her hood, then stepped quickly out into the wet and danced her way over to her chosen nest.

Robert pulled his cloak tighter around his shoulders, leaning close to the fire for one last whisker-searing kiss of heat. Then, with a booted foot, he kicked the coals out into the rain.

They hissed, smoked, grew dim, and began soaking up the water. Robert lay back, closed his eyes, and thought how like the coals they were.

He woke in the morning. It felt good, waking in the morning rather than in the middle of the night. His watch would fall again tonight, but there were enough Thanes that not everyone had a watch every night.

It wasn't morning in the strictest sense, since the sun wasn't up, but the hint of smoke in the air meant Robert wasn't the first awake. He reached for his flint, then rolled into a squat and hooded up instead. If he hesitated any longer, he was going to lose his nerve.

Warest and his sister, Nilico, had holed up closest to Robert. Hugged tight to the lee of an overhanging boulder, neither appeared awake, but Warest sat up on one elbow as Robert approached. Robert squatted close. The rain had slackened to a drizzle, but there was no use soaking it up when he didn't have to.

"Morning, sunshine," he said.

"Good morning, sleepy," Warest replied, his south-western accent thick. "I thought you would never wake up."

Robert laughed. "Good morning, Nilico."

"It is raining and it is cold," Nilico said without opening her eyes or rolling over. "It is not a good morning."

Robert was glad they were both still trying, even if their cheeriness sounded as hollow as his own felt. "Hey," he said, dropping his grin, "let's meet up under that big pine in about five minutes, OK?"

One of Nilico's eyes popped open, and Warest nodded almost eagerly. Which, for Warest, meant that his head moved a little instead of just his eyes.

Robert stood up.

Kialo, Lutho and Toledе were hunkered around a low fire nearby, already searing a wild onion on the end of a pointed stick.

The smoke smelled sweet, and filtered slowly through the dense cedar umbrella they had nested under. Water had leaked through on Lutho's cloak, it appeared, and the stone set of his eyes above his pudgy cheeks looked a hair more dangerous than usual. Robert made it brief.

In five minutes he had made his rounds and they had gathered, stomping their feet to get the blood flowing again and shaking droplets of water from their cloaks. There was tension in the misty air beneath the pine, and excitement. Had they been less than Thanes, they would have been bouncing their knees and shifting from foot to foot.

Robert was going to do his leaderly duty. He was going to give them direction. Whether they would listen or not remained to be seen.

Robert guessed that many of them didn't know themselves whether they would listen. He had been chosen leader because the rest of them were too stricken with grief to function. Whether that meant he really *was* the leader, when they didn't agree with a decision, was still very much up in the air.

They warmed themselves and waited patiently. Robert took deep breaths.

Did he want to do this? Wouldn't it be better, safer, just to wait?

No. In King's Table, when the stakes were high, you always felt the temptation to play it safe, to defend, to minimize further losses. But when you were down pieces, you had to make a move.

"The Band is gone," he said. Eyes that had been casually eyeing the ground or the smoldering campfire looked up, and winced. "Scattered and killed," Robert repeated. "Gone."

They knew it to be true, but he wanted to drive it home. They couldn't hold on to the hope that most of the Band had escaped somehow, that they were waiting for them somewhere, that there were Marshals building a new camp with new training grounds and new missions.

The Band was gone. Their fate was in their own hands.

"The Huctans are marching on Jardon," Robert said, and they winced again. Too many blunt statements like that and there would be bitterness, but sugarcoat it and he'd lose the point. "You know it and I know it," he said. "It's happening now."

Taking a deep breath, Robert spoke solemnly and slowly, concentrating on simply enunciating the words that needed to be said.

"Things have changed," he said, "and we can't just sit around gathering information anymore. We can't just wait around to be found again, or worse, to not even be *worth* finding again. We can't just watch Jardon fall, watch Botan's chance pass her by, and grow old wishing we had done something. That we had at least tried."

They were silent as they watched him, but as Robert spoke he found himself caring less about what the Thanes were thinking of his words and more about what he was saying. He felt sick, and yet he felt excitement too. They weren't *going* to grow old and full of regret. They were going to try, and that meant that they would either grow old with pride or not grow old at all.

"As much as the weak and worthless side of me would like to wait just a little longer," he said, "we can't. War is coming whether we like it or not. There will be war, and Botan will be a part of it."

The forest might have been empty but for the rain. All eyes were fixed on Robert, and they were not blinking. No movement, no sound.

Last chance, Robert thought. He spit it out before his knees could buckle.

"There are thousands of Botani men," he said, "trained and armed. They were kidnapped and beaten and scared. Timothy and I were among them, and I can tell you that many of them have been broken. Many are now more Huctan than Botani, and would kill their own countrymen as well as fight Jardon for the Huctans."

He felt sick as he said it, but it was true.

"I can tell you this, though." Robert felt himself step forward a little, felt his eyes grow hard, "Some of them are *not* broken."

He could have stopped there. Nick was nodding already. Selena, Tolede, Kialo, Diane... all of them had the signs of immediate comprehension and eager acquiescence written on their faces.

The words came to him easily. He had thought it out and he wasn't at all sure of it, but he had *decided*, now, and that was some relief. He told them that there were trained Botani soldiers in the Huctan armies who were not broken, maybe enough to make a difference. He told them that these were their countrymen, and that now, while the Emperor's eye was pointed toward Jardon, was the time to set a spark to the tinder pile.

"How?" Kialo asked.

"It's a logistical nightmare," Nick said.

Robert explained that they couldn't build the fire themselves. The wood was already stacked, and the efforts of a few young patriots weren't going to make it any drier or wetter. Their job was to strike as many sparks as they could, and, if the wood caught fire, to fan it before the Huctans could quench it.

"How?" Kialo repeated.

By rebelling, Robert said. Not by thinking about rebellion or planning rebellion, but by robbing Huctan guardhouses and attacking Huctan supply trains and burning Huctan outposts. They were Thanes. They did nothing better. They had been trained for nothing if not this.

"Yes," Lutho said, "and people will hear about what we do, and finally pull their thumbs out of their mouths to do something."

Word had to spread, Robert agreed, but it wouldn't spread because they made their rebellion public. It would spread precisely because they would be secretive. There were frowns at this, but he pressed on.

He himself had at first envisioned Huctan bodies hung across roadways and barracks burned to the ground in broad daylight. But that would be an obvious cry for attention, and it wouldn't work. Rebellion that was advertised would seem cheap, a stunt, propaganda. By its very visibility it would lose power. Nothing hushes up a rumor like everyone knowing about it.

And nothing spreads one like secrecy.

So they would be secretive, trusting that even their best secrecy couldn't hide it all. Money would eventually be found missing. People would grow incredulous when a sleeping guard happened to lose his sword, a cougar hamstrung three Huctan horses without taking any meat, and yet another patrol went missing. People would think they were seeing through something, perceiving what was supposed to be hidden, and they would proclaim it from the hilltops. The stories, instead of being laughed aside and minimized, would grow larger than the deeds themselves. One raid would get the publicity of ten. Four dead Huctans in the woods would spark rumors of hundreds already fallen to a guerrilla army.

The Thanes were nodding before Robert had even finished.

Some of them were smiling.

Robert told himself, later, that the Thanes accepted his plan because it was the most logical, because Timothy and Jesher and every escaped fragment of the Band would be in hiding, because the time was as perfect now as it ever would be. He told himself that they had thought it through, as he had, and that they were as un-thirsty for blood as he was.

But when they put their hands together beneath the pine, in the drizzling spring rain, Robert knew that they loved his plan because it was a desperate one, because it would most likely fail, because they would most likely die.

They had spent many years following the safe road, only to see all they had worked for destroyed in a single day. Now they were ready to take as many Huctans down with them as they could.

They were ready to be reckless.

CHAPTER 29

They said later that the flatlander took the people's guilt upon himself. Someone had to pay for the death of the Huctan on the mountain, and if not for the flatlander, it would have been the people.

Some said he admitted to killing the Huctan on the mountain. Others said that the body was found and the soldiers suspected him. Some—and these were quickly shouted down—claimed that the flatlander picked a fight without provocation.

But all agreed that whatever happened *ended* on a snowy day in Moure. All agreed that at least four Huctans were killed, and that the flatlander killed them.

Two were already dead before they cornered him in the square. The chase had gone long enough that the city was in uproar. For three stories people craned heads out of windows, looking down on the toppled tent work and overturned goods. The merchants had cleared the square in seconds when the soldiers poured in from three sides, yet they lingered and crept back to watch what would happen.

There was blood on the flatlander's hands. He had no fur cloak, though one was later found below some broken tiles on a rooftop. In the silence of the square, some claimed to have heard his breathing even at the windows they watched from. The snow seemed to melt before it touched his steaming skin. His breath was like smoke.

He made to jump up to a balcony as they closed in on him. No one was surprised when he did not reach it, though some swore they had seen him reach higher when he had been trapped in an alley minutes before. He fell and rose again to his feet, hands on knees, waiting as the soldiers came.

There was little color in the square. The snow had been falling softly all day, and had coated the sun-faded tarps with dry white. The chaos had shifted some of the snow, revealing some blues and greens and grays, but the wind was blowing and the white falling faster now. At times it was difficult for those on the far side to see even the crimson of the circling soldiers' cloaks.

No one remembered what the flatlander shouted. It was in a strange tongue, and muffled by the wind. The Huctans approached him slowly and with caution, though there were six of them and one of him.

The wind blew hard and a shower of snow dislodged from the rooftops. Some missed the flatlander's start and only caught the movement a moment later, several yards away, as one of the Huctans screamed. One crimson cloak remained on the ground while five others converged on the flatlander. He made for an unguarded street, tripped, and turned. A crossbow fired, and no one saw whether the flatlander was hit. If he was, it did not stop him from fighting.

Steel clashed. The crimson surrounded the gray now, and with the snow it was difficult to see. One red cloak stumbled back, straightened, and then slumped suddenly to the ground. There were shouts. The gray broke free of the red, then tripped again.

Some took it as a sign, when the snow slowed suddenly to reveal the flatlander's final stand. The Huctans closed, and every eye saw clearly as they fell upon him. There was another shout, this one in Huctan and later rumored to be a command to keep the flatlander alive. Spears were turned butt-first and thrust, again and again.

The flatlander tried to rise twice. He did not cry out. As his struggling stilled and the crimson circled, he moved suddenly and flung something at the nearest windows. It clattered against a wall and fell on a balcony.

Another spear butt struck the flatlander, this time above the eye, and he fell limp. The crimson closed around him.

As the snow fell harder, silent and heavy, a young girl picked up the spear point the flatlander had thrown onto her bedroom balcony. When her parents asked if she had seen what the flatlander had thrown, she lied. Hiding it under her bed, she vowed to treasure it until the flatlander returned.

For he *would* return. Everyone, in the childish part of his heart, agreed on this. Some denied it with their mouths, even to themselves, but every Botaño and Botaña in Moure that day felt something change.

There was hope. The flatlander had stood against the Huctans. Botan's spirit was alive. There was still green in the old tree's core.

Strange, how such a small spark lights such a large forest.

END OF BOOK 1

ACKNOWLEDGMENTS

Mom, for starting me on this journey.

Vance, Barry, Deena, Dan, Shannon and Laura Bow, Melissa Oestmann (both of them), Andrew Peterson, Andrew and Brittany Stevenson, and Anthony and Jessica Robertson, for reading and editing at various stages of the book.

God, for giving me breath.

Thank you.

ABOUT THE AUTHOR

Travis grew up in Reno, NV (where he raised pigs for FFA), earned engineering degrees from Oklahoma Christian University (where he broke his collarbone in a misguided Parkour attempt) and Stanford (where he and his bike were hit by a car), did R&D for Nikon (where he earned several patents), and now works on medical robots in Reno. He has two wonderful children, one beautiful wife, and one loving God.

Made in the USA
Las Vegas, NV
26 September 2021